Praise for The Barre Incidents

"Lauren Bolger continues to propel herself forward as one of the most interesting and finest voices in horror with her sophomore novel, *The Barre Incidents*. She excels at weaving the intangible, like familial relationships, trauma, and existential dread, with the in-your-face and gripping terrors of the kinds of creatures that will haunt your dreams. I think it's safe to say *The Barre Incidents* has cemented Bolger as the Cryptid Queen. Do not sleep on this novel."

—Michael Bettendorf, author of *Trve Cvlt*

"Lauren Bolger's *The Barre Incidents* is a thrilling mystery about family, love and grief blended with a deep dive into world mythology. The book delightfully interweaves the voices of friendly residents of a small town alongside ancient and otherworldly voices. A strange and thrilling tale!"

—Ivy Grimes, author of *The Ghosts of Blaubart Mansion*

THE BARRE INCIDENTS

Lauren Bolger

For Hannah and Ryan

I

Death Comes to Barre

The only reason Kara showed up to her parents' house after the funeral was for her dad, who was in a box under a fresh bed of dirt and couldn't care less.

As she lay miserably on the sectional in the den, those two inanimate objects—dad, and his shiny pine coffin—were settling deep for the long haul in the belly of Hope Cemetery.

That body wasn't her dad, actually. Kara didn't like to get existential, but sometimes that clawing dread climbed over her without her okay. It preyed on her in moments of quiet, opened her up, and then ushered the panic in. Now, since someone she deeply cared about, really loved, had traveled to the great beyond, the great whatever, the great . . . nowhere, probably, that panicked feeling let itself in again.

All she wanted was her dad back. And for that feeling to go away.

The shiva, as her dad had requested, would only last a couple of days. A week was the official time frame in the Jewish faith, but lots of folks thought that was too long. Too much.

To Kara, him dying was too much. Anything beyond that was ridiculous.

At some point she had sunk into the couch and just decided she couldn't get up. She closed her eyes, let her body slavishly mimic the contours of the cushions, the anxiety of the forever unanswered question, *where did he go* pulling up on every muscle inside her. *He was always here. How can he be gone?*

When things were horrible, her dad, Jonathan Lenker, always made things better. If it were anyone's funeral besides his own, he'd be sneaking her a stack of cookies. He'd creep back and forth from the kitchen, until half the serving dish was empty. She'd protest and he'd stuff some in her purse and walk away all casually. He'd make sure she was laughing before he went off to mingle again. When she got all morose, her mom retaliated by getting pissed off, and her dad was usually softer. What would she do now?

Her eyes stung, and she shook it off. Tried to refocus. One arm up on the couch back, she stared at the built-in dark mahogany cabinets and shelves that belonged to her father. As people came and went from the room, she emitted half-assed greetings from closed lips. Since she refused to make eye contact, most of them just shuffled by, probably figuring they could give their condolences to her mom instead and then fuck off into the night feeling good about themselves.

In life, Jonathan Lenker collected comics, as well as many historical books about their hometown of Barre, Vermont. She zeroed in on the one where dead Superman saw his temporarily dead adoptive father in heaven and they went on an adventure together.

That was a weird one, she thought. Superman, an alien, died, and somehow quickly found his human father who'd just had a heart attack. How nice they just happened to end up in the same place. She found herself resenting this fictional character who had a wholesome life built for him in the minds and hearts of billions, and who, after death, got to say hi to his dad.

Such a royal kiss-ass anyway, she grumbled in her mind. *Linebacker-looking, laser-eyed bastard.* The contempt was mostly playful, since she'd read all these comics happily growing up, but somehow the mock-abuse was proving cathartic.

Vaguely, she remembered Superman's dad was also named Jonathan. Her tired eyes settled on the book next to the comic. Fat and green. *Weird Trees of North America.* The lettering looked a few points too big for the spine.

Kara sat up, squinting at the book. Why didn't she remember that one? And why was it shoehorned right in the middle of all the Superman trades?

She stood up slowly and shimmied, smoothing the fabric of her dress with both hands. She should fix the book. Put it back where it belonged. Maybe it had something in there about Red Tree Hill, the hill with the gnarled red tree behind Hope Cemetery. She could check. Then she'd re-shelve it with the other books he'd collected about Barre's history. Their hometown.

She reached for the book, and the lettering on the spine twitched.

Blinking, Kara drew her hand back. Now the book looked normal again. The crying had blurred her contacts. Her tears were just making shadows, or something.

She canvassed the room, realizing she was alone in here now. Then she rubbed her eyes and stared at it some more, backing away, sizing it up.

The words pulsed, now. Growing, then shrinking. Beckoning, even. The letters stretched further and further, wrapping around the spine, like a hand caressing something beloved. Drilling into her: No, you're not just seeing things.

Kara shut her eyes and turned away, fighting the vision with every fiber of her being. Everyone in Barre seemed obsessed with phenomena. Just like any old town where the cemeteries encroached on their neighborhoods. Poltergeists. Cryptids. UFO's.

Life was complicated enough. She didn't understand why worrying about what someone claimed they saw behind a dumpster in the dark could make things any easier. And here it was, threatening to rub off on her, too.

The letters reached like fingers, stretching into the shadows the books made.

"What's happening in there?" Kara whispered. There, in the thin, flat, invisible space. Where it was dark. Where eyes couldn't reach.

She thought about Dad in his coffin again. When he was all dressed up, and she was alone with him this morning, right before the service, she'd sworn there'd been a thunk.

It couldn't be, though. It was the ducts in the ceiling. Only she'd backed up, terrified, and she could swear the coffin was wiggling on its stand. She stood there for minutes, maybe three, maybe five, and she swore something was keeping it going awhile, though she'd only heard the sound that one time. She'd stayed there until the movement stopped. She didn't want to alarm her mom, who had had her own weird-enough moment here a few days before.

"You done?" she'd asked him, staring at his face like he might answer, her arm half-extended toward him. She curled and uncurled her fingers, wanting to touch him but being afraid to at the same time. She let out a high, nervous laugh that went on just a little too long, and then her eyes had filled. Those were her last moments with his body.

"Hey, Kare!" Kara's heart leaped into her throat, and she let out a choked half-shout, turning toward the kitchen doorway. Her two aunts practically hovered in the entryway to the kitchen, like Kara was a starved lion, and people-meat was fair game. Kara had to force her breathing to deepen, then slow down. Her Aunt Sara stepped down into the den, closed the distance easily with her luxuriously pantsuited long legs, and placed her hand over Kara's.

Kara's contempt ebbed for a second, and her heart swelled. "Your hand is warm," she smiled.

"How you holding up, baby?"

"Oh, y'know." She pressed her lips tight, squeezed her eyes closed. "It sucks," she said quickly, then shut up again.

"Shit," Aunt Sara said. The "i" was elongated a little, the extra sound warming her with familiarity. Sara paused. "Hey, please know you can call me like you always used to when you were little, okay? And if you don't, I'll call you on Tuesday. I'll be doing some cooking and I'll drop you off some things to eat."

"I can't say no to your cooking, Auntie."

"And if you did, I wouldn't listen."

Kara laughed. "I know, I know."

"Baruch Dayan HaEmet," her Aunt Edna said loudly from the kitchen.

"Is that a drive-by condolence?" Kara called back, smiling tersely.

"I don't want to bother you. You seemed deep in thought."

"Don't worry Aunt Edna, you don't have to come in here."

Edna descended the single step into the den and stayed right there. "I want to, though."

Kara made her mouth a straight line and nodded, almost imperceptibly. "Thank you." Silence yawned between them, but Edna didn't budge. The discomfort stretched on. After a few seconds, Kara sighed quietly. *I guess nobody's going to talk, so I'll have to.* "What does that mean, anyway?"

"What?"

"Baruch Dayan HaEmet? I never learned that in Hebrew school. Or I did, and forgot."

"It means 'Blessed is the true judge.'"

"Okay, and what does that mean?"

"In so many words? It means God will take it from here."

"Take what? What's 'it'?"

Edna's mouth was open, eyeballs floundering around in her stubborn skull. "It being Jon's . . . your father's soul, of course." She blinked rapidly, then furrowed her brow.

Kara's blood heated. "Oh, sweet," she tried, but her voice wavered. *What a stupid thing to say. That clearly doesn't work for everyone, and everyone knows I'm agnostic. It doesn't help me.*

Maybe she genuinely thought it'd help though. A small war boiled inside her.

Despite herself, she continued. "What about me, though?"

"What do you mean, what about you? I said it to you, *for* you. It's a thing people say to make loved ones feel better."

"Yeah, but I just—" Kara started. "Nevermind."

"No, what were you going to say?" Edna's eyes were wide and still, pink pricking her cheeks.

It would be awful to laugh right now, Kara thought.

She laughed anyway. A hot, angry, uncomfortable kind of chortle. "It really feels like *I* took it from here if we're talking about real life. My goofy sweetheart of a mom, as she does, lost her shit, tried to be the . . . guardian person for dad's body. You know, the person to watch it overnight? Keep the soul company?"

"Shomeret," Edna advised, pursing her lips.

"Ah yes. The shomeret."

"I don't think Christians can act as shomerim."

"Yeah, normally. But we're talking about Lola Lenker, here. Tirelessly, she fought the funeral director for the honor until he gave in. Made me bring her toothbrush and clean underwear for overnight.

"Then, an hour in, Dad's body made a noise. And she freaked. Screamed bloody murder while the director was outside on a cigarette break. He called me, clearly rattled, and sent her straight home with her skivvies and her overnight things, like a kid who couldn't handle their play date." Kara sighed. "So she spent the weekend lamenting, and I planned everything myself."

"That must have been hard for you." Edna had gone practically robotic. She'd all but exited this conversation already. It was par for the course with her, but about something like this?

"Hard?" Normally, Kara would ignore it. But today? Impossible.

"Sure," Edna said.

"Hard would be a shrunken hat balanced on top of the overstuffed head of what that was like. I'm tired. I'm stressed. I miss my dad." Tears sprang to her eyes. All of it made her angry. So angry. She covered her face and sobbed, shaking her head. "Ugh." She felt her Aunt Sara sink down next to her on the couch, but it hardly helped. Sara wrapped her arms around her shoulders and head.

"My brother; your dad . . . he was something, wasn't he?"

"Yeah."

"I miss him too," Sara whispered into her hair. "We'll grow into the hurt, I promise. Just you wait and see."

"Aunt Sara?" Kara whispered between gasped breaths.

"Yeah?"

"I'll be okay but I'm gonna go for a bit."

"Sure you'll be okay?"

"I think, yeah. Just gonna drive around."

"Do what ya need, my girl. Do what ya need."

***

For Kara, the answer to the question, "where will I go," would always be home, or wherever Alec was.

She waited, all jittery energy now, for the car to warm, shoving multiple sticks of gum in her mouth as quickly as she could unwrap them, pressing the heel of her hand to her mouth, which comforted her—somewhat—as she waited for the cold stiffness to soften and warm.

Kara closed her eyes, trying to let go of everything that clung to her from today. But her hands stunk of multiple strong hand soaps, fighting for dominance. One was from her mom's house, sharp and biting, like an overpowering potpourri. The other one, a sick-sweet flowery scent from the funeral home. Lilies, probably. Ugh. The smells converged, conspiring, locking her in with that foul, lonely, hopeless state of being. The kind of feeling that made her want to call her dad for comfort, which reminded her again of why she was here, compounding the despair. It stuck to her ribs like a bad meal that wouldn't digest.

Next, her brain would search for reason and respond to itself by calling up her dad's eerie stillness as she stood there alone in his hospital room, waiting for the nurse. Then the funeral. The gravestones. The stillness they had to navigate around to get to his grave—like traffic cones, but still, sentient, and gray.

15

Her skin stiffened. She shuddered and opened her eyes. Closing her eyes hadn't done her any favors. Better to move.

Kara gunned the ignition, then pulled and released a long, labored breath. What would she say to Alec when she got there? Almost undoubtedly, he'd make fun of her for leaving the shiva early to come get him, in the most dramatically outdated phrasing he could offer. Something like: *Couldn't hack it, huh?*

In other words, something delightfully distracting and perfectly stupid.

***

She stepped in to a loud restaurant but a virtually empty bar. Charlie Foley sat there alone, hunched over the counter, his fleece hat lopsided and his stick-straight brown-with-silver hair fighting its way out. He nursed his usual Sprite with extra ice.

"Hey you," he said, just barely turning, like he'd read her footsteps. "You're not in your fatigues today."

"Fatigues?"

"Just making a joke. I'm used to the work uniform. White polo shirt? Apron?"

"Oh!" Kara shook her head, pressed her palms to her dress, as if checking her wardrobe. "Yeah, I'm off, what with the dead dad and all." She headed toward him, leaning her forearms against the back of a barstool. "Alec come up for air lately?"

"Nah, not that I saw. Very busy cooking. It finally quieted down just before you showed up. Almost everyone here is eating now. You look terrible, by the way."

"Yeah thanks a lot. I'm playing hooky from the shiva. It's still going on, now. I'm exhausted." She pulled out the stool and sat down. The leather upholstery in the seat had been refurbished recently. One of Darla's favorite things to complain about. Upgrades. Money well spent, but none of the regulars ever noticed the difference. And the stools, like everything else, felt permanently and vaguely sticky, no matter how well Kara wiped them down every night.

"What's a shiva?" Charlie asked.

"Like a wake, but Jewish."

"Ah, gotcha. You didn't bury him already, did you?"

"We did. We do it fast, so they can hurry up and rest."

"Is that shiva thing almost over? Too late to pay my respects? I really should. Did you know: back when you were small, before you worked here? When I used to drink—"

"My dad would drink with you here, after you guys finished your shift at the quarry. I know, I know."

"It's funny, I thought I'd told you that, but it feels good reminding you." Charlie smiled sadly. "He was great. Weird. Loud. Funny as hell."

Kara laughed. "A very honest, very true assessment. Anyway, you can still go tonight, or tomorrow. You've got time."

"That's good. Does your mom still live at that big old Craftsman remodel all on its lonesome up on Merchant Street?"

"Yep."

"Huh. Ever experience anything weird growing up over there?"

"Charlie," Kara warned.

"What?" he asked, his face soft. Equal parts innocent and earnest.

She shook her head slowly. "I'm no different than anyone else in Barre. All of us live somewhere near Merchant. It runs straight through the damn town. Literally everything is off of Merchant."

"Yeah but you lived *on* it. It's different."

"Hardly."

"I noticed you didn't actually answer my question, though."

She paused, then shrugged. "I'm just bracing myself for the next one."

"Are you worried you're going to see him?"

"Worried I'm going to see my dead dad doing a zombie march with the other dead miners from Hope Cemetery, down Merchant Street, to Rock of Ages quarry to go back to work?"

He paused like he'd planned to try and put it more delicately than that. Then shrugged. "Yeah."

"Everyone I know says that's just inmates from the state corrections facility picking up trash. If someone seems sure they've seen someone, I'm sure that's all it is. The location makes sense. All they need is an active imagination and the desire to make something totally unrelated all about them. I swear, everyone here wants Barre to be just like Roswell."

"You think the inmates collect trash in the middle of the night, though?" Charlie raised his eyebrows at her, sucking on his straw.

"I dunno." She smiled playfully and shrugged. "I don't run a prison. But anything makes more sense than dead people walking, right?"

"Not if you got an open mind."

"Really? Is *that* what you're saying you have? You're asking a bereaved kid about her undead dad because you've got an open mind?"

Charlie raised his eyebrows in response to her snark. "Just concerned is all. Also, you're hardly a kid anymore, are you?" He tapped his fingers, mouthing numbers, calculating her age.

"Thirty-six, Charlie." She smiled sadly. "But I'll always be my dad's kid." God, how cheesy. She shifted her weight and set her purse down on the bar. "Why do you believe this stuff, anyway?"

Charlie sighed. "A few years back, Barney Conover was driving North on Merchant, saw the miners walking toward him. He said his brother Gavin was with them, jaw slack and eyes glowing like a deer's."

"Niice." Her eyebrows shot up sarcastically. The minute she did it, she felt bad.

Charlie laughed a little, scandalized by that response. "Hey, this is for real! He was really shaken up!"

"You really believe him?"

"If only you'd have seen his face." He shook his head. "Barney's a sad, quiet kind of guy. And when he talks, people listen. I'm the only one he told, too. He wouldn't talk about it anymore. To anyone. I don't usually tell people about it, either. If you can believe that with the way I run my mouth."

Creepy. Kara chewed her lip. "What did he do—" She paused. "What did he *say* he did when he saw it? Did he pull over?"

"He did, but by the time he got out of the car, everyone was gone. Like they got spooked by the car, then took off running."

"Then what?"

"Barney, he looked around a little while, but didn't find anyone. Said he could feel eyes on him though. Then the air got really cold, and he thought he heard the trees crying."

"*Trees* crying?" Kara's heart sped up.

"Yeah, like the sound of crying, but really high up. You know how tall they are up by your folks' house. The sound was just echoing around, way up there. Like it was bouncing between the treetops and the godforsaken sky."

Kara shifted abruptly, then stilled in her seat. "Right by my parents' house?"

Charlie slurped down the rest of his drink. He set the glass down gently and leaned back, folding his hands to his chest. "Lots of guys who work at the quarry say they hear that sound by their house at night. Miners living all over town, even the ones who live right on the outskirts. Like they're a heart attack and six feet away from the same fate. I have yet to hear other locals claim they've heard it."

Why did such a specific sound spring to mind when he said trees crying? Like a scream stuck at a fever pitch? *How can I literally hear it? Feel it, right now?*

"What are you saying to Kara?" Alec's voice came suddenly from the kitchen, low and threatening. So scarce, it just barely cut in front of the clattering of steel on plates.

Alec's jaw was stiff, and he shifted a little to the side, which meant his patience had basically fallen quickly off a very high cliff. She'd known him since grade school, and though his childhood hadn't been the easiest, she'd still only seen this look a handful of times. This time, it was in her defense.

Whatever paper-fake happiness she'd taped up since her dad died torched itself. Something else entirely swelled inside her. An unspeakable, giddy, pining ache. She smiled a hello, but the smile felt too big, especially for all that was going on today. What they were talking about.

"All okay?" His throat sounded raw. His green-gray eyes were already set on her, waiting. Searching, checking her reaction to the conversation. A pained expression, framed by his longish dirty blond hair. He rubbed his jawline, his hand making a scratchy sound against his close-shaven beard, then set his mouth in a hard line.

Alec quirked an eyebrow when she didn't answer right away.

"Yeah. I'm okay." Her guts melted. *What the hell is going on?* She tugged absently at the zipper on her jacket.

"You probably heard enough to know what we're talking about," Charlie said.

"Maybe now's not the best time to tell her this." The gravel was present in his throat this time. He crossed his arms over his black apron and white t-shirt.

Charlie doubled down, gently. "If you believed, you'd be on my side, Alec. But with stories like that? The crying sound, and the marching dead? I hate to say it, but that's what I believe is gonna happen to me when my time comes."

"Why don't you just move? Or find a plot at any other cemetery? Do you have a plot at Hope?" Alec asked.

"I don't have any savings, Alec. I can't retire. I can't afford to move. I can't afford another place to be buried. I've got nowhere to go."

"There's always cremation," Alec offered.

"Cremation!" Charlie made a disapproving noise in the back of his throat. Alec shrugged.

Kara scrunched her forehead. *Trees crying.* Mom had said that sound was just stray cats. She pressed her lips together, trying to smooth the shake in her lower lip. "You don't need to defend me, Alec. We've all lived here long enough to be used to these bullshit stories."

That's it. All of it. All bullshit. Bullshit, bullshit. *It wasn't stray cats, though. The sound careened down the fireplace. Made my teeth ache.* She remembered those nights, and how long they were. She had to avoid the creaky board in the threshold, or she'd wake her mom. She'd sleep in the sleeping bag laid out by their bed. Dad would have his arm over the bed so she could hold his hand, know he was there. It was the only way she could keep her eyes closed without panicking. It went that way almost every night when she was a kid.

How tired he must have been. He'd fill that two-quart thermos to the top with coffee every morning. But he didn't seem to mind his job of helping her. Watching over her. Making her feel safe.

She thought about the coffin moving before his service. *You done?* she'd asked him. And she thought about the idea that the noise by her house was fate, calling for his eternal soul. And now whatever made him who he was, was *gone.* Forever gone.

And the worst of it all: his body. The one that walked in her house, with that slow and heavy gait down the hall. The one that laughed at her bad jokes. That held her hand when she was scared, was now a slowly rotting instrument that lurked the streets of her town while she slept. That wasn't something she was willing to accept. *I can't just sit here. I gotta do something.*

"Hey, Kara, I'm just looking out for you." Charlie reached for his glass, remembered it was empty, then withdrew his hand awkwardly. "You don't believe me, I understand. I just wanted you to hear the whole story in case you hadn't. Do what you want with the information. You're your own person."

You done? The phrase echoed. Her mind was a vindictive child, toying with her. She'd waited in the hospital until he had moved on. In the funeral home, she'd waited until the coffin stopped moving. What if he wasn't done? What if he was stuck? Couldn't move on?

"I don't need you to tell me whose person I am." Kara couldn't believe she was going to do this, but was also sure she had no other choice. She was going to head back to the cemetery, alone, to check on her dad.

If he wasn't sleeping, well, she didn't know what she'd do.

2

DEATH DAY

The day Kara's father died was the last weekend of September that felt like summer. Not only was it hot, but the air was oppressively thick. It pressed itself inappropriately against her and smelled strongly like cracked pepper. Whenever she wasn't working at the restaurant, she spent most of her time at the hospital with him, on the outskirts of town.

As she had throughout his long illness, she'd take occasional breaks outside to eat a couple granola bars and have some coffee. The back of the hospital had an overlook similar to something a hotel might have. A small meandering creek ending in a gazebo and a pond. The whole area was graced by a grove of mature oak and fir trees. When she grew distraught, she'd sit out back in one of the splintered old deck chairs and stare without seeing, only vaguely aware of her surroundings.

She'd turn his ring around and around her finger. The circle in the ring was formed by a snake eating its own tail. A morbid image, but with two tiny, gorgeous, turquoise eyes set in its head. And the act of spinning his ring, feeling the worn metal against her skin, and caressing the small interruption of the eyes with her thumb, stilled things, somehow. Like a wordless mantra. Smoothing the ripples of her soul.

Being late September, the cicadas shrieked their usual chorus. The way they ratcheted up, then wound down reminded her of the sound of her father fighting for the breath that he knew would soon leave him.

That day, she felt like they were jeering. The sound hurt her ears.

At the time, she didn't know it would be his last day.

3
HOPE

Kara would never get used to the size of Hope Cemetery. So elaborate. They called it a *museum of monuments*. Miners, townsfolk, rich and working class: all reserved their plots here in earnest. Yet in the dark, the pressing silence blanketed the place, easy as you please, just like any other graveyard.

Getting to her dad's plot was proving to be a damn chore. It felt like it took longer at night. Maybe because she couldn't see her endpoint in the dark.

Alongside and all around, giant arched pediments spanned six graves wide. Angels in every style imaginable loomed like a band of mismatched sentinels. At night, even the more modern graves—racing cars and airplanes—seemed to float in some ghostly space, in their own universe, wiped of any suggestion of roaring engines. Of fire. Of life.

They were stone, and stone was devoid of all that.

Pondering Angel, Dad called this one. Chin in hand, elbow resting against knee. Tonight, it didn't look like pondering. It looked like waiting.

"Who waits at a grave?" she asked out loud.

As soon as she'd spoken, she wished she hadn't.

"*I'm* not waiting," she raised her eyebrows at the angel, clarifying. "*I'm* just visiting."

"Two visits in one day," a voice came from close by. "I should be so lucky once I shuffle off to my eternal rest."

Kara clamped a hand to her mouth, muffling a scream.

Immediately after, she recognized the voice. "Alec!" she shouted. "What the hell!" She stared at him for a full minute, just scanning his face, as though making sure it wasn't going to change on her.

"Hey," he grinned wider. "You okay?" His eyes searched hers. His face dropped, forehead knitted in worry.

"I *was* okay until you scared me!"

"I did, huh?" He pressed his lips together. He looked down, then back up at her. "Were you really okay, though? Before I scared you?"

"Uhh," she chewed the corner of her thumbnail. Considered telling him.

"Cause you're walking around a cemetery at night—where your dad was just buried—and you're talking to statues."

Kara sighed. "Well, all I ever do is give Charlie shit for his stories. He was telling me about the zombie miners like he tells anyone who will listen. But then he mentioned something about the trees crying by my parents' house, which made me think. I had trouble sleeping at night when I lived there as a kid. I used to hear this ungodly sound, way up in the trees. *Every night.* I didn't even think of it as crying until today, but it makes total sense." Her heart was in her throat again.

She rubbed her face with her hands, exasperated by how absurd she must sound. "I know it's weird, but I need to check on my Dad." She left out the part where she needed to learn what could make that sound. And what it could want with her dad and the other miners. "You followed me?"

"Yeah, I did." Gently, he made a fist and held it in his other hand, then took a step back. "Sorry. Was it too presumptuous to assume I should come?"

This was too weird. Could she ask him to come with her to her dad's grave? She raised her eyebrows.

He nodded, his face set, then looked at his shoes. Like he thought she didn't want him there.

"If anyone was going to follow me, I'm glad it was you," she said, her face heating.

What was wrong with her? Why did she say it like that? Like she was flirting? Was she like, sad-randy or something?

"Yeah?" he asked, holding his lip between his pointer and his thumb. He always did that when he was thinking, or focusing.

Wow. Hot. "Yep." Ugh.

He let his hand drop. "In that case, I'm glad I skipped out on work. Sorry again."

"Hey, you offered me an out, right?"

"Yeah."

"So, we're good."

Alec made a small "hmm" sound in agreement. They stood quietly in front of another large statue.

She waved her hand vaguely toward it and then folded her hands in front of her. *Saint Lucy*. The statue was wrapped in robes, holding a bowl and a palm branch. The stone where her eyes should've been was blank and smooth. Despite having no eyes, her expression made her look indifferent, almost like her face was shrugging. That seemed a strange choice for any saint, with or without the eyes.

"What's in the bowl, do you think?"

Kara smiled, pressing her lips tightly together. "Her own eyes," she said quietly, then smiled at him, waiting for his reaction.

Alec turned the corners of his mouth down and nodded slightly. "Ohh, her own eyes," he said casually, then looked at her, eyebrows raised. He appraised the statue's face, then looked at Kara. "That's pretty messed up," he whispered.

"Isn't it?"

"We should probably get to your dad's grave."

He started walking again, turning sideways a bit to make sure she followed.

"Do you have to get back to work?"

"No." His voice lilted up at the end like it was a question.

She laughed, taking a few tentative steps forward. "So why do we have to hurry up?"

"I don't know. I'm tired."

"You're rushing me through my graveside visit?"

"No."

"Alec." She stopped dead and crossed her arms, waiting for him.

"What?" He sighed, rubbing the back of his neck.

"You're not rushing because you're tired. So why are you rushing? Spit it out."

"I just thought this might not be the best place right now."

"And why is that?"

"I dunno. I don't know that I believe Charlie's stories, but I was worried about you hearing things like that and then being out here by yourself. But then I didn't want it to come off like I was telling you what to do."

"So you don't believe?"

"I've heard stories, but it's hard to believe."

"I remember hearing that these things weren't always happening. My dad said back when they were first digging, before masks and all, the miners were breathing in that granite dust. Getting Silicosis and dying. That's when things got weird. Everyone was scared, especially anyone who knew someone working in the quarry. But they couldn't just leave. It was the town's lifeblood. The activity started around then." She paused. "Or, that's what they say."

"Wasn't enough to convince your dad to keep his mask on at work, though, was it?" Alec said, sadly.

"Yeah, a lot of them put comfort over safety. And for that haunted-town stuff, people like Charlie seem to be so adamant." Kara shook her head. "And you know I've never believed it before. But I guess after Charlie said what he said, this is the closest I've ever listened to a haunted Barre story. I guess I came here hoping to confirm that absolutely nothing is going on. Nothing at all. Whatsoever."

"So can we say hi, and get out of here?" he whispered back.

"You forget that I'm here to make sure nothing is happening, right? Because if I leave, my dad doesn't leave with us. So if I hurry up, that defeats the purpose, right?"

"Right. We're almost at the gravesite though, right?" he asked, a little too lightly. A couple crickets chirped, with a bunch more chiming in right after. She realized she was sweating in her jacket.

"Yeah, it's just up ahead." She slipped out of her jacket as she walked, tying the sleeves around her waist. The moon was full, or practically full. She could never tell for sure, but it was bright and it glared down at them, playing over the fog that felt its way slowly across the grass and between the monuments. The moon brightened the fog, making it look almost solid.

"Yup," he took another breath and held it, as though he was going to say something else.

"What's up?" she asked gently.

"Even before tonight you've seemed a little distant. Is there anything else you want to talk about? Like, solid-earth missing-your-Dad stuff? Or just generally processing?"

"Well, besides . . . all the other stuff?"

"Yeah, if there's more, tell me."

She stared at him for a minute. The air smelled fresh, like when it's morning and the dew is soaking the grass.

She thought she could smell the mud, now. A wet, earthy smell.

"That last day in the hospital, my dad didn't talk to me at all. His breathing was getting worse and worse, and he wasn't conscious. Sometimes he made mumbling sounds or moved around, but he never addressed me or anything. It was upsetting and honestly, a really long, sad, boring day. He died around dinnertime. And when he went, yeah, the heartbeat monitors went flat and everything, but it just felt like he'd been trapped inside his own body that last day. Like his body was suppressing him. And when he finally died, I could feel him slip out of there, and then just hover about the room. Not a ghost so much as a general presence, I guess."

"You didn't tell me you were there when he died," Alec said quietly. He lifted his hand toward hers slightly, turned his palm toward her, and extended his fingers.

"I called you right after to tell you he died, but I guess I left out the fact that I was there. I think I was still processing." She stared at his hand. It was an invitation, she knew. There was nothing else this could be. But what if it was something else and she just grabbed his hand and it got weird?

Don't think, she commanded herself. *Just do it.*

She caught him by the fingers. They were big, and rough, and warm. She shuddered.

"You okay?" he asked.

She took a deep breath, held it, and looked up at him. He was watching her eyes. She bit her lip and looked down, smiling, still grasping his hand. Her blood chugged in her temples.

"Sorry, you were saying?"

"Yeah, so," *what was I talking about?* She shook her head. "That feeling stayed with me until the funeral. Once we buried him, though, I couldn't feel him around anymore." She sniffed. "So I came back here, hoping I could get that feeling back. But I wanted it to be peaceful, and not . . . like what Charlie described."

He laced his fingers through hers, cocking his head to the side. "And how do you feel now?"

She hummed in thought. "I feel like, if you hadn't found me, I'd feel very alone right now."

Kara's head had gone dizzy. Looking at his face this close, with the night sky behind him, while touching his hand, felt alien. At least *partly* due to the setting.

Again, that warmth enveloped her, and her stomach turned softly, in a feeling akin to homesickness; but that homesickness was for Alec, while he stood right there. It was like everything would go dark if she didn't get even closer.

He turned his body toward her, rested his other hand over her shoulder, as though honoring her silent prayer.

The crickets went silent.

Her guts dropped. But this time, it was the way the darkness shifted just five yards behind Alec. It parted to produce a hulking pale shape, performing a fast, crooked, clod-footed march.

"Ah!" she choked out, trying to react. She pointed too late. As impossibly big as the shape was, by the time Alec turned his head, the figure had slipped silently behind the Saint Lucy statue and disappeared.

A loud cracking sound came from in front of them. An unfamiliar feminine voice materialized.

> *The heart of the world thrums*
> *Loud and uneven, a heavy stunted bass line.*
> *You'll feel it, you'll see it in the ground.*

Kara screamed, grabbed Alec's arm and backed away from the statue. The ground roiled at their feet, dirt turning and rolling over itself, the grass folding under. They looked around in the scant light. The sounds, the movement, covered the entire cemetery for as far as they could see.

It stirs the dead who aren't sleeping,
They rake the dirt, they turn the earth.

The earth rumbled loudly, yet the voice was even, steady, sure, like it played in her own head.

Kara's heart was in her throat. Her hand had gone sweaty. She pulled at Alec and looked into his wild eyes.

"Let's go." Panic throttled her voice. "There's something behind Saint Lucy. A *huge,* white . . . thing." There was no right word for it.

His eyes were wide and disbelieving. He nodded. "Let's get to a more open area," he shouted, gesturing to the tall monuments that could topple at any second.

No sooner had Alec pointed, than the shaking stopped. He let go of her hand, venturing back toward the monument in a quick jog.

"Alec, *stop!*" Her voice was hoarse, terrified.

Alec gave Saint Lucy a wide berth and walked around to the other side of the statue.

Kara gasped.

He shook his head. "Nothing's there." His voice was shaky, like he hadn't been sure what he'd find until he checked.

"I'm afraid to even ask. Did you hear the voice?" Was none of this real? What was wrong with her?

"I didn't hear a voice, no." He furrowed his eyebrows at her. "What did it say?"

"Something crazy about the heart of the world stirring the dead." She paused, heading toward the statue with shaky steps. "What happened here?" Saint Lucy's arms were broken off at the wrists. The bowl lay in the dirt, hands still attached.

"Hm," Alec said. "Must have cracked off in the earthquake."

Her gaze darted around, frantically. "The eyes are gone."

"When you told me about the eyes, I just assumed they were *symbolically* in the bowl."

"No way. Testa & Orlando Monuments? They don't leave anything to the imagination. They *carved* the eyes."

"Seriously? You've seen it?"

"*Yes,* Alec," her tone was sharp. I've *seen* the eyes."

"The earthquake cracked her hands clean off; maybe the eyeballs rolled away or something?"

"I don't think so," she said firmly, then felt bad. "This is all too weird. Let's just get out of here." Kara's eyes darted everywhere as they walked quickly back to the parking lot. The figure, the thing that may not be real, wasn't anywhere around that she could see, but there were so many places to hide.

***

Kara tossed her keys in the bowl by the apartment door, rushing straight for Tennyson's room. Every second alone felt like an emergency.

"Heya." She put her hand against the doorframe to Ten's room. Her whole body trembled.

Kara stepped all the way in the room, double-checking the dark hallway behind her. She wanted to talk about anything except what had just happened. With a shaky foot, she poked at a pile of crumpled clothes in the doorway. She cleared her throat. "You ever gonna get these dry cleaned?"

"Eventually." Ten stared down at her phone. "All my patients only want to do phone calls lately, y'know? So I haven't gone out, really." Her eyes met Kara's, and she tilted her head in concern. "Are you doing okay?" She sat up in bed, holding her cell phone to her belly. Her room always smelled like fake raspberries. A sweet, soft smell.

Suddenly, Kara *did* want to talk about it. "Eh, nope." Her voice shook some more. "Did you feel the earthquake?"

"An earthquake? No. That's . . . rare."

"Yeah. I was at the cemetery with Alec."

"Yeah, I know. We all were."

"No, like, again, tonight."

"You and Alec. Alone at the cemetery, tonight?"

"Tonight."

"Just now?"

"That's exactly what I mean. Yes. Just now, *to*-night. That's not the point I'm getting at, though."

Ten wobbled her head side-to-side and grinned. "What are you getting at, then?"

"Well, I guess you could say I kept running away from my problems, and they kept following me." What could she even say? "I was at the shiva, then I got upset and went to see Alec at work. Then Charlie was telling me about the dead miners urban legend thing, so I left."

"Why?"

"To check on my dad, I guess?"

"To make sure he was still buried?"

"I know. It sounds stupid."

"Don't use that word. *Stupid*. It's . . . stupid."

"Is that what you say to your patients?" Kara managed a shaky smile.

"A little more formal, but yes."

"Do your patients hear voices? See stuff?"

"Some do, yes. Why?"

"Any tea to spill about that topic?"

"Can't spill any tea, but you're *very* funny." Ten put her phone facedown on the bed. "Why?" she pressed.

Kara's phone buzzed. "Oh, it's Alec." She let go of the doorframe and headed for her room.

"Ughh, saved by the bell. Alec, huh? You better go somewhere *private*," Ten crooned.

"Hush please, Ten," Kara sang back. She answered the phone, walking down the hall to her room.

Alec's voice was low and quiet. "I got home *really* quickly."

"Well, there's not usually much traffic at 9 p.m." She walked across her room, decorated with the heavier, darker furniture her mom had gotten rid of ten years back. An old traditional sleigh bed stained so dark it was almost black, with a dresser to match. Thick rope-twist moldings ran across the edges of the headboard and footboard. They were abominations, clearly designed to be Traditional but with the dark color and elaborate details, they looked almost Gothic.

She loved them. The only thing that bugged her was the fact that they both flirted with being too big for the space. She jabbed her toes regularly on the stupid corners if she tried to rush around her room too quickly.

"I'm not talking about traffic," Alec said. "I started the car and got on the road and straightened the car out, and like, I was home immediately. I totally blanked out on the drive home."

"What are you talking about?" Kara scrunched her face at herself in the mirror as she sat on the bed.

Alec paused. "I dunno. Did you *just* get home?"

"Yeah, why?"

"Because I got home and had to sit and wait twenty minutes before calling you. Because I knew you'd be driving."

"Alec, I can talk and drive—"

"That's not the point. My ten-mile drive took me *seconds*.

"Jesus."

"Something weird is going on. I just sat there, shocked for a few minutes."

This was worrisome. What was next? They left the cemetery but the weirdness followed them. "That's really scary." She glanced at the coat at the foot of her bed. Her dad's dark green battle jacket. Extra large. A small half-gasp escaped her throat, a silent sob. The hollow feeling in her chest expanded.

Alec hadn't heard her. "Also, on the way out, did you see the statue of Gabriel?"

She took a deep breath, clearing her throat. Resetting. "What statue?" She stared absently at her nails, avoiding looking at the coat.

"You know, that sculpture of Gabriel, with his horn?"

"I didn't." She let out a sardonic laugh, then whispered: "I was running for my life."

"Well, his horn was gone. Not on the ground. Not nearby. Just gone."

"Oh, hell." She shoved back her hair with a hand and sighed.

"Anyway, though, you need rest."

"I suppose."

"Tell me you're gonna be okay."

"I'm gonna be okay."

"You're working tomorrow, right?"

"Yeah, Wednesday morning, always."

"Okay well, see ya there."

"Oh hey, Alec?"

"Yeah?"

What could she say? This was all so messed up. Kara was terrified for her dad, but didn't want Alec to think she was being weird. She wanted him to believe her, and help her figure things out, but you can't *make* someone believe something like that.

And there was this new thing she was admitting to herself. She was into Alec. Wasn't she? She couldn't stop staring at him back at the restaurant. And at the cemetery, when he'd held out his hand, her heart did backflips. And then the minute they touched, all hell broke loose.

She used to feel like things were good. She had everything under control. Best friend. Roommate. Dad: alive and not being zombified by some strange magic.

What the hell do I even say about any of this?

"Sorry about everything tonight." *Christ.*

"S'okay. Your dad died and we were in an earthquake. You get a pass."

"Sleep good, okay?"

"You too."

Kara stretched toward the footboard, dragging her dad's jacket over herself. Lying on her side, she tucked her knees into her chest and let the jacket cover everything but the tips of her toes. The acrid smell of diesel oil floated over her, calling the memory of him back so heavily, it made her throat tight. She could practically hear his hoarse voice when he put the jacket over her shoulders for the last time.

She and her mom were in the parking lot of the hospital, dropping him off there to start hospice care. He'd insisted he didn't want to die in the house. As though him dying there would make it haunted. As though the place could ever feel right with him gone, anyway.

It was such a short drive the car hadn't had the chance to warm up yet. Her dad was winding down from another coughing fit. Sometimes she'd listen to him go, thinking the spell was about to end, but then it went on for another ten minutes. Other times, he'd sound about to die right then and there, but somehow stopped abruptly. Every time he coughed she sat there, evaluating it, wondering how much time he had left. She couldn't help it.

Her mom was turned away from her then, breathing quietly, deeply, staring out the passenger side window, clearly trying to hide the fact that she was crying. Kara saw the shake in her shoulders; the little visible hitch in her breath. She couldn't look away.

"Kaa'aa'raa," Dad had whispered playfully from the back seat, the tone peaking in the middle, all sing-song. He had seen her watching her mom. "She'll be okay," he said, putting a hand on each of their shoulders. "You guys will take care of each other."

Kara looked up at him, smiling weakly. Her mom faced forward now, dipping her chin to her chest, listening. "We will," Kara whispered.

"That's an order." He slung the jacket over her shoulders. "This hospital is hot, and I'm always getting hot from coughing. Hang on to this."

"It smells like you," Kara had said, matter of fact.

He laughed. "Oy. I'm sorry."

"No, it's good." It didn't smell like astringent. Like the hospital. Like the past few horrible weeks. It smelled like the quarry. Their life together when she was younger.

It smelled like the memory of Dad coming home.

His clothes held the smell of the diesel trucks they moved the stone with. When she hugged him, he smelled musty. Like rock dust mixed with dried sweat. She tried not to think of that same dust entering his lungs. Corrupting that human machinery that let him be around.

Kara squeezed her eyes shut, waiting for unconsciousness to come so she wouldn't feel the tickle of hot tears dripping off her temple and onto the bedspread.

***

Light and shadow shuddered across Kara's closed eyelids as she tried to fall asleep. She opened them and saw her pale, blank walls and cluttered dresser. The dark blue blinds against the white walls. She closed her eyes again, and the dancing shadows returned. Like a dark room with an ancient projector going.

Her hand twitched, then her foot, and she drifted off.

She was at the Rock of Ages quarry where her dad had worked. The quarry that supplied the granite for Hope Cemetery and half the world. A glow emanated from the stone, and from the milky turquoise water at the bottom of the quarry.

The moon is the quarry's nightlight, she thought. The air was quiet and still, and the air felt fresh on her cheeks, just like at the cemetery.

The loud, deep ringing of a bell rose from somewhere deep in the quarry. Somewhere she couldn't see. Her skull vibrated as if she'd been struck violently by the bell's mallet.

The second it quieted, and despite the violence with which it shook her, she realized, viscerally: the moment she was experiencing was *now*. Her body wasn't there, but she was watching the quarry in the present.

The bell rang again.

Everything in her shook. But now she possessed a sharp awareness of her own body, motionless, in her bed. She was still asleep, but the bell was pulling her body to get up. To come find it. To pick up her tools.

The bell quieted.

Tools? Do I have tools? Her memory answered her. No. This call is not for you.

Again, the bell rang. She was returned to the quarry, where she watched from above.

Fear joined her there, immediately.

"The things your father took from me," a voice half-growled, half-roared. She couldn't understand why. It was as though a lion had learned to speak.

"Who's that?" she asked, her voice muffled, as though it was only reverberating in her own head.

"He set my eyes into your ring."

"This is a dream."

"A dream is reality, living in your head," the voice snarled. "You mustn't touch that man again."

"What? Who do you mean? Don't touch Alec?" The black sky thundered. *Where's the lightning?* she wondered.

"Yes."

The lightning came late. Kara's entire field of view was white, except for a hulking, robot-like shape, metal framing stuffed and upholstered in something smooth, buttercream-white, and shiny. It stood on a platform of granite, so low that lake-water puddled on its surface. None of the granite had been mined that far down. That would take hundreds, or maybe thousands of years.

Just as she realized it could be sentient, it *moved*, ever so slightly. Its faceless head tilted stiffly, regarded her. It gestured next to it. To a giant, black triangular structure. Like some kind of ship.

Fear blossomed hot in her skull, spilled out her ears. She touched the strange liquid.

The fear was the same color as the figure.
Her eyes were heavy and warm.
The voice came again:

   "Remove these human feelings
   that fester in your head.
   Everything has changed. Look upon him again?
   You will see in his face all the faces of the dead."

4

ALL THE FACES
OF THE DEAD

Kara woke up to her blaring alarm and a muted white sky outside her window. The cemetery and the dream had settled tight and heavy in her chest.

Her goal last night had been to quell her fears about where her dad was buried. Since she'd visited, she vacillated between thinking she was losing it, and thinking a giant monster had stalked her and Alec in the cemetery—and later, in her dreams.

Could all this stem from the stress of losing Dad? Maybe not the churning dirt or the missing stone, but the weird dreams and what she hoped were hallucinations? The fear gripped her by the throat. Her stomach felt sour.

"I should ask Tennyson," she said aloud. Pushing her hair back, she shuffled to Ten's room.

Tennyson was out cold, but she looked like she'd wrestled something in her sleep; her black fleece blanket had fallen nearly all the way off. Her breathing was so loud it filled the whole room.

"After work, then," Kara said and ducked back out.

By the time she got to the restaurant, she was so anxious to talk to Alec that she almost called him when she didn't see his car. The thing he'd said about being transported immediately home unsettled her, too. She had to force herself to put her phone away.

She got inside and checked behind the bar. About ten pint glasses needed to be cleaned.

"Charlie," she groaned quietly. Was he worse drunk, or sober? He'd stopped drinking before she started working there, thank god. But still, whoever worked the bar last night must have been sneaking off to the kitchen to get a break from one of Charlie's routines, and hadn't finished washing everyone's glasses. She remembered him slurping down his drink last night. What was that, his third? Fourth? No doubt that's why the bar was untended when she came to visit.

She didn't usually mind Charlie so much, but he got to the others, lording his personal tastes over them, as though his top ten everything was a trophy that nobody could live up to. Shouting at them if they hadn't heard of Captain Beefheart or some bullshit.

Cleaning the glasses didn't bother her, though. It was the least she could do for the poor soul who'd worked last night. She tried to remember who was on the schedule Tuesday nights but couldn't.

"Whatever, it's all the same," she grumbled, and got to work filling the sinks. She dropped the blue sterilizer tablet in the third one and stared at it, willing it to dissolve. She liked the morning routine, especially because it was quiet. The calm before the rush. But this morning, as she worked the soapy glass over the oscillating brush, her mind raced. Wondering where

Alec might be, right now. *He's fine. He's safe. He's on the road and will turn right at the gas station at the corner. Any second, now. Then I'll hear the door and it'll be him.*

What do they call that again? It's a thing, I think. A time slip? What happened on that stretch of road that Alec didn't remember experiencing? How had no time passed from when he got on the road to when he got home?

Oh, fuck it. She clapped down the glass and wiped her hands, grabbing for her phone. Inside her waitress pouch, her finger swiped something small and metallic and she unearthed it. The ring she'd been holding onto since her dad got to the hospital. She slipped it over her thumb, and smiled sadly at how much room there was still to spare. She turned the ring with her pointer finger and looked at the gaping mouth of the snake that held its tail, closing the circle. The turquoise crystals that were its eyes gaped at her.

Dad's ring.

She wished she'd gone back to the hospital with it on a necklace so he could wear it again. Before he died, the thing had hung off his finger. If he kept wearing it, it'd slip off and he'd lose it.

For a minute, she pictured him before he got sick. Fuller. Fleshier. Louder. Back when the cough was just a sound that announced his coming down the hall, instead of the death knell it became.

He hadn't even ever used the word: Silicosis. When he'd gotten so sick he missed a bunch of work and needed help getting up to eat and go to the bathroom, what had he finally offered her? Just a "Whadayou think it is?"

She couldn't blame him, though. He was tired. Angry. She imagined that, even though he sometimes didn't wear his mask, even though he'd watched his friends die, there had to be a certain shock to it when the doctor confirmed it. When she grilled her mom, she'd said he'd only known for a week, but Kara was sure it was months.

So many people working in the quarry met the same fate. But that was the job, and the cost of it for many. She'd been so busy for the two weeks he was in hospice, and then the days after, planning the funeral.

Kara almost had to remind herself that her dad wasn't still waiting there at the hospital for her to come visit. She stared down at the electric blue sink water. The tablet sat at the bottom, being stubborn. Still only three-fourths dissolved.

Her phone buzzed, pulling her from herself. Her brain trilled with excitement. *Alec.* She slid the ring on her thumb and grabbed her phone from her pocket.

A notification from a delivery app. *Okay. Not Alec.*

She stared at the water again, then at the cups drying on a towel.

She poked at Alec's name on the screen and put the phone to her ear. Five rings, then voicemail. *Shit.*

"Darla? You up there?" she shouted.

"Mm-hmm," a muffled voice hummed from the loft area upstairs. Every morning, Darla sat up there in her too-hot office with her Excel 2007 spreadsheets and her crystals (green, for energy. Blue for *serenity!*) and her wax warmer. She was forty-fiveish. Weird, lovely, hilarious. And she sure knew how to pick a good scented wax. When she came downstairs, there better not be any horsing around.

"Can I come up please," Kara asked in monotone.

More muffled speech.

"I can't hear you! Can I please come up?"

"Yeah! Sure!"

Kara shuffled through the kitchen, offering a hurried hello to the prep guy, and ran up the narrow stairs to the stuffy second floor. The high windows threw sunlight up there like hot balls of fire. She passed between the shelves, stocked high with salad dressing boxes, liquor bottles, boxes of syrup for the soda machine. Old candle centerpieces collecting dust. By the time she'd walked the ten yards to Darla's office door, sweat prickled her forehead and she had to work for a deep breath.

"God, lady, how do you *stand* it up here?"

"You know me, I love the heat."

"What, do you not sweat or something?"

Darla smiled down, close-lipped at her spreadsheet and shook her head slowly, doing a slow little dance in her old wooden chair. "I glow, baby."

Kara sighed loudly. "Must be nice." She leaned an elbow on the doorframe, fiddling with her dad's ring.

"What can I do ya for?"

"Um, well. I didn't want to get Alec in *trouble*, per se, but—"

"What'd he do?"

"No nothing, I—"

"Are you *ratting out* your best friend?" Darla gasped facetiously, finally turning to Kara from her screen, eyes bugging.

"Of course I'm not. I just wanted to *ask you* if he happened to call in or anything today. Or like, maybe he's coming in late?"

Darla removed her hands from her mouth. "Nope. He's on the schedule this morning. And he did *not* call in." She checked her watch. "Oh hell, he's twenty minutes late already. He's never late."

Kara popped her lips, nodding. "See? That's what I'm saying."

"Did you try calling?"

"I did."

"Hmm, I don't know. Maybe try one more time?"

Kara nodded and unlocked her phone to call.

"Hey, what's that?" Darla pointed to the ring hanging off her thumb. "Those crystals are so pretty."

"Oh, it's—" Kara paused. "It was my dad's ring." She looked back down at her phone without calling. "Thanks for stopping by yesterday. It really meant a lot to me and my family."

"Oh of course, honey. I know how rough it is losing Dad."

"Yeah," Kara kicked at the ground. "Wanna see the ring?"

"Yeah, sure!"

Kara handed the ring over and dialed Alec.

"*Oh.* This is an ouroboros ring."

"Huh?" Kara scrunched her nose at Darla.

The phone rang once, and then stopped abruptly before the second. "Hey, Kara?"

"Sorry," Kara mouthed to Darla, holding up a finger. "Alec! Jesus! Where are you? You scared the shit out of me."

Alec laughed loudly. "I'm sorry! I slept through my alarm, can you believe that? I'll be there in ten, I mean, um," he cleared his throat. "Possibly no minutes."

"God, okay, good. I'll see you." Kara turned to Darla. "Hey. Sorry, I gotta go see him about something. He's almost here."

Pocketing her phone, she rushed down the steps and through the kitchen. Her heart raced. She realized the dream had really affected her, made her feel off.

Just seeing Alec would reset everything, she knew.

She thought about the time they first met. Kindergarten. He was the kid with the hand-me-downs who didn't talk to anyone at first. The first week, she bought a carton of milk, and then asked one of the cafeteria workers to warm it for her. She didn't think it was weird. Her mom always did that for her, for some reason. She liked it warm. The lady behind the counter asked her to repeat herself. She was sarcastic. The last thing Kara needed after staying home with her Aunt Sarah and never going to preschool. Aunt Sarah had taught her numbers and letters, kind of like a governess. So she hardly knew anyone except her close neighbors, and some family friends.

Alec laughed at her, too. At first. But when he saw she didn't like it, his expression grew serious. "Warm milk is probably okay," he told her in front of everyone. "My grandpa drinks it a lot. And he knows a lot about food."

"Are you saying I'm like an old person?" she asked, cautiously. She'd been on the brink of tears but it was subsiding.

"Some old people are cool. Others aren't, but some are cool," he informed her.

Later that day, he told her he didn't have any siblings, and never had anyone to play with. They were each others' advocates from that day, navigating the halls of public school together.

And she never did learn to like cold milk.

Kara threw open the restaurant door and ran across the covered bridge to the parking lot. She slowed as she saw his car door open, then suddenly felt stupid. What reason could she give him for running outside to greet him at his car? That was kind of weird.

I'll tell him I was worried. That's all. It'll be fine. He won't care. She walked closer to the car, until she was just a few yards from it.

"Hey Alec!" She tried to make her voice sound breezy and relaxed but she was breathing like a runner in a marathon. "Did it happen again?"

"Yep," Alec turned to face her, and she froze. Her hands shot out automatically in defense.

"Alec?" It wasn't quite Alec who stared back at her. A dirty white skull with big, dark rings around its eyes ending in two wide swoops, where the cheekbones quit. The eyes were set deep in that blackness, a greenish-gray with light brown around the iris, just like Alec's. It was even dressed like him.

It had ears, too. The skin was sort of there, but translucent, like the skull itself were a death mask, floating into focus. The nose insinuated itself gently over the gaping cavity in the center.

It wasn't possible. The thing's jaw dropped open a little as it walked casually around the back of the car. It laughed, gently. In Alec's voice. "Kaaara?"

She didn't respond. She was completely frozen.

The skull face staring at her in the middle of a parking lot, in the early morning daylight, grinned.

"Are you okay, Kara?" It took a step closer.

She backed up. She couldn't find one word to reply with. Who was it she'd be replying to?

"Hey!" Shadows gathered where his brow lines lived, showing concern. "What's *wrong*?" A few more slow steps.

"Wait, stop." She moved away again. How could she explain what was going on? It felt like it might actually be him. But why was this happening?

The jaw was loosened now, a glistening row of top teeth parted in response. Confusion, maybe. The sunlight shot through the opening in his cheekbone, reaching down, molesting his shadow.

The thing took a step toward her.

She shuffled backwards further. "Please, *please* stay where you are."

"Can you tell me what's going on? Please?" He sounded scared now, touching his face cautiously with his fingers. "Why are you staring at me like that?"

Because her best friend was late, and now he was dead. He was clearly dead. He drove here, *dead*. Right? And somehow, also standing right there, asking questions, unaware of how dead he was.

She had to get someone. She had to bring someone with. To have them confirm . . . what exactly? That it was true? That he was dead? Undead? Or completely alive and fine, and she had lost her entire mind?

She couldn't look at him like this anymore. She ran across the covered bridge. Yanked open the door to the restaurant.

"Kara," his voice was soft and pleading. "Stay here with me. Don't leave."

She stood behind the door, watching him through the glass.

"Take a breath. And tell me why you're looking at me like I'm going to kill you. *Please.*"

"Alec, your face is a skull, man." Kara held her mouth and sobbed. She couldn't believe the words that came out of her. Couldn't believe what her eyes told her. But now that he'd asked her to stay, she couldn't run inside. Couldn't leave him. She came out from behind the door again, but kept her foot there as a stopper. Just in case.

"What are you *talking* about?" He felt his face again, apprehensively. "My face is a—" he stilled, putting his hands out in front of him. "Okay, I don't feel it. But I believe you. I believe that's what you're seeing. I'm staying right here. Go get Darla. We'll see what she says. You're gonna be okay, Kara. I'm fine, and you're gonna be okay."

Kara wiped her nose on her sleeve and sniffed. She half-turned to walk through the door, then looked back at him. She pictured coming back out for him, and he'd be crumpled to the ground, real-dead. Or just disappeared. Gone forever.

"You're real, though? You're really you, and you're real?"

"Kara, listen. I look weird to you, right? But I'm breathing." He put his hand to his chest. "I can feel my heart beating. I'm alive. Literally nothing could make me leave this spot before you come back."

She took a deep breath and held it, then exhaled and spoke. "Goddammit," she whispered, closing her eyes. "Just come in with me."

"Are you sure?"

"Yeah. Come in with me. We'll go inside and say good morning, and we'll see if everyone acts normal, or starts screaming."

Alec laughed one of his easy laughs. "I like that idea."

***

The entrance of the restaurant was still deserted. Darla hadn't come down yet to fuss with the liquor bottles or straighten the tables. "Let's go in the kitchen," Kara said.

She turned, and Alec was *directly* behind her. Her breath hitched and her hand shot to her chest. The lights were low in the bar area, all the blinds were still shut. His skull glowed, softly. The darkness around his unblinking eyes made them look bigger and rounder, like he was gaping at her.

"Sorry," he whispered.

"S'okay," she managed. Speeding toward the kitchen doors. A dull ache had settled in next to the fear. She missed his face, horribly.

One problem at a time, she told herself.

They entered the kitchen. Nobody was up front by the grill station, either. Kara rounded the corner. Hugo was mixing a colossal batch of spinach pie filling with the mixing machine. She'd always marveled at how big the thing was.

"Hey, Hugo." She bit her lip and clasped her shaky hands together, wrestling down her nervous energy. It felt like a fifty-fifty shot how Hugo would react when he looked up. She didn't know what to say. "God, how much garlic did you put in that? It smells amazing."

"You don't want to know, and I don't want to remember." Hugo peeked up at her and smiled. "Lots of crushing." She watched his eyes intently, her heart racing. He must have noticed her expression, then caught the form standing next to her. She looked back at Alec and stepped away again. The fear held her by the throat this time. She hated turning around and seeing that behind her. It was like being startled all over again.

"*Hey,* man!" Hugo's eyes widened. "What's wrong with you?" Kara's breath caught as he grabbed a white dish towel off his shoulder and slapped Alec with it. "This filling is a family secret. *Get* out of my part of the kitchen. I'll call you back here when it's time to work the dough."

Alec laughed, harder than he normally laughed at anything Hugo said.

He's nervous too, Kara thought. *He was scared Hugo would see what I saw.*

Still grinning, those wide-open eyes were on her again.

Momentarily, she was mesmerized by how weird it looked. Then, she started to feel queasy.

"You know what? I'm actually not feeling that good." Kara's forehead was sweating. "I think I'm gonna call Ellie and see if she can come in early, work breakfast and lunch today."

"Oh, whaat, you smell my food and now you want to vomit?" Hugo held his hands out, his breath still short from his last gut buster.

Kara tried to smile. "Don't use that word, Hugo, please?" Kara pushed her hair back, trying to cool down. "I'm gonna sit down," she mumbled to Alec without looking at him. "Can you get me some water?"

"Yeah. I'll call Ellie for you. Anything else?"

"Nah," she whispered. Handing her phone over, she headed for the bar and climbed into the nearest chair.

She rested her elbows on the bar and her head in her hands. What the hell was happening? Would his face ever go back to normal for her? Her life had been completely derailed by her dad's death, but now this, this outlandish, insane thing blocked her from returning to normal. Was this punishment for going straight back to work? She felt sick when she looked her best friend in the eyes. She pictured the normal Alec. The way his eyes smiled when he looked at her. Closed mouth, longish blond-brown beard. Like his eyes were—

A glass dragged along the bar. "Thanks," she croaked, and sipped at the water.

"Ellie was very happy to help."

"Of course she was." She held her hands back over her eyes, avoiding looking at him. "She's a doll." Removed her hands to take another sip, but kept her eyes focused on the glass.

His voice sounded level, serious. "Kara, you should really take a few days to rest."

She didn't know how to answer. She was pissed he'd suggested it before she'd announced it. Now she couldn't take credit for the idea. "How many is a few?"

"Three days. A week, maybe."

Bullshit. One or two, tops.

She couldn't look at his face, so she stared at the tattoo on his left bicep. Gjallarhorn. An old illustration of the Norse horn that Heimdall blew to signal Ragnarök. He'd been worried people would equate the tattoo with white supremacy, somehow. She'd laughed and told him nobody would know what the hell that thing was.

Alec's arms flexed, and . . . she was staring. Even without looking up, Kara could feel his eyes on her. She shook her head at him. "Taking a break doesn't make sense here. What about solving this problem? Figuring out why all this is happening?"

"I have no idea. All I know is, I should start work, you should probably rest, and Ten doesn't work today, right? So she can hang out with you the whole time. And I can call and check in on breaks."

"Alec, it's nothing, really. I just feel like shit."

"Yeah, you feel like shit, *and* that other thing, where you can't even look at me."

"I feel like you're treating me like a child."

"I'm sorry. I don't want you to feel that way. But your dad just died. And now, frankly, you're seeing parts of me I never even gave you consent to see." He hummed a small laugh. "Seriously, though. It's what you would tell me to do if this happened to me."

Kara pictured the situation in reverse. "Yeah, but you wouldn't listen."

"You'd *make* me listen."

"Hmm, yeah. I totally would."

"Just take a few days off. You literally took *one* day off for his funeral. And that was yesterday."

"Okay, okay, I get it. I'll ask Darla."

"Ask Darla what?" Clanging noises sharpened from the kitchen as Darla pushed the door open, leaning against the threshold between kitchen and bar.

"Can I take a few days off?"

"Girl, I was waiting for you to ask me that. You're so stubborn. *Why* are you so stubborn?"

Kara laughed. "I was born this way." She lifted her head and looked at her boss. Darla smiled with her head crooked, like one would smile at a puppy who kept pissing the rug, but was also incredibly sweet.

"I'm proud you gathered enough sense to take a few more bereavement days." She walked over to Kara and worked her fingers open, placing her dad's ring in her palm. "And can I be extra nosy and suggest you put this ring on a chain or get it fitted so you don't lose it? You just buried the guy, maybe it'd feel good to keep his ring with you."

Kara closed her fingers around the ring, pressing it against her palm. For maybe the thousandth time that day, she thought about death.

Sunday, she'd lost her dad. Today, death was quite literally everywhere.

5

INDRID COLD

My name is Indrid Cold.

That is the name I give myself on this earth, and in this body. This body that sweats and whose mouth tastes like the stinking primordial orifice it crawled out of on its birth date. I am driving through a town where the trees are young. Though really, to me, even the oldest of trees are young. Life on this earth is an incessant and infuriating pounding of a drum. A collective heartbeat that will not quit; not in this moment, of course, but in the next. Maybe by the time these fledgling trees grow and then perish.

To the trees, I do bear reverence, but for the humans, I hold a disdain. It is their disgusting costume I must wear. It is their language I must speak. These strange pitches and how the skin flaps inside must vibrate for me to make the proper sounds.

I feel I am getting closer. I will have to speak again soon. I groan, which also vibrates the flaps of flesh. So I sigh, and open the window. The breeze blows clean and the tips of the lazy reeds ripple like the waters of this place, with the same rustling and hushing sounds.

My lungs fill with a much better oxygen than what I'd been breathing in the vehicle.

My, I'm cranky today.

In this body, I must bare my teeth to hold the skin on these sallow cheekbones. Those who see me react in fear, yet they also see that I'm grinning. I should forgive them, for what do they know? But as I explained, I am very old and I rarely forgive, even when it's due.

I'm a bit lost now, but I'll know my heading better when I grow nearer. The twins. The one who chooses the dead and the other who guides them. It is inconsequential to I. I am here to witness the prequel to a great event, the one that the death twin dreamt of.

But for now I must drive these two horrid vehicles: the meat, and the metal.

Ah, well.

6

DEPOSIT

"You're right, it is pretty peaceful here."

Tennyson Davies sat with her legs pretzeled, flicking rocks into the pond near the hospital. "It doesn't bug you that your dad died right over there?"

"It's on my mind, yeah. But not more than it was at the funeral."

"Did this help at all?"

"Huh?" Kara turned back to Tennyson. She was flickering in and out of being able to focus on Ten. Mostly, she was spacing out, staring at the railings on the gazebo. "Sorry, did what help?"

"Hello?" Ten chuckled quietly. "Did *coming here* help? Do you feel any more at peace?"

"Well, I woke up feeling like complete garbage and I guess I feel spacey, but less garbage-y?"

"That's something. Are you missing Alec?"

"I am." Kara could feel Ten stealing glances at her. She was afraid to meet her gaze. Instead, she hunted for more tiny rocks to whip into the water. A startled frog dove into the water and then, for a couple of minutes, all was quiet.

"I was waiting to find out who was going to bring

up the skull thing," Ten started. "And you haven't yet, and I'm feeling nosy, so I'm bringing it up first."

Kara turned toward Ten, but her gaze was stuck on a bald patch of dried, cracked dirt, where the grass wouldn't grow.

She hugged her knees and kicked her heel against the ground. "Yeah, I was definitely avoiding bringing it up," she said quietly.

"You know, I have patients who go through that stuff, too. I'm a good listener."

"Yeah, but it's different, isn't it?" Kara rubbed her face, scruffing up her hair and eyebrows. "I'm not your patient and I really don't want to talk about it."

"You don't want to. Doesn't mean you shouldn't," Ten pushed.

"I don't like feeling like I'm your patient. Is that really going to help me?"

"No offense, but yes, obviously. As opposed to not talking about it? Talking about it is supposed to help."

"Well, you already know what happened, sort of."

"Sure. Alec told me. But can he really tell your story? He couldn't see it, could he?"

"No, I guess not." Kara's hands were shaky again. She grabbed them tighter, hugged her knees closer. "The reason I really don't want to talk about it?"

Ten tipped her head, inviting her to continue.

"It's because I'm afraid to ask what it means."

"You mean the fact that you saw something that wasn't real?"

"Yeah."

Ten shrugged. "It can mean you're just going through a really tough time. Times of really intense stress can cause that. Or, you could have developed something more permanent." Ten shrugged. "But whatever it is, it's like anything else. It sucks, and the best way to make it better, or . . . less bad, is to do something about it. Get more information." She paused. "Talk to *me*, and find out how to deal with what's happening to you."

"So I'm not going crazy though?"

"Crazy?" Ten snorted. "You know I don't like that word. So, no. You're not going crazy. You're just going through some shit, is all. Everything is people going through varying degrees of some shit."

"Yeah, I guess."

"Is that the first weird thing you noticed? The skull?"

"Well, no! The graveyard stuff, *hello?*" She waved her hand in front of Ten's face, mimicking the same thing Ten had pulled earlier.

She smiled, but it was quick. Then, right back to business. "And you're sure that was real?"

"Yeah. Alec was there with me. And, I mean, it was an earthquake."

"Remember, I didn't feel any earthquake."

"Yeah, but it happened. I know, 'cause it turned all the dirt in the cemetery. And I heard a voice, and saw that . . . *thing*."

"Did Alec hear or see anything?"

"No. But we both felt the earth shake, and saw the dirt turn, until the grass was swallowed down inside it. Then, two of the sculptures were broken with parts missing."

"So, the voice. Auditory hallucinations. You're sure you *both* saw the broken statues?"

"Yeah, I'm sure. I didn't even see the second sculpture; Alec did and told me about it after."

"Okay." Ten's face got really still and serious like she was processing all this.

Kara sighed, rubbing her eyes. The sun was beating down on her, and it stung her cheeks a little. The pond water had that dead bloated-fish stench. Why would she think talking this out with her therapist best friend would do any good? All it was doing was separating shit she was pretty sure really happened from crap that definitely happened because Alec had seen it too. "Yeah. It made sense at the time. Hey, can we take a break from this little therapy session? It feels more like a grilling than a session."

"I think that's a good idea. I might be a little pushier with you than with my patients." She smiled and nudged Kara's hand with hers.

Four large black-and-white birds landed in the water right in front of them, wings flapping violently, agitating the water. Kara and Ten shielded their eyes from the spray, their expressions bunching.

Kara squinted at the birds, wiping her mouth with the back of her hand. "Are those barnacle geese?"

"I dunno, I've never heard of those before."

"Yeah, they have that weird look to them. Their faces look kind of like puffins with the white faces and the black around the eyes and neck. I've been bird watching at this pond, on my little outside breaks, and I've never seen this breed here before.

"Man, normally I hate geese, but the feathers on their backs are so cool! They look like roof shingles or something."

"I know, right? I love the way they look."

"And there they are, making a deposit."

"What do you mean?"

"Well, they probably frequent multiple ponds. But when they stop in different places, sometimes they'll snag some fish eggs or plant life in one pond, then land in another, and deposit the eggs there. So yeah, they're like, placing some other fish's babies in another place, and that's how you can get all types of ecology introduced into a pond. I guess it's sort of like cross pollination. Just with hatching instead of blooming."

"You know what that makes me think of when you say, 'making a deposit?'"

"No, what?"

"Pooping." Kara took a large bite of a Red Vine in her fist.

"I definitely did not mean pooping. And where the hell did you get that Twizzler?"

"Not a Twizzler. Red Vine. Much more delicious," she said, holding a half-chewed bite in her cheek. "Had it in my pocket." She stuffed the other half in her mouth and kept chewing.

"Anyway," Ten rolled her eyes. "You like avoiding my point today, don't you? It's strange: we build ponds and stock them and then just assume they'll stay the same forever. And when we're proven wrong, our brain freaks out a little, and struggles to find something to grab onto. I bet your brain just glitched out a little, there. Your dad's gone, but now you've been assured that Alec's still kicking."

"Bad brain," Kara grumbled, rubbing her eyebrow.

"But you got Alec and me, and your mom."

"Ech, my mom. Don't remind me. Also, you forgot to mention my Red Vines."

"Yuck." Ten snorted and shook her head. "Those things give me a stomachache. Was there anything you wanted to do today?"

"Yeah, I was going to go buy a chain for my dad's ring so I can wear it."

"See? That's a great activity. Closure, and comfort. All in one. You're the new bearer of the ring."

Kara laughed and elbowed Ten. "Okay, I get it. Thank you. It's all wrapped up in a nice little package now."

"Feeling better already, I know." Ten winked at Kara and smiled. "You're welcome." They stood up to go. Ten hugged her from the side.

Ten was good at her job. And an incredible friend. But with Kara, she'd also been known to give safe answers when the real one was less than safe. And Ten talked about weird occurrences sometimes. She believed some of it. Wouldn't allow a Ouija board at their place.

Ten bit her lip and let her eyes flicker to the ground. Kara noticed.

7

THE RED TREE

Something was very wrong with Alec.

Kara's fist thumped against her chest as she speedwalked from the parking lot to the restaurant, gripping the ring tightly, its new chain hugging her neck. Alec's car wasn't there, but he said this was where he'd be. He'd answered her calls while she was off, but he wasn't very open.

She could guess why, though. All her calls were thinly veiled attempts to check up on him. How was he feeling? Did he believe her? No, *really*, did he? He'd insisted over and over that he felt fine, and that she needed a break dwelling on "all this." She'd pushed back, saying that she'd rather not take a break from "all this" if "all this" was tied up in any way with Alec's last days on earth.

He hadn't said so, but she knew he'd thought it: she was going crazy. Being off work wasn't helping, at least not past that first day she'd spent with Ten. There was nothing concrete to distract her. She found herself wanting to go to the cemetery again. To look for some sort of clue. Something, anything that could lead her to an answer. A projected end point to this. A guarantee things were going to be fine. Anything.

She entered the front door, heard Charlie stop in the middle of one of his loud gaspy laughs that was usually reserved for off-color jokes. He sat at his usual spot at the bar with some other regulars. She didn't acknowledge him, instead pushed her way into the kitchen. She had to find out which sucker had answered Alec's call to trade shifts, and why.

"Kara, that you?" Alec's deep, familiar voice came from behind the door.

The metal-salt scent of fish guts hit her like a wall. She held her breath, but it was too late. Her blood surged, delivering a full host of memories. Early mornings alone with Alec. That time she threatened to "cook his keys" and dropped them next to a hot pan, and he made this weird choked yelling sound. Like it was stuck in his throat and his body wouldn't let it out fast enough. They laughed until they cried. Until her chest hurt. She bit her lip to keep from laughing, but then stopped. Now there was a new companion to those memories: a heavy, burning sort of ache.

"Kara," he said again, low, like he was calling for her now instead of asking.

The honeyed tone of his voice saying her name is what did her in. Kara froze in place for a full twenty seconds. Finally, she stepped through the open door and saw Alec behind the counter, where he always worked.

"Hey, Alec." Her face melted into a grin. His face was his face again. He wore a worn-out wife beater, stretched and a little crooked at the shoulders. His arms, still muscular, still *insane*, tensed when he sliced at the fish in little, precise motions. A curly lock hovered over his eyes; his dark blond waves looked slept on, then swept carelessly aside, the strands climbing over each other, his thick beard trimmed shorter than when she'd last seen him. Her churning blood coupled with a familiar queasiness. Why did it feel like it had been so long since she'd last seen him?

"Damn, it's good to see you smile."

Her heart exploded. "I—who, me?" she squeaked.

"Does that bewildered look mean my face is back to normal again?" He paused his prep work and watched her steadily.

"Yeah, thanks to who-knows-what."

"I don't know who we should thank, but it's good to see you. And I'm glad I've got my friend back to normal. Smiling at me instead of wishing for a bucket to puke in." He looked back down at his work and sliced a codfish clean through its belly.

"Yepper." Kara bit the inside of her cheek. What the hell was her problem? First the skull, and now this?

It's just relief hormones.

Relief hormones? What the hell?

That's a thing, right? This will totally pass.

Come on. Focus. Task at hand, woman. "I had to come by. I couldn't get any answers out of you over the phone."

"Yeah, you would talk about that stuff all day. I need a break from that. Take your coat off. Stay a while. Don't you want to rejoice in my beautiful face-flesh? Maybe take a break from grilling me?" He grinned again. "You cut your hair. It really suits you."

Are things okay again? Please let them be. She touched the ends of her short wavy hair. Couldn't be helped. "How come your car's not in the lot?"

He laughed quietly, ignoring her question. "Nothing's the same without you around." He said it matter-of-factly, as though talking about his favorite set of knives.

"That so?" She cocked her head. *Hello? I asked you a question, buddy.*

"Yeah, Nancy gets all the good tables now. You know how she's always been pushy with Darla about the section by the windows."

"Ha-ha." Her stomach dropped. He was totally avoiding answering her question, just like over the stupid phone.

He smiled warmly and tipped his head up to look at her, his eyes lifting at the corners. Her stomach flipped. His ever-expressive eyebrows rose. He switched knives and sliced the fish into strips for frying. "Hey. While you've been gone, I've been thinking a lot about the other night. You ever give any thought to what happened at the cemetery?"

"Obviously! That's why I've been calling you."

"No." He paused in his chopping. "I meant you and me." His voice had grown low and quiet, his jaw loose. The words leaned back in his throat.

She didn't answer at first. She'd been nervous about forcing him to talk about his magical car problem. She knew him so well; she was sure she had every possible move of his blocked. Every argument, every evasive tactic. But now, he wanted to talk about the hand touch. Here he was, all warm and wide open. It was agonizing. She made a croaking sound.

He set the knife down and looked up at her pained expression, then flushed. "Sorry. You don't have to answer that."

"No, it's okay. I—"

He looked dejected. "I shouldn't have asked. You just caught me off guard is all." He looked up and wiped his hands on his apron. "Showing up all of a sudden." He smiled wide with his big, adorable kind-of-square teeth.

She literally didn't know what she'd say about that, even if it were physically possible to form the words. She scrunched her entire face up. She literally couldn't even acknowledge it. Her stomach churned. *He's gonna be pissed at me, isn't he.*

"Where's your car, Alec?"

He rolled his eyes, big.

Ah, hell. She'd killed the mood.

"Hugo drove me."

"How come?"

"My car was acting weird."

"What was wrong?"

"It wouldn't start."

"Yeah, but was it making a noise? Clicking? Screeching? What? I could've come and fixed it, you know."

"I dunno, you were busy 'relaxing.'" He made sure to use air quotes. "It just wouldn't start."

"You don't know what happened when you turned the ignition?"

"No, I don't know what's wrong with it."

Kara groaned. "It's okay. I'll come by after your shift. You can drive my car home after work. Drop yourself off at home."

"If you're offering to pick me up, you can just drive me."

"No, you're driving. That's what I need help with. I need to see this time slip thing."

"Hell, no. I mean, no thank you. I don't want to drive," he held his hands out to stop her. "But thank you for offering." He wiped his hands on his apron. "You know what? I just remembered. I need to talk to Darla about something."

"About what?"

"Purchasing stuff. Inventory." He walked quickly to the back to wash his hands at the sink.

"You never want to talk to Darla about inventory."

"Yeah, well." He grabbed towels out of the dispenser, barely wiped his hands on them, and threw them away.

"Can you just stop lying to me? It's infuriating."

"First, I tried telling you I don't want to talk about it. That didn't work. Then, I tried being vague. I'm trying lying now because I've run out of ideas on how to deal with you *pushing* me like this."

"Alec, come on, you *know* me! I wouldn't push if it weren't truly important. It's like you think this is some kind of *joke*."

"It's very much the opposite of a joke to me, Kara. That's the thing. Which is why I'm not keen to just jump in this reality-blinking car and give it another spin."

"You never told me it was 'cause you were scared."

"I'm not scared." He stared at her.

She stared back.

"Okay, let's say I'm scared. Why *wouldn't* I be scared?"

She stared at his shoes.

He pressed his lips together and nodded, then headed back through the kitchen, toward the door that led to the bar.

"Hey wait! Don't go out there!" Damn, damn, damn. He'd brought up the *hand touch* for god's sake, the one thing that'd been good about this week, *really* good, in fact, and she'd gone right back to her mad science experiment.

He stopped, fingers splayed out against the door. "I'm going out there. You'll have to stop pestering me if I go out there."

She racked her brain on how to make this lighthearted again. Just get him back in here. They could talk about something else.

"Like hell I will. I'll say weird stuff in front of Charlie. He eats that shit up! I'll get him talking about it all night and leave you to deal with it."

"You won't. And I think you're forgetting *you* work in the dining room. I work in the kitchen, away from that bonkers shit that spews from his face-hole."

She thought. "Yeah, but the bartenders will come hide from him in here and bother *you*. You hate that."

"You're right. I *do* hate that," he said, and pushed the door to the bar and dining room open all the same.

Kara took a deep breath and sighed loudly, staring at the door as it swung, open and shut, open and shut.

Now, alone in the kitchen, her heart pounded from the confrontation. She wished he could see, could know how he made her feel. She'd liked other guys while they'd been friends. But not like *this*.

No way was he thinking about her like that after this conversation. She needed a different conversation, now. Some kind of distraction.

She sighed again and followed him through the swinging door.

***

From the bar, Molly's cigarette-ruined tenor pulled Kara back to reality. "Look who's here. And she cut her hair! Almost didn't recognize ya, Kare!" She sat among four other regulars, including Charlie at the bar. Some were hunched forward on their elbows while others leaned in to talk to each other over the generic jazz music turned just a couple notches too loud.

"Yeah," Kara smiled and palmed her short curly locks gently, self-consciously. "I like it better this way, actually. Easier to deal with."

"Not me. I like a woman who keeps her hair long." Charlie Foley raised his eyebrows.

"Charlie," Alec growled disapprovingly.

Kara turned. "It's okay, Alec. Charlie forgot for a second that nobody fucking cares how Charlie likes his women." She glared at Charlie.

He ducked his head like a scorned dog, which surprised her. "Jay-zus, Kara. Having a bad day?"

"So far it's not great," she sighed, looking pitifully at Alec. *Pro: has a face again. Con: Everything else.*

Alec bit at the corner of his lip instead of looking at her. *Ouch*, she thought, with bruised sarcasm. She turned back to Charlie, directing all her anger at the only willing recipient. "And you should know that was a shitty comment to make."

"Now I got *you* snarking at me. Funny, you're the only one here who's always been nice to me." His voice cracked. She flushed as she noticed his eyes immediately teared up.

The pity thing was a bit below him, though. She shook her head. "Apologize, and mean it. Then I can be that again."

"Sorry, Kara." He said, covering his forehead with his hand.

Molly slapped lazily at Charlie's shoulder, startling him. "Take it easy Charlie. You're just hungry is all."

Kara sucked in a deep breath and held it. She'd never seen Charlie show remorse before, or any sort of shame. He'd always been rough like this. And he never relented, never apologized. The years must have caught up with him at some point.

"Where's Darla?" Kara asked no one in particular, attempting to end the weird exchange and unwilling to give up her dogged pursuit of knowledge.

"I dunno," Alec replied. He made no move to go looking for her. They locked eyes immediately. His face was somber now, and his eyes hunted back and forth, searching her face like fingers feeling out a dark room.

All it took was one look from him. Her heart throbbed, which annoyingly caused her anger to flake away at the edges. She figured it was better to just bother Charlie for a while instead. Now that Alec's face didn't scream immediate doom for her, she could stop driving him crazy for a few minutes. His argument did have merit, after all. She was pushing him hard about something he wasn't ready to deal with.

For now she'd ignore the fact that not knowing what was wrong with him was driving her to absolute distraction.

Plus, Charlie knew the town's freaky hard-to-believe history. And he clearly owed her one, now. She touched her hair again, and her anger returned, but for Charlie.

Kara made her way toward Molly. She offered Alec a small smile as she placed her hand on the back of Charlie's chair. "Were you guys eating soon? Did you want to grab a booth?"

***

Molly and Kara were a few beers in. Charlie was happily distracted playing his usual ridiculous game with Molly, asking her if she'd seen some random movies from his favorite genres and then playfully berating her for not having seen them. This time, the movie in question was *Once Upon a Time in the West*.

"I don't watch that shit," Molly protested over and over again, growing louder each time. "It's not my fault I'm not into your garbage movies, Charlie."

"It's not garbage, it's good," mumbled Alec, playing with the cord on the blinds. Kara wasn't sure Charlie or Molly even heard him. He'd been gazing out the window the whole time, just nursing his

77

water. As if they'd forced him to sit with them. Like he hadn't followed them to the booth while he was on the clock. What was he thinking about right now?

Whatever. Kara picked at the paper napkin wrapped around her cutlery. She had to think of a segue from Charlie's movies, back to the topic they were on the other night.

"Charlie, do you like any zombie movies?" She blurted out, lamely.

"Which ones?"

Shit. She'd never seen any zombie movies.

No, wait. One. "*Shaun of the Dead*?"

"Shaun?" his eyes bugged out, incredulous, apparently, at the movie name. "Who's Shaun?"

Kara rolled her eyes. "The main character. In the movie, obviously. How have you *not* seen *Shaun of the Dead*?" she said loudly, catching Molly's signal she was playing Charlie's usual game.

Molly looked at her, expression blank. She'd clearly never heard of the movie, either. But then she brightened. Sat up straighter. She got what Kara was doing, now. "Yeah, Charlie! What, are you from another time? A damn *dragon* in disguise?"

Charlie eyed Molly soberly, evenly. "Dragons aren't real, Molly. So no, I'm *not* a dragon in disguise."

"Oh, you're right. A dinosaur. I meant a *dinosaur* in disguise."

"*Anyway.*" Kara smiled, resting her forearms against the bar, her paper napkin ring now battered to hell. The attempt at some kind of pretense wasn't working, so, forget it. "Charlie," she said, her voice flat. "Did you hear about anything weird happening at Hope Cemetery the night before last?"

"Besides the fact that you were going to go haunt that place like a spook past your bedtime?" He shook his index finger at her, then straightened. "Wait a minute, did you see something?"

Everyone at the table was watching her now.

She was suddenly embarrassed. "Oh, I dunno," she shrugged. Alec leaned gently into her, his bicep touching hers. He raised his eyebrows, encouraging her to go on.

She took a deep breath and continued. "Some statues got broken. Everything was shaking, like an earthquake, but nothing was reported anywhere else in town at all. Things just felt real weird there."

"Ah."

"So what else can you tell me, besides that story about the walking dead who go back to work?"

Charlie folded his hands and furrowed his brow. "You sure you wanna know?" He eyed Alec, like he was trying to get a gesture of permission.

Annoyance prickled behind Kara's eyes. "You don't need his approval. I've invited you to speak."

"Oh, I know. But if Alec wants to start something with me, he will. And he won't ask *your* permission."

"Alec? Do me a solid. Give him a pass on this." She chewed her nail. "Don't worry about him," she said to Charlie. "You know you want to tell me."

Charlie sighed, looking tired. Played counter hockey with his water glass. She had this. He was a half-step away from the edge. Didn't even need a full shove. What had she tried to segue for? This guy was always poised with his fingers licked, hovering a page flip away from Barre's supernatural underbelly.

"Besides the zombie stuff," he clarified.

"Besides the zombie stuff, yeah."

"Try weird animals hanging around that place at night. They're big, like people, and walk on two legs like us, but they're animals."

"Are you talking about dog people?"

"Yup."

"I've heard about those," she said, glancing at Alec. His eyes were trained on her, sober, but not giving much else. He inclined his head slightly, encouraging her to continue. She turned back to Charlie. "Anything else?"

"Dog people aren't strange enough for you? I can give you a list of people who say they've seen 'em. How about Shelby Sammons? Been working nightshifts as a paramedic for fifteen years. She's seen them on multiple occasions. I've got plenty more."

"No, I get that. But I mean, like, more first-hand accounts of things going really strange."

"Kara." Charlie's face had gone dead serious.

"What." *This isn't going to be good. It's what I wanted, but, not good.*

"*I've* seen them, too."

"Is that so?" she said. Her heart sped up but her face played poker.

"They got my friend, Sammy."

"Where is Sammy now?" she asked.

"When I say they 'got him,' I mean he's gone," he said. He held his arms open, his eyes half-closed.

Kara's breath caught in her throat. "Gone? As in—"

"Dead."

"Wait, are you serious? This wasn't recent, right? It had to have been years ago. I didn't know about this."

"Uh-huh, when we were teenagers. It happened at Red Tree Hill, you know, outside the woods, behind the cemetery."

"I know the place," Kara said slowly, soberly. "I don't go over there, but I know of it." She glanced at Alec, whose knuckles were white around his glass. He had that doomy look on his face again, narrowed eyes trained on Charlie. But he didn't speak.

"So you've never seen it up close?" Charlie asked her.

"Walked up to it and looked at it? No."

"I have," Alec said, his voice low. "That tree is messed-up looking. It looks a thousand years old."

"Some say it's that old, or older," Charlie said.

"It's all twisted and creepy. Then the lower trunk is all scraped and chopped up by pocketknives. Kids who messed with it."

"That was my generation," Charlie said. "You kids never go near it. You're smart."

"My parents told me I couldn't," Kara commented absently. "Said there are bears in those woods."

"Bears? Or something else?" Charlie said, looking thoroughly haunted. "I'll tell you why your dad really kept you away from there. Last time me and him saw Sammy alive was in that field, by the tree. It was me, Sammy, your dad, and Sammy's girlfriend, Jamie." Charlie rubbed his jaw, remembering. "We were drunk as skunks, playing flashlight tag. I was 'it,' and Jamie was running like hell. She was the fastest of the four of us, so I probably wouldn't've caught her. But she slipped in some fox shit, and did a weird sort of flip. Like a half cartwheel, then just flopped over. We couldn't stop laughing. We were doubled over, our sides aching, while she wiped her shoe in the grass. She was swearing at us. That girl swore like a sailor. Some of the worst language you could imagine.

"But then we heard a noise. Kinda like a galloping horse. It was pretty dark, but we all turned to each other like, 'what was that?' We set our flashlights in the direction of the sound. The sound paused, and we realized if it started walking quietly now, we'd have no idea where it was at. Or if it was coming toward us. At that point I stopped looking for it. We all high-tailed it out of there, fast as we could.

"But I just remembered something before that. If you look at the base of that tree, you'll see some real bites in the side of the trunk. That night, Sammy took an axe to that tree. We'd started the game of flashlight tag to distract him, 'cause he was starting to freak us out. Still, he wouldn't get off it 'til he'd gotten himself good and tired. He had pretty good aim, actually. Gave it a good ten whacks in the same spot. That takes a lot of stamina and precision. Like golfing." He pantomimed swinging a golf club. "Your dad kept laughing, all nervous and squeaky, telling Sammy to stop. I knew he must have been real upset, 'cause I never heard your dad get like that. You know him. He knew how to make people listen. He had that deep voice of his since he was like sixteen. But we figured out pretty quick Sammy was beyond listening.

"Anyway, eventually he got tired and sat down. He sat, and the rest of us were laying under the tree. The moon was full, and it lit up the clouds a little; made it look like they were glowing. Soon as I noticed that, the sky started spinning.

At the time, I assumed it was 'cause I was drunk, but in hindsight, it was different. Like it wasn't my head, it was the world outside it. Starting in with the spinning, there was a loud screeching sound. Like that old blood-red tree was angry, and just scratching away at the stars.

"Then the clouds curdled, like milk gone bad. I could *taste* it. Sour."

"Tasted, sour?" Kara asked.

"I don't know, yeah, that's how I remember it."

"Were you doing drugs that night or just drinking?"

"Just. Drinking." Charlie gave Kara a leveling gaze. "You gonna let me tell the story?"

"Absolutely." Kara held her arms out, encouraging him to continue.

"So anyway, I assumed the sour taste was because I had drunk too much. I got up to stop the spinning, and that's when I suggested flashlight tag. I think I wasn't sure what was going on but wanted to get away from that tree, and get Sammy away from the axe.

"So yeah, back to the running part. We couldn't see what was behind us. And we were scared. Like, good and scared. We were running back toward my car, which sat at the little half-drive of asphalt where the gates are closed." He pointed, vaguely. "You know, back where it says, No Trespassing. There were a few streetlights that way but they were real dim, so it was more like random spotlights dotted down the road.

And what comes crossing that road, arms forward, fingers curled forward like a damn T-Rex? Some huge dog-thing walking on its hind legs. It walked just like a person, 'cept its biceps was close to its sides and it had like, paws, and claws held out in front of it, like I said, like a damn tyrannosaurus.

"It got across the road, across to *our* side of the road, and stopped. It looked at us, and it let out this ungodly scream, like a human would if they were on fire.

"That point, we were frozen. We stopped, and heard there was still footsteps behind us, too. We knew at least one of us was fuckin' burnt-ass toast. But most of all, we knew we had to try to get to that car. I told Sammy, I said, 'Sammy, don't none of us stop.' I told him and Jamie and your dad to just fuckin' *get* no matter what happened to any of us."

Charlie let out a loud sigh. "So, we ran. And . . . it got Sammy." He took a deep breath and covered his mouth with a shaky hand, then rubbed his chin and continued.

"As Jamie and I made it to the car, we heard this loud shuffling, some grunting on the ground nearby. Then a long dragging sound. It'd grabbed him and then drug him off to the woods. I know it, 'cause that's where they found him. We went right to the police station and told them what happened, and they found him within the hour.

"I assumed the things were hungry, and they were gonna eat him, Discovery Channel style, like lions on a zebra or something. But when they brought me in to ID the body, it was just part of his ear chewed up, and bite marks on his face. So I asked did he hit his head or something? And they said no, no signs of trauma.

"Wasn't until a couple weeks of pestering his family, they finally came out and told me. His heart was gone."

"*What?*"

"Yep. Not a heart attack. Not eaten by those animals. Just, his heart fucking disappeared."

"That's not possible, though, right? Like, medically?" Kara shook her head. What was she even asking that for? Obviously it was medically impossible.

Charlie shook his head. "Not that I know of. There's no way for it to be. It's unexplained, like spontaneous combustion or something. And like a lot of other things here. And what's more," he rubbed his hands together, "I did a lot of reading. Obsessing about this for years. Why would I not, you know?"

Kara nodded.

"I was dying to know why they didn't eat him. Why did they leave him alone? I spent hours at the library researching. There's no breed of dog, wild or otherwise, that wouldn't jump at the opportunity to eat something that's already dead. They don't have to kill it to want to eat it. So either they're more intelligent than actual dogs, they're well fed, or someone or something forced them away from Sammy before they could really tuck in."

Kara shivered. She was cold all over. "Did you ever figure out which it was?"

Charlie shook his head slowly. "For all I know, it could be all three. This is what I'm telling you, Kara. This place is fucked. And I've told you why."

Kara's heart sank. What was she going to do with this information? It didn't seem to explain what happened. What she saw. "Is there anything else you can tell me that might help?"

Charlie sighed. His eyes were swimming again. "Help with what, kid? You haven't told me anything."

"I told you about the graveyard—"

"You gave me a vague idea, but nothing I can work with."

"I guess it's hard to talk about."

Charlie fought a frown but his wet eyes shone with mirth. "Welcome to the club. I've been keeping my story pretty close to the chest for what, forty-five years now?"

"Yeah, you sure as hell never told me that," Molly said quietly. Her mouth was turned down, eyes grave..

Kara thought. "Well, when that earthquake happened in the graveyard, I heard a voice talk to me, tell me the dead aren't sleeping. And I've been seeing things."

"What did you see?"

Suddenly she realized: With everything that'd happened, she now fully believed Charlie's story. She shivered, as the reality of everything agitated her that much more deeply.

She imagined the one screaming, like he'd described. Felt like she could picture exactly where it stood in that field. She'd driven by so many times. Sometimes slowly, daring herself to stop. Now she pictured one of those things standing there, turning to the sound of her car approaching, looking her in the eyes.

Wanting her, this time.

Her skin stiffened. She took a deep breath before speaking. "Someone walking by in the cemetery. Someone really tall. It didn't look human." Kara shook her head. "It's not like anything you've told me about. And," she rubbed her jaw gently, "and Alec's face as a skull."

Charlie shook his head slowly. "That can't be good."

"I just don't know what any of it means."

"I'll tell you one thing." His eyes found hers. "That ring was your dad's, right?" He gestured to the ouroboros ring around her neck.

She looked down, as if checking it was still there. "Yeah."

"Whatever that ring was, whatever it did or didn't do, it was important to him. He told me once that it made the crying go quiet."

"The crying?" Her blood surged. "That sounds familiar."

"Sounds it, because it is. Don't take that off, whatever you do." He shifted in his seat, placing the knife on his plate, turning toward her. "You see those turquoise eyes set in there?"

"Yeah." She held the ring in her hand, staring at them.

"I was there the day your dad found those two gemstones in the quarry."

"What? He found these in the quarry?"

"Yep. Was the oddest thing, too. I didn't see him dig them up, but I'd seen him that morning. At lunchtime, he would always sit by himself, but this time he wasn't there. He hadn't called off early or sick or anything. Just bailed. Some guys mentioned he found those gemstones and just pocketed them and high-tailed it home."

"Did he come back the next day?"

"Yeah, he was back the next day. Looking like he hadn't slept for a second. And he was wearing that ring."

"I always thought it'd been in the family for generations." She touched the ring. Followed the etchings along the body of the ring, the slim hatching pattern that suggested the texture of the snake's skin. "He never took the thing off, not even to shower."

"I assumed he forged it himself. I don't think there's a jeweler in the world who'd agree to that fast a turnaround."

"I guess that tracks." Kara stared at her shoes. Her dad had a full workshop in the basement and used it frequently, always making things for her and her mom. Something crawled back to her. A memory trapped behind a clouded window:

Her dad's back was to her, and the sky behind the basement windows was black. She'd been woken that night by the sound of moaning wind. Almost like those crying trees she used to hear, but something was laid in front of them, drowning them out.

The room was hot. So hot she shivered. The howling of the wind drowned out the crying, and a hammering sound acted as percussion.

She came around to the side of her dad, saw him set down his mallet. He held a silver ring on a mandrel. Picked up a sharp metal tool, started scraping. Making a hatching pattern on the body of the snake.

Wind lifted her old yellowed drawings taped to the deep freezer. The room sang songs that were turquoise, like the eyes in the ring. Like the lake in the quarry.

"What are you making, Dad? Who's that for?"

The wind was too loud. He couldn't hear her. His face was worked over with sweat. Spread slick across his forehead, beading around his temples, streaking down his jaw.

She watched him for a long time, wondering why he didn't notice her. Realizing the windows to the basement were old; their metallic housing was rusted shut.

Where could the wind be coming from?

Kara rubbed her hand over her face. "I remember, now. He made it in the basement." She pressed the ring hard into her palm. She could almost feel her dad there, knowing she had the ring. Rejoicing in it.

Her heart was an engine, overworked.

She gasped, and now her eyes were swimming like Charlie's. Her eyes stung and her chest bloomed with heat. She'd never felt good, and fear, and love, all in the same breath until now.

8

THE CHAOS STONES

Kara sat at her kitchen table with Alec, an open wine bottle, and two half-drunk glasses, nose still running from the tears she'd cried since Charlie's story. She held the ring in her hand. It was late, and Ten had gone to bed.

"I can't stop wondering what my dad meant when he told Charlie the ring quieted the crying."

"Yeah," Alec said quietly, his voice grave. He took a drink of wine.

"Remember how I told you I heard a sound like that too, back at my parents' house?"

"The other night at the cemetery. Yeah, I remember."

"Yeah." She palmed her glass and took a drink, then shook her head. "It was horrible, you know. Sometimes low and angry, like a braying. Then other times high and mournful, like a cat."

"God, Kare." Alec's eyebrows knotted. "That's terrifying."

"Yeah. My dad used to let me sleep in their room when I was little, but my mom would get frustrated from me coming in there so much. Waking her up.

Then when I got older, like eight or so, I just got used to falling asleep with my headphones on.

"But whenever a song would end, that horrible sound would just go on and on. These days I think I'm a little hard of hearing from the headphones."

"Oh, I believe it. You *never* listen to me." Alec smiled at her.

"I do, though. To every word you say."

"Hm," he laughed, resting his chin in his cupped hand, twisting the stem of his glass between finger and thumb.

They smiled at each other. Kara close-mouthed, Alec biting his lip. They watched each other for what felt like endless minutes. Her heart kicked, reminding her it was there. Her face heated. *Is he thinking about me what I'm thinking about him?* she wondered.

He'd asked her about the hand touch back at the restaurant. In that moment at the cemetery, she'd been so ready to just go for it. Now the need wrestled with the fear.

Is he breathing heavier? Alec's breaths came deep and slow. His lips parted a little and he let out a shy laugh. His fathomless eyes were hooded. He looked at her lips, back up at her eyes and down at her mouth again.

She took a deep breath. Pressed her palms against her thighs, straightened her arms. Her heart was in her throat.

Her fear won out again. "So anyway, I keep thinking about my dad's ring. What it could mean."

It was as if she had broken their trance; Alex's eyes looked lost. He took a big breath and let it out slowly before speaking. "What'd you come up with?"

"I don't know, just toying with meanings, I guess. You know how my dad's Jewish?"

"Yeah."

"And how my mom is super weird?"

He nodded, slowly, smiling a little. "Yeah?"

"So I told you how Jewish people bury their—sorry, *our*—dead quickly, right? So they can be at peace? "So, another custom we have involves just, like, returning the body to the dirt, the way we came from it, biblically."

"Ashes to ashes, dust to dust."

"Well, we don't cremate. We aren't even supposed to really get tattoos or piercings. Our body is ours while we live in it, but we're not supposed to alter it. Now, plenty of Jews do. You know *I* do. But in Jewish cemeteries, it's kind of frowned upon. You're born, you die, you go back to the earth. We think of it like just the natural way of things."

"But Hope Cemetery isn't a Jewish cemetery."

"Yeah, that's true. My mom had him buried in a non-Jewish cemetery, of course, so they could be buried together. That makes sense, right?"

"Yeah."

"So it's all fine, that was the plan. My dad knew about it. He worked in the quarry and a lot of those guys get buried at Hope Cemetery. It's got all that Barre Gray granite in the monuments. The showcase of their life's work."

"I mean, yeah. You know I know all this stuff. I grew up here, too."

She nodded. "Anyway, my point. I was looking up the Ouroboros ring. Trying to figure out why my dad took two little stones from the granite and decided he had to forge a snake ring and set the eyes in. The problem is, I can't stop seeing all this in the context of my dad's death, and I don't know if it's skewing my ability to reason.

"But the Ouroboros is one of those crazy symbols depicted in a million different religions, philosophies, parts of the world. You get it.

"The big takeaway for me was how it represented eternal cyclic renewal. Life, death, and rebirth. It's kind of just speaking this concept we all understand. No matter who we are, where, when we're from, we all understand this common truth."

"And that all boils down to?"

Kara got up and poured herself a glass of water from the cabinet above the sink. "I dunno. It's like he took this event, this unexpected chaotic event of finding two tiny identical stones in a quarry—" She dipped her head, interrupting herself. "That isn't a thing, by the way. I looked it up. Random stones don't show up in colossal granite formations. So he took those little chaos stones, and set them in this strong image, this fact of existence. Like taking chaos and reminding it how small it really is in the scheme of everything. Of the way of things.

"So, that makes me wonder. If he used the ring to tell chaos to go fuck itself, and then he stopped hearing the voices, what would happen if I take off this ring?" She sat down next to him again, gripping the chain in both hands and pantomimed lifting it over her head. "I'm not wearing it on my finger, but I'm still wearing it. Would I see your face as a skull again? Is this just me, now, and the ring is just helping me focus on what's needed?"

"No offense, but if we're starting to experiment again—"

"—what, Alec?" She tried to hide the impatience in her voice.

"If we're starting to experiment again, I want you to know that, just like my blinking car trick you want me to perform for you again, we are potentially flirting with death, here. Or worse. And," he looked away, then right into her eyes, "I don't ever want to see you look at me the way you looked at me that day."

She offered him a sympathetic smile. "I must have looked so strange."

He didn't return her smile. He rubbed his eyes. "Kara. You looked at me like I was everything bad and wrong about existence. I've never seen you that upset in my life." He married his hands and pressed his forehead against them, elbows resting on the table.

"Alec," she whispered. "I'm sorry." She scooted her chair close to him and hugged all of him close. The full range of his bent arms, sagging shoulders, everything, and breathed him in. Pressed her head against his neck. He felt warm. A soft smell like cedar and oranges, and some kind of soft human smell that wrapped her in a feeling of home. "You're not ready. I get that now."

"I'm not, and I won't be."

"We'll talk about that later."

He stiffened a little, no longer returning the hug. "That doesn't sound encouraging. So you're not gonna drop it?"

"Again, it doesn't make sense that I'll wear this necklace forever until I die, and that you'll never drive again. What, are you going to sell your car?"

"Kara," he groaned. "I'm tired."

"Okay, okay." She backed up, put a hand on his bicep for comfort. Felt awkward. "Sorry." She removed her hand again. *Don't say anything else,* she told herself. *You don't have to warn him this is going to be talked about again. Now's not the time.* "Need a ride home?" she offered, realizing this might be why he'd stayed so late. He was afraid to ask her to drive him.

"Yeah, I'd love that." The tension vacated his face, which made her feel better. She'd been so caught up in all this that she'd forgotten to check in with him. See how he was feeling.

He leaned back in his chair, watching her. She stared at his chest, watching it expand, collapse, repeat.

This ancient universe, this impossible place. And here they were, now. Living in this century. An unthinkable body count of all who had lived, and then died before this moment. And the fact that the same inevitable fate awaited them.

But for now, they were here. They were alive.

9

THE RED TREE
IS HER THRONE

Kara's shrill ringtone pierced both the night and her dreamless sleep. The necklace caught under her arm and tugged at her throat as she slid the phone across the nightstand toward her. It showed a local number.

Disoriented, she put the phone to her ear. "What?"

"It's Charlie," he told her. "Your mother gave me your number."

"When? Why?"

"Just now," he said. "I'm so sorry. Can you come over?"

"Over. To you? Your place?"

"Yep."

"Why? What's going on?"

"I gotta show you something."

She rubbed her face. Checked the clock: one in the morning. She'd only been asleep an hour. "Where do you live? Are you still at the apartments behind the high school?"

"Yep. Don't ring the bell, just text this number when you're here. Molly's asleep."

"Why can't you just tell me?"

"Just come over. Please hurry."

Fear and exhilaration throttled her violently. She got his unit number, hastily tossed up her hair, and brushed her teeth.

She pulled up to a silent building, tall and foreboding, with crumbling brick, wrought iron balconies, and a mansard roof. Her body felt weak. What could he possibly have to show her at one in the morning that he couldn't just tell her on the phone?

She came up the front walk. Once she passed the streetlight, she saw the sky was a dark blue against the black roof. The wind was still, but the leaves trembled. She shuddered.

The second she creaked open the heavy metal door, the buzzer sounded. She shouted in alarm, and an angry tension exploded within her. Kara wrenched the second door open.

The lobby was clean, but outdated. A massive cream-colored leather sectional sat in front of floor-to-ceiling windows. She stared at her reflection beneath the dim overhead lights. All she could make out was the permanent exhausted shrug of her shoulders and the double slouch of skin beneath her eyes.

Mercifully, the elevator had no mirrors. The pull of the contraption, lifting her body away from the ground floor, the familiar sounds it made, soothed her until it delivered her to Charlie's floor. The doors scraped open loudly, stating the journey's end in their own language.

His door was the second one on the left, and it was ajar. Kara knocked on the giant metal thing, painted either dark brown or dark red. Too dim to tell.

She heard the scrape of a chair, then a quick shuffle toward the door.

It swung open, and there stood Charlie in the dim light. Same clothes as earlier. His face was drawn, eyes tired. The foyer was big and open. His home smelled clean, like vinegar. Not what she expected. *He's lucky he's got Molly,* she thought.

"There you are," he whispered, looking relieved.

"This better be good." She tried to lift her features, show she was kidding, sort of. But when she saw his face fall, she knew she'd failed. "So what is it you wanted to show me?"

"I saw her once."

"Eh? Who'd you see?"

"The one, the thing who did this."

"Did what? What are you talking about?"

"I saw her that night. In the tree. The night Sammy was killed. She's responsible."

"But I thought you said the dog thing took Sammy, not some lady?"

"But like I told you, his heart was missing. That wasn't the dog people. I think it was *her* that took the heart."

"Why do you think that? And why didn't you tell me this earlier, at the restaurant?"

"Because I forgot." He sniffed, then continued. "I think she made me forget."

"If you forgot, how are you telling me? And, sorry, but why did you make me come out here?"

"I have to show you something." He motioned vaguely with his hand, shuffled off down the corridor, and turned right into a dark room.

She hesitated. "Charlie!" she whispered. Her heart was pounding. She didn't want to go in there.

Charlie didn't respond. A switch clicked on in the room. Light shot out into the white carpeted hallway, and Kara followed.

The room was small. It smelled acrid and dusty, like an old abandoned closet. A desk sat directly to her right. Straight ahead, a TV wall unit, the top of it covered with framed pictures. To the left, Charlie sat on a striped futon, bent over an open book sitting in his lap. He smoothed a creased sheet of paper over it again and again. At first it looked like random scribbles. As she stepped closer, she registered what it was: An angry, dark penciled figure. Severe swirls collected around each other, choking each other. Radiating darkness.

Kara sat down next to him. "What *is* that?" she whispered, lifting her gaze to his face, which was still turned down. Her neck prickled. She realized suddenly that she didn't want to look at it anymore.

"Sometimes she has a body, and sometimes it's just ... raw flesh and muscle." Charlie was quiet for a whole minute. "Earlier today, when we talked, you said you saw something unnaturally tall in the cemetery. Something clicked on in my brain. I got home and this memory of me scribbling something in pencil, late at night, kept repeating in my mind. The memory was wrapped around this desperate feeling of dread. It made my head throb. My mind felt . . . violated. Like something sharp had gotten in and scooped something soft from the side of my head. A voice kept repeating the word *bookshelf*, over and over again. I went through all my books, opening them, expecting something to fall out. I—" He laughed sadly, shook his head. "I have a lot of books, Kara."

"But then you found that." She pointed with a trembling hand.

"Yeah. And the moment I looked at it, everything came back to me. In the tree, she looked like, I don't know, a space robot or something. A head, but no face. Very big. Like a machine wrapped in smooth shiny cream-colored material. Like something someone built."

"Oh my god." Her throat felt tight, her breath short. She leaned a hand against the wall.

"That's what the tall thing looked like?"

"Yeah, that's definitely what I saw."

"Oh, Kara. Kara, Kara, Kara." He *tsk*-ed three times as though she'd invited any of this.

She shrugged. What could she even say? "I know."

"And the book I found this in, this is an old journal of my mother's. The page I placed the drawing in? The page has just three lines in it." Charlie pointed to big, thick letters. The pen had bitten down so hard on the page, it'd practically ripped the paper.

> The fleshless thing with bionic armor will wait forever.
> She needn't die, and she needn't move.
> For the red tree is her throne.

"So your mom knew about her too," Kara said. "It's got to be her. Both times, it was her."

"Seems that way." Charlie sighed. "So anyway, the thing I was made to forget? I remembered everything when I saw my drawing. One night I woke up, and she was standing in my bedroom doorway. I lived alone, then. It was way after I finished high school but before I met Molly."

"What did this thing do?"

"Nothin'. Just stood there. She had no eyes, but she was staring. No mouth, no nose, but she was breathing."

"What did she look like?"

"It's hard to say. It was like she didn't even have a body. She was just . . . messy looking. Like a sloppy, living oil painting. All big fat streaks of dark reds. Just leaning with something that could have been an arm against my doorframe. Every part of her was just shifting rhythmically, the streaks rearranging slowly in and out, in and out. That's the part that struck me as breathing.

"Soon after I saw her, she started moving toward me. All those weird streaks shifted like the weaves of a basket so she could move, and it made this scraping sound, like every part of her was rubbing against itself. I screamed, and she replied with a kind of roaring, screeching noise. That's when the dog came running. Whatever form she existed in, just folded up from the outside into the center of itself, making even louder sounds, and she was gone.

"After that was when I started drinking heavily. The nights just felt scary and full of . . . violent possibility.

When Molly moved in, it helped, but it also didn't. 'Cause then I was worried she'd come again and Molly would be at risk, which, actually, was even worse."

"I'm sorry."

Charlie nodded and put a hand to his head. "I'm angry so much of the time. Just, so angry. I hate how I feel when I think about that night with Sammy, I'll never know why she did that, or what she wanted. And why did she watch me, but not do anything?"

"She probably doesn't see you as any kind of threat, so that's good, right? I mean, if what you said is true, we know how easy it is for her to just, you know. End it."

"Well, yeah, but then why visit me at all?"

"I dunno. Think about what information she obscured from you. You forgot you saw that figure in the tree, and you forgot that you saw her in that . . . other form. So she doesn't care if everyone knows Sammy disappeared mysteriously, but she doesn't want you to remember having seen her."

"Mm."

"Think about it. Your mom put in that journal entry about her, so she must have heard about her or run into her or something horrible. But how come, with all that havoc she can wreak, you'd never heard of her before? You always knew about the weird things going on around here, but you didn't know about her until you found your drawing."

He cleared his throat and smiled ruefully. "I wish my mom were still around so I could talk to her about it. I hate to tell you this, but those moments where you'd do anything to talk to your parents again? That never goes away. At least if you liked them, that is."

"I believe it." She placed a hand on the paper. When he let go, she folded it back up, placed it bookmark-style back in the journal, and shut it gently. "At least you've got Molly to look out for you."

"Yeah, she's the best. I call her Molly Ringwald 'cause her name is Molly and she's the only one I've known who . . . becoming an adult hasn't touched her."

"Why, 'cause Molly Ringwald was in all those teen movies?"

"Well yeah, but mostly: remember that speech in *Breakfast Club*? About forgetting all that's important about being a kid when you become an adult?"

"Charlie, that wasn't Molly Ringwald. That was Ally Sheedy."

"Huh?"

Kara thought twice.

"Oh, nothin'. I said I'm really very sleepy. I'm going to head home now."

10

NIDHOGG

The memories I've hidden, the work I've done has been upturned, all because the mortal left himself a quaint little drawing.

I, Nidhogg, displaced Bastion of Hel, had to leave my Red Tree, my throne, to make him forget.

What am I saying? Red Tree is *their* word. The little villagers have no idea of its origin. Of its age. Human Science has named this tree a Great Basin Bristlecone Pine. There is another tree like it elsewhere on this continent that they named Methuselah, after a man who they claim lived a thousand years.

A human living a thousand years is nothing more than a comedy. What would they do with all that time? A sputtering match burning everything it tread upon to cinder. And these humans name my beloved as though it were a pet rat.

Before the humans, it was only Methuselah and me. We have shared countless revolutions together. I watched the sky split over the massive celebration of stone. Bore witness as the pieces of the sky fell like slow-falling snow, forever linking the tree to the rock.

Then, the humans came, making their own miracles with their steel toys and machines. They gathered in this place to mar the world's landscape. To create more of themselves who would do the same. Remove trees. Build shelters. Multiply themselves, and make things around them scarce.

All the same, they left us well alone. We believed they could sense the danger that would greet them if they interfered in any significant way. Those who visited us did so with awe and fear in their hearts. Always at night.

The people, I admit, are a little bit like us sometimes. They can see the tree is special, and they perform their own stupid experiments on it, with their little pocket weapons. They scratch their letters upon its skin, as though that will join them with the tree. As though that will make it theirs in some way.

When the evening blesses us, the animals stand watch at the edge of the woods. The ones that are special; my children. Human enough to listen to me, and animal enough to be my pets. The night I entered this terrestrial realm, I learned they can hear the working of my ideas, and they follow me. All I have to do is apply a little force to my thoughts. Just like the below realm, with my lost souls.

The tree became red when I tried to make it my own. When I heard the roots humming to the underworld and singing to the sky, and I tried to drink its blood and feed it my own.

The evening I met the man they call Sammy, I sat in the boughs of the tree, as I typically do. When I climb those branches, I can almost touch the stars. Not like a human child dreams *they* can, but because this tree truly can scratch the heavens. This is the furthest I can remove myself from this terrestrial space. My rightful seat. The branches are snarled and, in the night, threaten to rend one another apart. But there is a section behind the wildest snare of branches that forms a small flat place. A perfect spot for me.

My wild, my beloved, my throne.

I watched the four tall children, drunk with youth and spoiled fruit. They played. Stumbled. Laughed. Delighted at their own stupidity. But this wasn't new for humans. What was new was the tall thin boy with the long weapon in his fist. A stick with a sheath of steel. Like a large tomahawk. He leaned the handle against the tree, and continued his theatrics, of trying to catch the other three.

After a time, they lay down underneath the boughs of the great thing. I hummed quietly to myself, daring them to see me. Would be nice to further wrench more tension across those tight, clueless grins. Twist them, and then split them.

I was watching them, drinking the ill, churning curdle of the young. The skinny one in particular. He had beat himself into a frothy kind of madness, and he'd turned toward the ax, eying it like a low-flying bird. Like wet candy rolled in the dirt.

I'd say I knew what he was going to do before he did it, but it might just be the certainty of the warnings, quiet at the time, but in my own hindsight, deafening.

He grabbed the ax, and chopped. The tree's spirit buckled, its toothy bark grit tight. Clamped and grinding, in sheer agony. It couldn't move itself but its insides kicked hard, spinning the very stars, for nobody else but itself, those under and in the tree, and myself.

I wrapped my legs around the branches and held on.

That night, I swallowed my first *living* human heart. It tasted full, thick, and salty, like the gods had spit in my mouth. And despite how totally it filled me, that was the same night I came to hate humans completely.

I was there too, the night of the pairing, in that place where the dead are dropped in voids in the dirt. When the one called Kara and the one called Alec touched in that space, the earth trembled, and the gifts were bestowed.

A pairing isn't a one-time cosmic event, you know. Most who are touched by it don't even know that it's happened. All they know is they grew close, and the world around them shattered. So much so, they had nothing to celebrate, nothing to lean on but each other.

A pairing is a touch of the skin, turned magical. A marrying of souls. The universe, blessing a union and breaking something else. The stronger the bond between those two, the more of a threat it is to everything I do here.

More importantly, however, it is a celebration of all the pairings that came before it. And anyone who refuses to acknowledge the history of it all, to pay proper homage . . . frankly, they deserve an awful fate.

II

Cold at the Station

Kara jammed the spout into the tank and squeezed the handle, trying to decide whether to wait in the car or outside. The gas station was completely deserted. It was cold, it was late, and she was dead tired. Today had been a normal day at work. A busy double shift, but normal. She'd needed that. Alec had been normal. She'd driven him to and from work *without* commenting on it, saint that she was. She hadn't pushed him to talk about anything weird. They'd laughed. They'd joked. They'd eaten good food together on their break.

The wind picked up, a sudden gust with sharp, frosty edges, gentle at first, then strong. It flipped her hair up and over, undoing her part.

Kara muttered a few obscenities, wrapping her dad's green jacket more tightly around herself. Another comfort object for her. But her old jacket had a hood on it. This didn't. She made a mental note to wear a hoodie under it from now on.

"I'll wait in the car, then," she mumbled. Head down, she circled behind the car.

As soon as she reached the back passenger door, she heard the front door clunk open.

Quickly, she ducked down below the back window and froze, craning her neck, listening. A shuffling followed, and her blood ran cold. Something soft bumped against the open driver's side door.

Someone is stealing your car, she thought. *Nobody near here's awake, and someone is stealing your fucking car. What are you going to do?*

She backed up a few steps, blood careening through her temples. She turned and banged her hip against a plastic garbage can. Her stomach flopped like a beached fish. There was no pain, but she startled herself and was terrified she'd told the intruder how nearby she was.

Kara sucked in a silent breath. The shuffling continued, much louder than the noise she'd just made; they must not have heard her. She crouched, then crawled silently forward, ducking down next to the back tire. Her mind raced.

The sound continued as if nothing had happened. Shuffling, bumping. *What were they doing?* If they were gonna steal the thing, they'd have started the car by now. Her blood thickened, slowed. Terror mixed with anger. Her breathing came quiet and heavy. She lifted her head carefully so she could just see over the trunk and through the back windshield.

They. No, it, was hunched over. It was huge. It seemed like if it stood up straight, it would be at least three heads taller than the car. And its shoulders were a weird shape. Like they came up unnaturally high and arched forward. She squinted.

No. Not shoulders. They looked like . . . folded wings. The longer she looked, the more she was sure those fuckers were wings.

Kara ducked again and moved as low and fast as she could away from the car. She raced toward the pump, her mind shouting nonsense. A bird. A bird, a bird. What bird was that big? She reached the pump and grabbed the cement pillar, wrenched her body around it, and hid on the other side, face cold against the metal brace. *God, it's the size of a person No: bigger than the biggest person. And it's a bird.*

My god.

The shuffling stopped.

Kara took a sharp breath and listened. Readied herself to back away and keep running. Where was it?

Two steps. Two awful steps, little *tak-tak* sounds against the concrete ground. Talons. Talons the size of . . . what? *They're just big,* she thought, trying her best not to picture them. She wanted to back away further, but if she went too far, the gas pump wouldn't be hiding her anymore. She couldn't bear the thought of the thing seeing her.

Two more steps.

She couldn't stand it anymore. It could be coming around back the way she had come; coming to get her. She looked quickly around the pump.

Two glowing red eyes pointed right at her. Rent her free from reality. The thing took two massive steps around to the front of the car. It jumped and landed on the hood, puncturing the night with a loud crunch of metal. It stared at her for a fraction of a second, then leaped. Straight up into the godforsaken sky, like a helicopter. It didn't even flap its wings.

"Son of a bitch," was all Kara could say.

"You're getting it wrong," a deep voice spoke loudly, clearly from behind her. A man stood across the street, watching her. Fully unperturbed by the giant owl/man-beast that had been there a second ago.

"Excuse me? Are you talking to me?" Kara shouted. "If you are, I wonder why you might be standing there, offering your opinion when you didn't bother to help me with that *creature* that looked about to eat me just now." Her heart was slamming in her chest.

The man just stared.

"Oh I'm sorry," she spat. Her arms, her legs, everything shook. "Did you not see it? Was it hiding behind one of these little gas station pillars?"

"I was attempting to start a conversation."

Kara focused harder on the figure, and stiffened. He was grinning at her. The corners of his mouth extended sharply up to mid-cheek. Violently unnatural, as though the lips were held up by clothespins.

"You were born in a place where the light is bent. Wrenched crooked until it fashions a shape."

"What's that now?" Maybe she was distorting his face with her mind? She was tired. It was dark. He was far away. But why did he speak this way? Some people hung around the front of this gas station sometimes, but she'd never seen this guy before.

"A triangle with three points. A vortex."

"What's a vortex?"

"A triangle."

Oh, forget this conversation. "Ah, okay. Hey, I'm sorry, I've got to leave. Nice to meet you, though." She turned to go.

"The ring of your father's," he said.

"My father's ring? Wait, what ring?" she tested him. Her blood crashed heavily through her.

"The snake, eating its tail. That is a circle."

She gasped. Her breath came quickly. "What *about* the ring?"

"You dropped it. It is on the floor of the seat next to yours. That is what the Mothman was trying to take."

"Mothman? You're telling me that was Mothman? Like, famous cryptid harbinger of doom, Point Pleasant bridge collapse, *that* Mothman?" It certainly *had* looked like Mothman. "He wasn't trying to hurt me?"

"He did not harm you. He was searching your car, yes?"

"Yes."

"You see? Mothman cares not for human flesh or violence. He is only following her orders. He must. I can hear her whispers, but he, the lowly creature, must obey them."

"*Her* orders? Whose orders?"

"You will learn in time."

"Does she look like you? Or maybe . . . a robot with no eyes?"

"A robot?" He breathed rapidly, as though laughing. "She is wearing that suit of mine?"

"Please. This isn't funny. I've seen terrible things." She paused, realizing he didn't care. The fear in the next question throttled her words: "Are you going to hurt me?"

"I have no reason to do so right now. But she may."

"Can you tell her to talk to me? Not to hurt me?"

Rapid breathing again. "I would not do that, no. I cannot help."

"You can't? Or you won't?"

"I have helped you enough already. You must use your gifts. I do not concern myself with these things. I am only here to watch. This is your job, not mine."

"My job? What is my job?"

"You are the death twin."

"I don't know what that is. Please help me. Please tell me what that is."

The thing made the laughing sound again. "I don't think so. I would rather just watch." Its milky dead eyes shone in the streetlight.

Kara's stomach turned. She groaned quietly. "Would you please stop smiling at me? It's very unnerving." She started to back away toward her car.

The thing limped quickly across the street toward her, one arm stuck at its side.

She bolted to her car. The minute she shut the door, he reached the passenger window.

"Stop smiling?" it said between parted teeth; its lips did not seem to move. His skin was stiff and lifeless, like a cadaver dressed for a funeral. The pungent stench not unlike a city sewer overpowered her.

She cried out. Locked the doors with shaking hands. The thing leaned its face into the passenger window, pointed down into the floor of the passenger seat. "Take the ring," it said, the voice stunted in speech, its tongue and throat doing all the work.

Kara screamed. The man tapped repeatedly at the window. His grin began to melt. She launched herself over the middle console and looked at the passenger side floor. There was the ring, as he'd said. She realized she must have broken the chain when she was putting her dad's jacket on in the car. She thought she'd felt something tighten, and then loosen again when she'd put it on. She leaned over, careful to join the two ends of the chain together and clutched it to her chest. Everything was still intact. The clasp must have failed when she pulled on the chain.

His face had fully relaxed now. Lips parted, cheeks drooping. The holes where the eyes belonged were displaced now. Shiny pink rings of underflesh showed under the little bit of eye whites that were still visible.

Half-groaning, half-screaming, Kara gunned the ignition and drove off.

12

HORNS

Kara knocked at Alec's front door, staring at the blond wood deck with white lattice railing panels, sniffling against the chill breeze. The horrible grin of that *thing* was seared into her, and now that she had some distance, she realized who he made her think of.

The Grinning Man. Indrid Cold. She thought back to the time when she'd first learned about him, back in high school.

***

Even now, she could practically taste the coppery bite of rust from the farming tools hanging in the small barn. The breath on her neck in the darkness of Alec's shed. The hard-lipped, graceless kiss his cousin Tyler had clearly been *so* confident she'd return. When she didn't, he'd locked her in there for what felt like an hour after telling her to go fuck herself. To which she'd yelled *thanks, with relish,* and thought about the movie *Grease*, and wished she'd had some gum to chew loudly right after, or something to say that made her feel less stupid.

She'd never told Alec, just settled in haughtily, sickened and angry, her heart pounding, not letting herself think too far ahead to how long she'd be stuck in there. If she'd struggled, she felt sure that Tyler would somehow know, and that he would feel he'd succeeded in upsetting her. For all she knew, he was just outside, waiting for her to bang on the door and implore him to let her out; or in other words, ask him for a favor. She refused to offer any satisfaction whatsoever, in any form. However, she would definitely be avoiding both Alec and Tyler for the rest of the summer, or the whole five weeks that remained of it. The thought of that pissed her off, like Tyler had stolen Alec from her.

Which implied Alec belonged to her.

She rubbed her face. At the time, the thought hadn't bothered or alarmed her. It just was. She'd reminded herself that, as fall crept toward them, Tyler would be forced to go back home, and Kara would have Alec all to herself again.

She felt along the wall until she bumped into the small bench by the doors. She ran her fingers down the shelves. Found one of the many flashlights in the top drawer, loaded it with batteries, feeling for the springs in the flashlight, and the nubs on the batteries, matching them up, and turned it on. She pointed its beam upon the books, on the shelf above the chest of drawers. Alec didn't have a bedroom, so he kept his books here. His childhood home was small, threadbare, one bedroom for his parents, and an open space with kitchen, living room, TV and couch, which he slept on. A hard-as-hell thing, the argyle lines so faded it was practically a solid reddish-brown.

And there in the shed, among issues of *Asimov's*, books by Ray Bradbury, Mary Shelley, Shirley Jackson, and Peter Straub, was an old, battered copy of *The Mothman Prophecies*.

There's where and when she'd learned about the chaos in Point Pleasant leading up to the bridge collapse. Strange inhuman figures dressed as people, posing as intelligence agents to get in, gain information, their voices sounding like a tape recorder played backwards. A giant bird-like creature with glowing red eyes, stalking locals, appearing on the tops of buildings or the hoods of cars, sometimes racing alongside vehicles.

And Indrid Cold. The interdimensional being. Always grinning. Showing up in a "lamp-looking spacecraft." Calling residents day and night, hour after hour, asking bizarre questions. Knowing things nobody could know. He would visit that same person again and again, tell them things, show them things, allegedly take them to his home planet, Lanulos. All the way up until their eventual demise.

The book had no pictures, but later, when Kara looked him up on her phone, the drawings of that grin, stretched wide beneath a pair of dull, bored eyes, violated, violently, the idea of what a human face should be.

All that activity went on for months, until the Silver Bridge collapse in the sixties. Almost fifty people had died. And all the activity petered out, trickling to occasional visitations at best. Like the disaster had slammed that door shut.

***

If that's who I saw tonight, she wondered, *what does that mean for us, and our town?* She shuddered, trying to push away what she'd just seen and heard. Staring at the railing panels of Alec's porch, she tried to wrap her mind around all she'd just experienced. Dog people attacking. A body without a heart. Afterwards, a creature made of nothing but muscle, threatening Charlie. And now—if she could believe herself—she'd just seen Mothman, and spoken to Indrid Cold. She squeezed her eyes shut and took a deep breath, trying to mentally start the conversation she was about to have.

Alec answered the door too quickly, though.

"Hey you." His smile evaporated the minute he saw her.

"This's new," she mumbled absently about the railings, hardly opening her mouth.

"Sorry, what?"

"Nothing," Kara growled quietly in frustration. "Can I come in?" she managed.

He nodded rapidly and gestured for her to enter.

"Where have you been?" he asked.

"What? Why?"

"You smell like garbage and gasoline."

"That would make sense. Listen, Alec. I think we should just sit in the car and give you a few minutes. And then I think you need to drive so we can see what this is all about."

"Kara, I think whatever this is, is dangerous. We can't just be doing this. We don't know what's happening. It's an unknown. And very intense."

"So what are you gonna do then?"

"What? You come over, unannounced, guns blazing, wanting every answer, and wanting it *right the hell now*. What do you mean, what am I gonna do? *Not* drive. That's what I'm gonna do."

"Why, though?"

"What do you mean, why? Do you not remember, not only was it terrifying for me to black out and appear in another place immediately when I drove last, but you saw my face as a skull? What if that happens again when I drive? What will you do?"

"The skull thing didn't happen from you driving."

"If you gave me just one reason why. Anything besides that it's a feeling you have." He watched her, steadily.

Okay, it was a hunch that one thing didn't cause the other. But a big hunch. She shrugged, moving on. "No, like, you're going to actively just never drive again? Just Lyft everywhere and get a little old spouse who will take you everywhere you'll ever go, forever?"

"I dunno."

"You're doing that thing again, aren't you?"

"What?"

"Like you did at the restaurant. This noncommittal *let's just wait and see*, see if it'll all blow over. And I can't live with that. I'm telling you that I will not let you *not* drive ever again. Not when." Kara stopped, her throat starting that tight sobby feeling again. "My dad." A chill rushed over her, hardening her skin.

"*Kara,*" he whispered quietly. Not admonishing. Just acknowledging her.

"The things I just saw. A giant creature, like Mothman. I think it *was* Mothman. And a guy. Indrid Cold. He told me it was looking for my dad's ring."

"Kara, Mothman and Indrid Cold *visited* you? *What?*" His eyes pleaded, as if he were asking her to tell him something, *anything* else besides this.

"I don't know." She covered her face in her hands. "His face was so fucked up. Like he was dead, but not. And Mothman. He shows up before these great catastrophic events, like the Silver Bridge collapse. Which makes me *really* concerned."

Alec's face was pale. "Yeah. I read that years ago. I still have a copy."

"I know. That's the copy I read."

He offered a small smile. "You're right. You mysteriously handed it back to me when I never knew you had it. Nicked it from my toolshed hovel."

"Mm-hm." She nodded. "I'm not sure which scared me more. The encounters with Mothman, or those aliens. Interdimensional beings. Whatever they were."

"The men in black freaked me out the most. Them, and Indrid Cold." He shuddered.

"Hm." Suddenly, she felt impossibly cold. Her skin was diamonds. She crossed her arms.

"I'm not going to ask you if you're sure that's what you saw," Alec said.

Her eyes filled. "Thank you." She held her breath, picturing her dad again. At Hope. In the ground. With all this craziness going on. What was he doing right now? Lying there dead? Screaming for help? Walking around somewhere? *He's not resting. I don't know what's happening with him but he's suffering.*

Alec's voice was gentle but startled her all the same. "What are you thinking right now?"

"I'm freaking out about my dad again." Nausea climbed her throat and settled around the spot where it threatened to convulse into crying again.

"Listen, just sit down for a minute. Sit down and just be here. Your mind is everywhere, just be here with me, hm? Did anything follow you here?"

"I don't think so." She walked over, sinking into the cushy sectional in that kind of forgiving walnut color that looked happy in the sun and cozy when only the lamp was on. She sighed. He grabbed a flannel off the arm of the couch and shrugged into it, covering up his Gjallarhorn tattoo.

She could practically smell light beer and buttered popcorn, and remembered when she'd gone with him to get the tattoo one fall break during college. He kept making a slight gritted-teeth expression whenever the tattoo artist looked away, pretending he was in intense pain. They'd come back here after and watched one of the Thor movies. He'd already discovered his love for mythology and had finished several classes, so that night, he jokingly played a bitter history buff, exaggeratedly pointing out all the ways the movies got the source material "dead wrong. *So-ho-hooo* dead wrong." It devolved into jokingly ridiculing every choice any of the characters made. There was a lot of laughing that night, the breathless kind, where her sides hurt.

Being here folded up her troubles; perfect, marrying the well-worn creases, like a map.

"How come you're staring at my couch?" he asked.

"Trying to measure with my eyes how old this thing is." How quickly she felt herself rushing back.

"Probably as old as you and me."

"Like it was made in the eighties?" She tugged a fleece blanket off the back of the couch and wrapped it around herself.

"No, like, I think it's been around since we met."

"Oh. Not quite as old, but still old." She smiled. "What's this?" A messy stack of pictures sat on the side table, some bent at the corners, the edges wavy with age and some kind of dried liquid.

"Oh, those are old too."

"Yeah, they look like shit. You should keep 'em in a box or something."

"I normally do."

Kara stretched her body lazily across the arm of the couch from her spot, practically in the middle, and snagged the pile with the tips of her fingers.

"Oh my god, our college graduation!" she squeaked, then pressed her lips together, surprised by how high-pitched the sound was. "Look at us!" She squinted at it. That was when he still had that crooked incisor, before the Invisalign. She missed the way it stuck out when he smiled. She looked at him now; he was grinning warmly at her. She realized she was smiling at him, too.

She stopped, biting her lip. "Why do you always make that face?"

"What face?" he moved his fingers near his cheeks, his eyes roving as if hunting for the answer.

"No," she pointed to the photograph. "Like, for pictures."

He laughed, cautiously and repeated the question. "*What* face?"

She made her voice deep and goofy. "You know, like: *huh-huh-huh. I can't believe you're takin' muh picture.*"

"Can you ever just not make fun of me?"

"No."

Alec rolled his eyes and dropped into the easy chair. He leaned forward, resting his elbows on his thighs, and ran his fingers through his hair.

"You have a really nice smile," she offered, with a grin. "I love your *real* smile."

He watched her, sideways. "Yeah, well. You force me to smile for pictures, that's what you get. I can't fake happy."

Kara's smile was real, but the corners were worrying back down, tucking it away. She had to make him do this. They needed answers.

"Alec, remember how the skull thing turned out all right?"

"I do, yeah. I don't remember really figuring out *why* it did, though."

"It's probably my ring that fixed it."

"'Probably' isn't good enough. You don't know for sure the ring fixed it."

"You won't let me test my theory, though. All it would take is taking the ring off for one second, and looking at you. And then we'd know."

"Okay, so you'd potentially see my face as a skull again and we'd learn something. But then what else would happen? We have no idea. There has to be a safer way to learn more. A safer way with fewer unknowns."

Kara shook her head. "What about the unknown I just grappled with? All by myself in the middle of the night? These weird things and people are appearing in our town, whether we do something or nothing. This Indrid Cold guy who scared me at the gas station? I was terrified. The skin of his face was . . . drooping. He was horrible, but he helped me find my ring, and he said 'use your gifts.' I think this is your gift. I need you to drive, and I need to be with you when it happens. I just need you to trust me."

"So you're going to trust that ghoul?"

"Not trust. Test his claim. Just like you're trusting this ring to protect me without knowing anything else. I didn't tell you that he came up to the car and told me I dropped it. Helped me find it."

"I get what you're saying. You have a point. But it just feels like you're asking me to trust you as I jump off a building." Alec shrugged. "I can't just make the fear disappear."

"Maybe I *am* asking you to jump off a building. Maybe I'm telling you to jump and promising you can fly, but you won't know until you do it."

He chuckled. "You're fucking kidding me, right?"

"I mean, I said that to make you laugh on purpose, so maybe."

"I'm laughing because this feels like an urban fantasy action film."

"Well since it's been your lifelong dream to be the main character in an urban fantasy action film, let's go." She got up from the couch and gestured for him to follow. "You're the one, Neo," she whispered. "Let's go."

He took a step toward her. "I swear I'm only going to do this so you can see how fucked up it is you're making me do it again." His voice had some mirth in it, but his face was weighted with equal parts darkness and fear.

She picked up the keys and offered them to him, flashing her eyebrows playfully. She realized the only way to shake him out of it was to push through it. "I bet I won't scream," she tried.

"I bet you will."

***

Kara plunged herself into the weird exposed metal smell of Alec's car, groaning as she wrestled against the hard, unforgiving seats. "God, this car is so old."

"Not as old as us."

"Cars age like dogs." Kara jammed the buckle in and shoved her purse straps down. They normally drove places separately, so sitting next to him in his car brought back memories of high school. Sharing their favorite bands. Singing together loudly. Messing up lyrics and laughing about it. Those memories were colored differently now that this crush had materialized.

She sighed. "What is this car in dog years?"

Alec whispered numbers to himself. He tapped a bent index finger up to his lips. "I got it in high school, so . . ."

"Who buys a car in high school, anyway? Seventeen, you somehow saved up enough for a car, and then, there go your savings."

Alec's mouth was a hard line for a while, then he spoke. "Glad you didn't tell my seventeen-year-old self that. He'd be crushed."

"Oh yeah, you really cared what I thought when you were seventeen."

"I did, though."

"Sure."

"No, I'm serious. And if I remember right, you were so impressed at the time."

"Not impressed, no. I was jealous."

"At seventeen? Impressed and jealous are the same thing, Kare."

"Mm, touché. How much life do you think this thing has left in it?"

He slapped the dashboard. "Oh, this thing? This thing is just *flirting* with death."

"Speaking of flirting with death." Kara slapped Alec on the shoulder, mimicking his dashboard slap. "Are you gonna start this thing, or . . . ?"

"Um," he took a deep breath in, and exhaled slowly. Tapped the ignition, then let go again.

She touched his elbow gently. Her breath quickened. She ignored it. "You know what my mom told me when my dad died?"

"No, you never said." His stare was intense; his jaw set stiff and off a little, in thought. At least she'd distracted him a little from the nerves.

"I'm the one who called her from the hospital to tell her he was gone. Of course she cried first. But then she said 'I'm telling you Kare, the universe and all the hard objects in it? It's only a matter of time before one of those things comes knocking. And whoever doesn't last to next year? It's not gonna think too hard on that question.'"

"That sounds a bit harsh, doesn't it?"

"Yeah. Being reminded of my own mortality right after my dad died? Pretty harsh."

"So that was *not* meant to comfort me, right?"

"No. Just . . . you know this whole gas station visit? Now, I know it as a fact: something's *clearly* after us. Exploring these things is only going to help us find out more."

"But how do you know the weird car thing and the skull aren't caused by that entity?"

"The minute stuff started happening, I had that dream. The dream where that thing said not to touch you again. I think the things happening *to* us might be a good thing. If she's bad, and she doesn't like this stuff, I think if we stick together and try to test these things out, that is the last thing it wants us to do."

Alec sighed, hand on the ignition. "So, where to?"

"Well, since we're speaking of Miss 'hard objects,' let's go to my mom's. I want to check out a book of my dad's. It's called *Weird Trees of North America.*"

"Ohh, because of Red Tree Hill. That makes sense. It's really late, though."

"Yeah, she never sleeps."

Alex breathed in again and held it. "Okay. Here we go."

"So, what'd you do last time?"

"I just started it up, thought of where I was going, and started driving. Then suddenly, I was there."

"That's fucking awesome."

"Yeah, *awesome.*" His sarcasm had teeth.

"Just do it."

"Hmm. Kay." His knuckles were white. But he twisted the key.

The engine turned over.

He growled, then smiled, tight-lipped while she laughed. Tension reigned, stretching taut between them. "Second time's a charm."

Alec turned the key again. The engine cleared its throat, then roared. He clunked down the gearshift and backed up, hand resting on the back of her headrest.

"Nice and easy, Al, you can do it." She had a small additional theory she needed to test. She shifted her gaze to Alec and then, staring forward, she removed her necklace, put it in her pocket.

He shifted into drive, let out a big breath, and drove.

Kara had watched very little science fiction in her life, but Alec's old Corolla had clearly slipped, or shot, or whatever, into warp drive. Her eyes were stuck closed. Her head was thousands of pounds, pressing violently against the hard-ass headrest, as her neck trilled in agony, pain ringing up her skull and battering her back.

She forced her eyes open, her hammering heart doing a backflip when she saw: not trees, or buildings, or anything rushing by; just a whitish-blue funnel shape, flaring out in front, like they were inside a horn and being thrown forward toward its opening.

The moment she regarded it, the need to breathe throttled her like a steel hand, and the inertia reversed, wrenching her forward. A brutal crashing sound of splintered wood, a joint impact. Kara sat forward, hair over her eyes, stuck in her mouth. She choked, shoving her hair back, breaths coming fast like a panicked rabbit.

Quickly, she pulled the necklace back around her neck and surveyed the damage. They had crashed into a giant stack of wooden skids. One had slid up the hood, still fully intact, and a whole mess of the rest of them made a wide, violent "V" where the car had made impact. They were in a giant yard, in front of a big Craftsman house with blinding outdoor lights, its sides and back hugged by a big "C" of forest. All around them was shorter greenery; big elaborate plant beds and trellises built up with wooden railroad ties, or repurposed brick, or . . . broken up skids. More than enough confirmation that they'd arrived in her mom's front yard.

The next sounds were muffled to Kara. Words.

"Oops. Shit, I'm sorry."

"Oops?" she spat the word, slapping her hand against the dash. "Could you have warned me?"

"Warned you?" Alec asked loudly. "*Warned you?* Kara, god, did I *ever* warn you! If it weren't for you I'd never have done this again! Didn't I make that clear?"

"But the w—" she stopped herself. "The warp drive thing? The giant funnel?" She covered her face in her hands. She sounded ridiculous. But it wasn't ridiculous. They'd just gone through that together, right?

Right? She touched the ring around her neck again, gently.

His face was drawn, exhausted. "Kara? Funnel? What the hell are you *talking* about?"

"Okay, please," she begged. "Just tell me, from *your* point of view, what just happened?"

"It was all the same as last time! Well, besides the fact that I crashed into *these* things." He gestured to the stack of skids. "The other times, I ended up in the parking lot, where I was supposed to end up."

"Okay. So the roller coaster to the fucking *basement* of hell, the goddamn *backwards tornado* kissing the windshield. You didn't experience *any of that?*"

"I mean, no. The seatbelt pulls me really hard at the end, but what you're describing? No. I don't experience that. It's really just like I blink and I'm there."

"Okay, well, that's very, very nice for you. I absolutely don't want to do this ever again."

"And that's fine with me. You're the new driver."

She stared at the dashboard, seething.

"You're mad at me, aren't you."

She took a deep breath, closed her eyes, and sighed. "I really have no right or reason to be. It was my idea. But yeah. Sorry."

"What can I do?"

"Just, wait with me until I'm less . . . hot with rage? Then let's go in."

"Okay. I can do that."

***

Kara rubbed her collarbone. She rotated her shoulder and it didn't make her scream. So, it wasn't broken. But the pain was seriously knocking.

"I crushed your mom's wooden skids." Alec stated the obvious again, sagging back in his seat a little.

"I'm sure it'll be fine."

He just stared at the skids. "Why are these even here?"

"Oh, she keeps these things when she gets furniture deliveries. Then does projects in the yard." Kara gestured all around her.

"That's a lot of furniture."

"Well, she sort of collects them from people in town, too."

"Nice hobby."

"Let's go in." Kara moved quickly out of the car and up the front walk. Alec rushed to keep up.

"Okay. Quick warning," she was already panting a little. Pitiful. "My mom's even weirder since my dad died."

"Beyond her great-at-math, bad-at-people shit?"

"Way beyond. It's been super awkward. She says inappropriate shit that upsets me, and then acts like a fucking robot, like she doesn't understand what my human problem is."

"I think I can handle it."

"Okay," Kara extended the vowel sarcastically. "But I warned you."

"She likes me."

"Yeah. You give her attention. Of course she likes you." Kara rolled her eyes. "Do me a favor, please don't let her bait you, okay? Like, if she says something weird, don't invite her to elaborate. I promise you we'll both regret it."

"I'll be good."

They climbed the porch steps up to the soft green Craftsman-style house with the natural stone pathway and red brick pillars.

Lola answered the doorbell almost immediately and Kara entered first. The smell of baking bread and maybe a tiny hint of burning hung absolutely everywhere.

"Hi Mrs. Lenker," Alec nearly shouted before he'd finished walking through the door. Kara shot him a cold look. He shrugged with his hands and mouthed *"What?"*

"Alec, remember, you can call me Lola. You guys are grownups now."

"Okay, Lola. Your hair looks nice, by the way. It's cool you don't dye it." He grinned smugly at Kara.

"Oh, my gray streaks? Thanks. I don't believe in using paraphenylenediamine."

"Oh, that. Yeah." Alec rubbed his neck and raised his eyebrows at Kara.

"What was that noise outside?" Lola scurried over to the front hall table and started sorting out clutter, as though they were still on their way and she could hide it all. "You okay, little bird? You seem disheveled," Lola asked from behind an armful of takeout bags and a big cardboard box. Her silvery-brown hair was wavy, still drying from the shower.

"Uhmm, I'm fine. I kind of bumped the skids out front with Alec's car." She was coming to the conclusion that forcing Alec to boomerang himself from point A to point B through a tornado might have caused this problem. So the least she could do was take the rap. She looked down at her shoes and kicked at the wood floor. "You haven't called me Little Bird since I was a kid."

Lola bustled into the other room. The garbage bag rustled loudly. She shouted from the kitchen. "Hey, I texted you after the shiva. We need to burn the Yartzeit candle, but you never responded. You sure everything's okay?"

Ah, yes. The Yartzeit candle. Kara was still a little pissed her mom forgot to light it. After Mom had insisted on sitting with her dad's body at the funeral home and then bailed, Kara had already had more than enough. Sure, mourning looks different for everyone, but these weird behaviors were beyond unacceptable. The first was overcharged with unnecessary drama, and the second, flippant. Like she didn't care at all. It's not like it was a distant cousin or something. It was her *husband*. You don't forget to light your own husband's Yartzeit candle. Was it normal for things to get this fucked up after a death?

No. Nothing had been normal since he died. Nothing.

Kara pushed her angst down. The garbage bag rustling had gone on for three full minutes now. She practically had to get on tiptoes, trying to shout and be heard. "Did you hear me about the skids? I crashed into them in the yard. And yeah, I'm okay." And shit, she'd forgotten about the candle too, after her mom and texted. What did that say about her? "Everything got to be a bit much. I'm really sorry."

Lola returned from the kitchen and aimed a leveling gaze at Kara. "Hm, that's a big ways to travel up into the yard. You don't *look* inebriated."

"Thank you?"

"I'm glad to see you're wearing his jacket. He wanted you to have that, remember? And . . . oh, *hello* there."

Here we go. Already past the big strange occurrence. As important to her as someone tying their shoe. Lola's eyes traveled down to . . . what? Kara's boobs?

"Huh? Hi? Oh."

Lola stepped forward and touched the ouroboros ring around Kara's neck. "I've been looking for that. I wondered what happened to it. I was going to wear it. Same way as you, around my neck. Or get it resized."

"Oh, shit, ma." Myriad shits. Could not afford to give that thing up, taking it off just threw her down a doom tunnel. "I really wanted to keep this. I'm sorry." Well done. *Very* convincing.

Lola stepped back and withdrew her hand, recoiling like something stung her. "Oh." Her eyes turned down at the corners. "I guess that's okay. Yeah, you should have it, then."

"I'm sorry, ma," she repeated. "What about, like, his wedding ring or something?"

She paused, biting at her thumbnail. "I kind of accidentally buried him in it."

Jesus Christ. "Mom! What do you mean, accidentally? *How?* Don't they double check for that stuff?"

"Well, I wanted *him* to have it. You know, to take part of me with him in a way. But they said they normally don't do that. I kept thinking, I'd be buried with my ring, and he'd be buried with his. So I used my persuasive ways until they relented."

Kara stared. She knew her mother's "way" all too well. Basically, she strong-armed them into going against their policy.

"Once he was buried I changed my mind and asked them to get it." She shrugged. "But I guess they frown on that," she said sarcastically.

"You didn't *actually* ask them to retrieve Dad's ring after he was buried."

Her mom didn't respond.

"That bothers me. Maybe we can find you something else you can wear of his, then," Kara mumbled. She was used to her mom being weird, even extra-weird, but this was awful. She actually asked them to exhume her father to get the ring back? That had to be made up, right? For attention, maybe?

"There was a death, you know. At the quarry."

"When? Recently?"

"No. When you were a baby."

"Oh, yeah, that. You told me about that before."

Lola continued anyway. "His job was so dangerous, Kare." She looked grave. "After the accident, I tried to get him to apply as a custodian at the university, but he refused. I told him that place was poisoning him from the inside out."

Poisoning him. Kara thought about that. The sound of his cough was burned in her memory. The relentless struggle to breathe. His body weak, rail-thin, so fatigued he practically sunk into his hospital bed.

Lola prattled on. "Of course, that did the opposite of convincing him to quit working there. Or to remember to wear his stupid mask. You know how he was. Never wanted to listen to me. *Especially* if I was right."

Everything in Kara's body cringed. She couldn't listen for another second. "Did you *hear* about the cemetery?" Kara blurted out, changing the subject.

"What do you mean? What about it?"

"About the broken monuments with missing pieces?"

"No."

"It's so weird. There was this earthquake that seemed to *just* be centered on the cemetery and nowhere else in town." She looked at her mom, who was eyeing her sideways over the swerve in conversation. Processing. Slowly grasping the subject change. Kara pressed on. "Then, Gabriel's trumpet from the entrance and the eyes of St. Lucy just disappeared."

"Gabriel's trumpet's gone? It'll have to turn up!"

"Why do you say that?"

"It has an infinite surface area!"

"This is another math joke, isn't it."

Her mom smiled big. The closed-lipped, amused, trying-not-to-laugh smile. Nodded, knowingly. "Yep. The Gabriel's trumpet paradox. That a horn or funnel shape in mathematics has a finite volume, but an infinite surface area. If you measure the curve of that horn shape on a graph, the point will never fully reach zero, so it continues into infinity." Lola pantomimed a horn, spreading her fingers and making a bird-like gesture with the heels of her hands to mimic the spreading of the larger end of the horn.

"Imagine, studying the nature of infinity," Kara whispered.

"I don't have to imagine," Lola said.

Kara stared.

"Kinda freaky, right? And when you marry that with the biblical meaning, it's symbolically connecting us with the spiritual realm."

"How?"

"Well, we are finite, but in religion we grapple with the nature of infinity. So that horn represents it well. It's a material object we can grasp, but its call reaches to infinity. Connects our world to a more magical one."

Kara tilted her head, studying her mother's words, rolling them around in her mind.

Alec cleared his throat and chimed in. "And the fifth angel blew his trumpet, and I saw a star fallen from heaven to earth, and he was given the key to the shaft of the bottomless pit."

"Alec?" Kara froze. "What the hell."

"Just a bible verse I thought was freaky as a kid. I kinda hunted around for the creepy stuff and memorized a lot of it."

Kara quirked an eyebrow at him.

"Church is boring." He put his hands in his pockets and shrugged. "And long."

Fear pricked the back of Kara's neck. Why did a bible quote feel exactly like what had been happening? None of this could end well. And while her brain barreled through the parallels, the Doom Tunnel sprang to mind again. She lowered her voice, turning to Alec. "That tornado. When you were driving. It didn't look like a tornado, really. It was smooth, just like a trumpet. And Gabriel's horn in math is literally a funnel shape with an infinite volume." She pantomimed wiggling the wheel of a car.

Alec lifted his bottom lip, which she interpreted as discreet curiosity.

"What are you guys talking about?" Lola was staring at them.

"Oh nothing. Something's wrong with Alec's . . . car. I'm gonna try to fix it later. Yeah." She made her face change, tried to look like she'd just thought of something important. "Anyway, I wanted to take a book of dad's, do you mind?"

"Be my guest."

Kara and Alec headed through the kitchen and into the den.

"So, what book is this we're talking about?"

"It's called *Weird Trees of North America*. I was spacing out, staring at it during Dad's shiva, and I saw the letters move."

"Huh. And you think *that* tree is in there?"

"I don't know. It's possible. He wasn't any kind of tree enthusiast as far as I knew, but he *was* pretty into our town's history. He used to blab to me about stuff all the time. You know, mundane nonsense like 'do you know how old this building is?' To be fair, it's probably really impressive, but you know how because it's your parent telling you, you just kind of hear things washed of all their color?"

"Yeah, I know what you mean."

"So anyway, I think Barre history, plus a book about weird trees, might equal stuff about the Red Tree."

"Do you think the Red Tree could be the cause of anything though? Like, the story goes that *dog people* attacked that guy, and his heart disappeared. How could a tree be responsible?"

"I really don't know that it could be responsible. But my dad was there, everything happened right after Sammy took an axe to that tree, and he kept this book on his shelf, so it's worth checking." Kara's heart sank as she finished her sentence. Almost all the books on the shelf she'd been looking at were gone.

"Mom!" she shouted, causing Alec to jump. "What'd you do with Dad's books?"

"I sold some of the comics. They were valuable!"

"Jesus!" she whispered angrily. "Already?"

"Not nearly everything, honey. Just one shelf full! I ordered a set of encyclopedias and needed the space."

"For god's—" she turned to Alec. "What does she want encyclopedias for? Has she heard of the fucking internet?"

"What's the 'fucking internet?'" Alec grinned at her.

Kara snorted. "Shut up," she said, swatting at him. She grabbed at the last book that lay face down on the dusty shelf. "What's this?"

"*Our Heavenly Visitors* by Tobias Carr," Alec read the title over her shoulder. "I've never heard of this guy. This is your dad's shelf? That does *not* sound very Jewish. The name *or* the title."

Kara shook her head. "It doesn't look like a religious text of any kind either, though, does it?" She flipped the book over. "Hah, okay, how confusing is this? The title reads like a religious text but look at the back copy." She handed the book to Alec.

Alec read the back. "'These heavenly visitors are anything but heavenly. The only thing that makes them heavenly is the fact that they come down from the heavens.'"

Kara's heart thudded faster as she read the next part. "It says they came from space."

"Eesh, that stuff creeps me out."

"Do you believe it?"

"I mean, I just believe that I have no idea."

"Right?" She sat down on the big sectional, laying her dad's jacket on the couch and setting down the book on her lap. She flipped back to the table of contents. Twenty-seven chapters, a list of cities and states.

"There's Barre," Alec said, sitting down next to her. Kara looked, moving the book toward him so he could see better.

Something slid from between the pages, landing on her thigh. It was a photograph: her dad, looking very young, and three others. He was in the driver's seat of an old car, his face close to the camera, selfie-style. Another young man leaned in from the passenger seat, and a guy and girl cuddled close in the back seat. Their eyes all had a wildly happy sheen to them.

"They look stoned," Kara mumbled, amused. She set the book against her lap, framing the edges of the picture with both hands, inspecting it further.

"You know who that is in the passenger seat, don't you?" Alec's voice shook a little.

Kara narrowed her eyes at the left-most figure. "Shit."

"Yeah, shit." It was Charlie Foley. Grinning. Acne on his jawline instead of the pockmarks there now. No deep creases across his forehead. Not a care in the world. She knew Charlie as someone who always joked around but in this picture he looked carefree. She thought about him now. Jaw muscles tight when he wasn't talking. His eyes wandering when he smiled, like someone was missing, just out of his reach.

"You don't think that's Sammy and his girlfriend in back?"

"Could this be from the night Sammy died?"

Kara's eyes filled. "Yeah, I think so. My dad had to have put this here for a reason, right?"

Alec nodded, his eyes wide. "Kara. This is too real."

She sighed. "Yup." She wiped the tears off her cheek and slid the picture back into the book. She sniffed quietly and saw Alec's face turn toward her. She held her breath, now, for a different reason. Stayed facing down at the book.

She saw his hand go to his face, thumb and fingers holding it, in thought.

She turned to him. He was holding his chin. Looking down. Biting his lip.

He reached behind her. His hand rested against her side, gentle but firm. He didn't pull her closer, just rested it there. A gesture, no pressure.

His voice had that gravelly sound when he spoke. It was deeper than usual. "You okay?"

"I dunno." Hm. About that. She felt the skin on her face flush. Her neck. Her stomach flipped and her whole body was warm, rolling, pins and needles. He was still watching her intently. *What does he think about when he looks at me like that?* she wondered.

He cocked his head. "Should we just take this with us and read it later?" His voice, still low, had dropped to a murmur. It felt intimate, like they were deciding something important together.

"No." *Definitely not. Not moving from this spot.*

The print with their town's name was bold and dark against a stark white page, and the font looked eaten away at the edges, an apt style choice.

Alec whistled, a surprised kind that caught her off guard. She jumped. He gave a short humorless laugh.

"I scared *you* this time." His face was grave. "So," he said quietly. "We're gonna read this now, huh?"

"I'm afraid," she whispered, turning the pages with a shaking hand. "Oh my god," Kara mumbled, flipping back a few chapters. "This book has a chapter on Point Pleasant, too. Mothman Prophecies."

"Good old M.P.," he said quietly. "That's our book." He smiled, close-lipped and his eyes were cast down.

She flipped back to the bookmarked page and started reading.

13

OUR HEAVENLY VISITORS

72   Tobias Carr

The month was August. The year: 1992. There were reports that a man named Indrid Cold had surfaced again, the first time having been in 1966, on the backroads of Mineral Wells, West Virginia. In chapter four of this book, we detailed his many encounters with the residents of Point Pleasant, West Virginia. Now here he was, doing the same in Barre, Vermont. A few local townspeople reported receiving calls from Indrid Cold, asking them if they worked in the quarry. If they knew where he could find the Red Tree. Other reports came in that during these calls, he stated he was looking for "the dragon with its wings shorn off." None of that made sense to anyone, of course, but they were rightly terrified.

Some were visited in person. They reported a grinning man, similar to previous reports of Indrid Cold. Those in Barre who saw him in person said his skin appeared "not to fit correctly," tight in some places, and loose in others. I have a theory as to the reason, which I will expound upon later. All signs point to the one encounter in Barre that ended in unspeakable tragedy.

All accounts regarding Cedro Testa and Dino Orlando indicated a fraught partnership. Their fathers had joined forces to found Testa & Orlando Monuments in the sixties. Cedro loved the business. He grew up wanting to run it. After his father passed, he spent hours on the floor putting in hard labor six days a week.

When Dino's father died, he urged Cedro to sell; but Cedro wasn't having it. So it went for a couple of years. Dino made some bad bookkeeping decisions and they had to lay off all their workers.

I was able to pay a visit to Cedro's workshop, which he nicknamed his "hall of masterpieces," but to the outsider, even with daylight shining through the windows, it invokes a certain quiet dread. Stone figures in repose, or serene contemplation. Indoors, though, they appear eerily lifelike. So lifelike, in fact, that they looked as if they might start to move or speak.

On this night, Cedro forgot something in the workshop, and drove the three miles back to recover it. When he walked in, those silent stone sentinels would have been waiting in the dark. If only they could have spoken. They could tell us for certain who did this.

Cedro needed something from the back office. Today, he doesn't even recall what that thing was. All he remembers is the entire room smelled like iron. That, and one other thing: the waking nightmare that greeted him when he flipped on the light.

It wouldn't be identified as Dino Orlando's body until later that night. To say he'd been ravaged would be a gross understatement. He'd been expertly and painstakingly skinned from head to toe. A cadaver of muscle and bone.

Cedro claimed the body was not resting, but frozen in place, stretched out in unthinkable pain: back arched, jaw opened impossibly wide, arm reaching toward him. Of course, when it had happened, the poor man was probably just trying to make it to the doorway. What a haunting image and memory to hold of the last time one saw their lifelong friend.

***

"Oh my god," Kara breathed. "Oh my fucking god."

"So according to this book, like—" Alec cut himself short.

"Yeah. They say Indrid Cold's been here." Her mouth went dry. "So really, that's actually probably who I saw."

"Kara, I don't want to say it but . . ." Alec fingered the right-most page.

"I don't want you to say it either." The light illuminated the page Kara held. A shadowed dark square from the next page showed through the current one. "Seriously. There's more on the next page."

"I know. I don't want to see it. It's gonna look like the living person. The one whose skin Indrid Cold took. The skin he's wearing right now."

"Well, I mean, maybe not." Alec's voice was low.

"How could it *not* be?"

"Not to be gross but, does skin keep for thirty—"

"No, you're right, that *is* really gross." Kara covered

her mouth. Was this real? Was this possible? Did he leave the skin behind somewhere, then come back for it? Or was he always here on this planet, dimension, *whatever*, wearing it? Did he soak it in something? Preserve it? "I really don't think he got a new skin. We were both apparently totally unaware of this story. If someone had been killed and had their skin removed recently, we'd have heard about it, don't you think?"

"I don't know."

Kara squinted her eyes, breathed in, held it. That sweet-sour smell of what had to be rotting meat returned to her nose, like smelling the ghost of that thing that made you sick, hours later. Holding her breath, she turned the page.

The picture was awful quality, a grainy photocopied thing. It was hard to tell the subject's age, but deep lines were etched down his face. His skin looked stiff, like he was working hard to hold his composure.

She nodded, slowly. "I think that's who he was using. I wonder when this was taken."

"Kara, his partner. Cedro's still working. At the same workshop by the quarry."

"Yeah, I know. Everyone knows that."

"Yeah. He comes into the restaurant. We've seen him."

"Well, maybe we can just wait until he comes back in."

"Kara."

"What!"

"Who's avoiding shit now?"

"I'm not." She sighed loudly. "Yeah, let's go talk to him." She closed the book.

14

ROCK OF AGES

"It's dark," Kara said quietly as they emerged into the cool night air. She could just make out the tree line behind the house, fanning out across the darkening sky. In this town, the night felt like a jungle. As if every living thing awoke at night to observe them from between the trees.

She couldn't stop thinking of her dad in the bookmark photo. Young, free-spirited, potentially stoned, with his friends. She was already older than her dad in that picture.

What did that night do to him?

All the history of this town was piling up. A skinless monster woman walking around in a robot suit. Indrid Cold stealing peoples' skin. Dog people. Mothman. And why was this happening now? She prayed Cedro would have some answers. That he would even talk to them, period.

"These woods feel very full tonight," she grumbled, walking toward the car. She felt like she could never walk outside at night in this town again without this new electric charge in the air.

"I know exactly what you mean," Alec said. "This place feels different somehow."

"Yup."

"You know what it makes me think of?"

"What?"

"That first fall bonfire from last year."

"We do that every year. Why last year?"

"Well, remember, last year was different? We usually do it at your parents'."

She brightened. "Oh yeah! It was too cold out. The frost had come early. We took my parents' logs to my place and used my fireplace." Immediately, she remembered the second detail. She covered her mouth and laughed silently, catching Alec's gaze.

He grinned so big his eyes crinkled at the corners. "Well, first issue, the flue was shut."

She nodded. "The fire alarm went off."

"And then, while you were waving the smoke away from the detector, I leaned in to open the flue, and there they were."

"The spiders!" She chuckled. "I still think it had to be more than one egg sac. Those things *carpeted* the floor."

"You wanted to kill them all." Alec shook his head, smiling as they both ducked into the car. Kara on the driver's side.

"I didn't know they were in there when I lit the fire!"

"No, I mean, after they started running out at us, your solution to the problem was to kill them all."

"I didn't know what other option we had!"

"Me either. But I wanted to find another way."

"You just grabbed my fleece blanket and all but like ten spiders hopped on a magic carpet ride out over the balcony."

"Yup."

"How did you know that would work?"

"I didn't. Believe it or not, I've googled it many times since it happened, and I still have no answers."

"Huh."

"Actually, from what I read, that should *not* have worked."

"That's interesting." She put the key in the ignition.

"Yup."

"So . . . why did you bring that up?" She turned the key. The car started up without any issue.

"Ah, yeah, my point. So, remember how overwhelming that was at the time?"

Kara hummed quietly. "I think I see where you're going with this."

"See?"

"Yeah, I get it. Just gotta have faith and assume the spiders will flock to the blanket."

As she clunked into reverse, he put his hand over hers and squeezed. "Exactly. In the face of weird impossibility, the one thing that hasn't changed is you and me."

Her blood raced again, even hotter and faster, because she felt it now, for sure. When Alec had held her hand in the cemetery it'd been dark, and they'd been distracted. Now, he glanced at her hand, then back up at her. He loosened his grip, letting go a little. The sudden absence hit her cold and fast.

"Thanks for driving," he said in a low, quiet voice, then turned the other way to buckle in. His shoulders were rising and falling a little faster than normal, like he was trying to catch his breath.

"You okay?" Kara asked.

Alec nodded, almost imperceptibly, and she reversed slowly from the pile of skids, down the small hill and back to the road. She looked at Alec while clunking from Reverse to Drive. He rubbed his thumb side-to-side against his lips, absently, and her mind reeled.

***

Of course Cedro was still there at the workshop as the clock approached nine. Where else would he be? Somewhere normal, like home? Kara watched him go from surprised, to excited and friendly, to awkward and quiet. As he tried vaguely to smooth his wiry hair, inspecting them curiously, she realized he didn't normally entertain company here.

They asked to see his showroom, not knowing when to broach the reason for their visit. He'd welcomed them in, seeming unsure of what to say, settling for complimenting them both on how much he loved the rolls they served with their soups and salads at the restaurant. Behind him, Kara and Alec raised their eyebrows at each other and shrugged.

They passed through the tiny lobby, with its worn brown carpeting and old leather chairs. Thirty years ago this place would have seemed updated, but clearly nobody had touched it since then. Kara stifled a laugh. They'd tried. But literally, everything was brown. All different shades of it, too, like a UPS fanatic having an estate sale.

The second Kara entered the showroom, she was surrounded by black, white, and Barre Gray granite statues. Life-sized female figures wearing hooded cloaks, hands steepled in prayer, robed bearded figures, graceful hands reaching up as they ominously regarded the ceiling, tables with smaller figures atop them and half-finished disembodied torsos stacked carefully underneath. Busts decorated the back wall.

The only light source—one metallic green shade pendant—hung like a sole flickering star in the center of a galaxy of black ceiling beams, and one table lamp at the back of the vast room.

Cedro excused himself to use the restroom, returning to the lobby. Alec crossed the showroom toward Kara, who stood staring at the light, mesmerized. She thought about Indrid Cold, who had stolen the skin of the man who'd worked here. What had led him here? What clues could even be found here?

Kara had once heard that animals were easier to skin when alive. That wasn't true though, right? She was sure she'd looked it up.

"Do you think he even knows anything?" she asked Alec quietly.

"I have no idea."

"How would we even broach the subject?" She felt stuck. No way Cedro wanted to be led down a path of weird questions about his murdered business partner.

"I dunno. I was planning to let him talk a little, and then bring up Dino kind of gently."

"He didn't say anything to reporters," Kara noted. "I tried looking it up and every article said he never responded to their requests for a comment."

"Weird. I wonder why he talked to the guy who wrote that *Heavenly Visitors* book."

"Maybe he was different. Like, super trustworthy or something. His motives were probably way more benevolent than readership-thirsty bullshit." She noticed a messy workbench at the back of the room and headed straight toward it.

"Kara, thirty seconds ago you mentioned the importance of gaining this guy's trust?"

"Yeah, but what if we try asking, and he refuses?" She hovered over the stool in front of the long wooden table. "Imagine what he went through with losing Dino."

"Poor guy."

Kara beckoned Alec to follow. "This could be the only way we learn more."

A thick layer of granite dust covered Cedro's workbench, a million fingerprints dragged through it. A worker's N95 mask, goggles, and a giant Shop-Vac hose lay just to the side of the work area. The figure Cedro had been carving appeared to be in robes, on its knees, with hands in prayer like many of the others.

"That seems like a weird thing to put as a monument."

"Barre's got all kinds of weird things. But isn't he just kneeling in prayer?"

"I don't know, the legs are more bent and askew. It looks like he's begging."

"Do you think it means something?"

"No clue. Probably a commission, right? It's creepy, though." Alec walked in a circle around the statue while Kara inspected the table, avoiding the dust, as if she might incriminate herself.

"Check the drawer with the lock on it," Alec suggested.

"But . . . it has a lock on it."

"Yeah, I have one of those. I put my sensitive information in there. I also never lock it. And when I do, I leave the keys hanging out."

Kara clucked her tongue. "You're so freakin' smart, you know that?" She pulled at the drawer.

The damn thing was locked, though.

"Well, shit," she said quietly.

"The key's probably close by." Alec looked nervously toward the lobby. "He's been in there a while. He's probably coming back any minute."

"I feel like we'll hear him when he flushes the toilet, though." She pulled open the other drawers, hunting for the key.

The top right drawer had a small, sealed envelope in it. It was the size of a thank-you note.

Kara turned it over. "Cedro Testa," it read in a thin, black, leggy serif, with no address.

She shook the envelope in front of her, fanning herself with it. "Someone either slipped this in his drawer and he doesn't know about it, or it was left or given straight to him and he's afraid to open it," she hypothesized.

"So what do we do?" Alec asked.

Of course, the god-damned toilet flushed.

Kara stuck the envelope in the back of her pants and tried a few different positions with her hands. What did she normally do with them? Nothing, that's what. She walked among the sculptures and inspected them, waited for her brain to go back to autopilot instead of telling her she needed to fuss with her hands.

She spun toward Cedro when he entered the room. "You okay?"

"Fine," he said, gruffly. "Why did you come here?"

"Well, ah," Alec had nothing, she could tell. "We weren't sure you'd be here, but—"

"We were thinking of starting a lost and found at the restaurant," Kara said lamely. "We wanted your opinion."

"She's just kidding," Alec laughed. "We came to visit the quarry, and knew you were nearby, and were just wanting to see if you were in the workshop. We thought we'd say hi if you were here."

"Why were you at the quarry, though? At night?"

"I was sad about my dad," Kara said. "I wanted to be somewhere where he spent a lot of time."

Cedro wandered over to a sculpture of a robed man, resting his hand on its hooded head.

"Charlie told me he talked to you, Kara. Why didn't you listen?"

"You don't understand. I have to—"

"No, *you* don't understand. You shouldn't be here. This is no place for anybody at night."

"*You're* here." Kara walked toward Cedro, picking through the maze of statues, looking for places she could step.

"I'm not talking about me. All my money, all my family's money, is tied up in this place. I can't go anywhere."

"Why are you here so late?"

"I never stay late. I was about to leave when you both got here. I didn't want to scare you, but I'd like you to leave, so I can, too."

"Cedro," Alec called, still standing by the workbench. "Any idea how these got here?" He pointed to a horn-shaped sculpture leaning on a table.

Kara picked her way back over to Alec. A pair of marble eyes were set on the table next to the horn. She gasped quietly, held her hand to her mouth, and looked at Cedro.

"Everything in here has been carved by me. Why, what's wrong?"

"Cedro," Alec paused. "These two were taken from Hope."

"Nooo! No, no they weren't. Those pieces that went missing?"

"Yeah, those."

"No, no. Those, well, I don't know where *those* are. These ones you're looking at, they aren't to scale. Too small. I had to scrap a lot more carvings when I was younger. Not like now."

"So you did carve the eyes and the horn that were in the cemetery?"

"Yep, that was me. When the pieces went missing the other day, the cemetery commissioned me to replace them. They're not even making the families pay. They just want it to be resolved quickly. So I pulled out my replicas from storage."

Alec reached out and touched the horn. A loud whooshing sound came, and a gust of wind blew back Kara's bangs. She watched Alec's hair do the same.

"What the hell was that?" Kara demanded. She looked around frantically, fixing her hair.

"How odd. That's what happens when I finish a sculpture."

"What, it gets windy?"

"Yeah, that little 'whoosh.' It only ever happens when I'm sure I'm done, just needs a little more sanding. With the last stroke, a stiff wind shows up. Like magic. Like it's dusting off the last of the granite. Then, I know I'm done. I take my mask off and I clean up 'cause that's it. But it never happened when someone randomly touched it like this."

"And you've never wondered why that happens?"

"I did when I was little. I'd ask my parents, and they'd say 'oo!' and go, 'that's the ghost of the workshop.' Dino and I used to joke about it."

"It happened then, too?"

"Oh yeah, it's always happened. Happened to my grandfather, too. It's, what do you young folks call it? It's 'a thing.'"

"Has anything else weird happened?"

There was a scraping sound directly above them. Kara jumped.

"What was that?" Cedro ducked his head, looking nervous.

"I dunno." Alec stood very still, craning his neck, looking at the tile on the drop ceiling. Nothing for a minute. Then, footsteps.

"Do you have an upstairs?" Kara asked.

Cedro's face hardened. "No."

Another shuffling sounded, closer. Followed by a charged silence. They stared at each other.

"Is your door locked?" she whispered.

"No." They regarded each other, then Alec and Kara made a beeline for the door, Cedro following close behind.

"There another door in this place?" Kara practically barked the question.

"No. Well, yes. But it's always locked."

"How do you lock *this* one?" Kara depressed the silver bar on the door, then let it go again.

"Back away, back away," Cedro said gruffly, but quietly. "There's a key here. It's attached."

Kara had to wrench herself away from the door to let Cedro take over. Her hands shook. She hoped his were steadier.

"Do you ever hear noises like this?" She asked, as he turned the key in the lock and shoved the metal bar with his forearm, testing it. The steps grew a little quieter, as though pacing back and forth, above and behind them.

"Not normally, no," Cedro said. His features were still hard, and seemed pale, but tinged gray.

As desperation crawled over her, the apprehension for asking Cedro questions dissolved. "Are you afraid because of what happened to Dino?"

"Yes." Cedro's eyes swam.

Boom. Boom. Scrape. The sounds were slow, loud and sure. They followed the path the three had taken toward the door, growing until the footfall punished them from directly above.

They looked up again.

Then, the footsteps stopped completely.

"Should we back away from the door?" Alec whispered.

"No," Kara responded. "We need to hear if he lands on the ground so we know where he is."

Alec tapped Cedro on the arm to get his attention.

"Is this door soundproof?"

"I don't think so, but I have no idea."

"Think about it. When you're in the lobby, can you hear people pulling in to the parking lot?

"Yeah."

They stood there a while, shifting impatiently from foot to foot. After ten minutes, Kara took a bathroom break. When she came back out, Alec and Cedro sat cross-legged on the floor, Alec leaning back on the heels of his hands and Cedro picking at his boot.

She checked her watch. 9:10.

"How long have we been here?" Alec asked her.

"I think, like, ten minutes?" she guessed.

"I think I'm going to go out and look."

"I really don't think you should."

"I dunno, Kara. I'm not staying here until morning."

"Me either," Cedro chimed in.

"Well, if you go out, I'm going with you." She tried to smile.

"You stay in here," Alec ordered Cedro. Kara wondered why Alec hadn't argued with her when she insisted on coming with.

She and Alec hovered a little too close to Cedro while he unlocked the door. As soon as he stepped aside, Kara pushed the metal bar slowly and quietly in. She let herself and Alec back out into the frigid air. It seemed at least twenty degrees colder than when they'd entered.

Kara took Alec's hand, and they inched backwards cautiously until they could see over the lip of the flat rooftop. He married his fingers with hers and she pressed her lips nervously together.

"You don't see anything, right?" Alec whispered. He was flushed. She wondered if his heart was like hers, doing backflips from fear, and frontflips from her skin touching his.

"No."

They backed up further. Still, nothing.

"Could someone be lying down?" Kara asked. "We'd never see them if they were lying down."

"Maybe?" he squinted at her. "Do you think it's him?"

"I don't know. I'm not sure who else it would be, right?"

"It's odd," he mumbled.

"What is?"

"The footsteps started as soon as I touched that horn of Gabriel."

Kara's breath caught in her throat. "God, yeah. You're right."

"What does that mean?"

"When you touch something magic, he can find us?"

The call of a giant bell reached across the quarry from the tallest shelf of granite, its voice, deep and bass-y. It reverberated in the endless pit. Absently, Kara let go of Alec's hand and stepped toward the open pit. She was certain she could hear the sound of men laboring against the rock, but nobody was there.

She looked up into a sky that wasn't sentient, but watched them all the same, and thought about her dream.

15

THE UNDEAD

"Does the quarry have a bell?" Alec bit his bottom lip and looked at Kara absently.

"Not that I know of." She squinted, trying to focus. They stood mid-height on their platform of well-worn gravel about 300 feet from the quarry's shallow lake, the tallest walls of granite meeting at a corner just across from where they stood. The tall stone across the water seemed to be glowing an ethereal cloudy turquoise, just like the lake below. "Do you see that?" she asked. She pointed to the tallest formations. So tall, they seemed to scrape the heavens.

"Where?" Alec looked to where she was pointing. His eyes widened as they reached the spot. "Oh my—"

Kara stared harder. Shadows played over the stone. Twenty bodies making big sweeping movements, with what looked like pickaxes.

"There are people working?"

"It's night," she said, shaking her head. "And those shadows we're seeing are across the tallest section of granite. In front of it is all water. Nothing could be standing at the base of that, let alone working, Alec."

They made their way to the small hill that overlooked the bottom, both knowing what they would find. They knew this place too well to have to look.

But still.

They got to the edge, and Alec rubbed his face. "Yeah. That's where the lake is." He nodded slowly. "So what are those shadows, then?"

"The only thing that makes sense . . . makes no sense."

"Yeah," he breathed.

"The glow is coming from a tower of solid stone. It's almost like they're *inside* the stone. But they can't be. Nobody has started cutting that, yet."

"How—" Alec said, more a statement than a question. "Oh my god."

Kara looked at Alec, who was still gazing out across the quarry.

"What is that thing?" Alec whispered.

Kara followed his gaze. Standing near the miners was another shadow, twice the size of any human. It seemed to be observing the others. Its body was comprised of strange shapes. Long, ungodly skinny legs, a strange oblong torso the size of a mini fridge. It towered above the shadows of the men.

You mustn't touch that man again. The dream voice tore through her, agitating like a fresh memory.

Kara gasped. "That's the thing from the cemetery, and from my dream. I can feel it." Her hand leapt to her father's ring. She held it between her fingers, rolling it back and forth under her thumb.

"What can we do?"

"I don't know," she whispered.

Something heavy sounded behind them, by the door to Cedro's workshop. A body dropped down, landing loudly. Kara let out a short scream.

The thing was bent over, breathing heavy, staring at them. Kara's heart thundered in her chest, trying to move her, but she wouldn't dare.

"No," Alec moaned quietly as it turned toward the door. The yellowed light from inside the lobby washed its skin a sickly gray.

Indrid Cold.

The figure shoved the big metal door open further and slunk inside. The door creaked slowly shut behind it.

Alec moved to follow, but Kara held him back. With her eyes, she implored him to pause. They watched the door shut, and a muffled cry issued from inside. Kara's mouth went dry and her heart squeezed. She let go of Alec, and they ran quietly to the door.

In the lobby, the grinning man held Cedro by the lapel.

"You took him from me. From us," Cedro cried openly. Limp with grief, he tried to shove Indrid, but couldn't move his arms more than a few inches. "How dare you come back here."

"Let go," Alec said loudly, evenly. He curled and uncurled his hands. They were shaking, Kara saw.

"I will not." Indrid spoke between his teeth. "Come closer and I'll mar him with the thorns of my jaw." He curled his lips back to reveal blackened gums and thin teeth that curled like a cat's extended claws. "Do not test me. I will bleed your friend dry."

"Why are you here?" Alec demanded, forging his way forward.

Kara followed close behind.

Ignoring Alec, Indrid lowered Cedro onto bent knees and dragged him deeper into the building, toward the entrance of the workshop.

"Your skin has kept well," Indrid spat. "Not perfectly, but better than your partner's."

"Why? Why are you doing this? Why now, after being gone so long?"

"Clearly, your friend's pelt has spoiled. Hold still, my child, hold still." With some effort, Indrid shifted his hold on Cedro, turning him away and wrapping his arms around the sculptor's chest. "Come, join me at the workbench."

"I'm not your child," Cedro whimpered, spit forming at the corners of his mouth as he spoke, his face reddening. Equal parts furious and pitiful.

"You are a child. A child of earth! They don't hardly let you age here before you join the forever sleep and succumb to rot. You couldn't handle living longer than your blessed shelled reptiles." He hoisted Cedro's body onto the table. Cedro wrestled against it, twisting himself sideways and sliding off.

"Now," Indrid repositioned Cedro. Ran a finger along his jaw. "Tell me about my friend. Have you seen her?"

"Your friend?" Cedro's body stilled for a moment.

"Yes, don't play stupid. Your other visitor. The one from below."

"You don't know where she is." Cedro's voice was still high and strung out, but a resolute amazement nibbled at the edges.

"Tell me what you know, child." Indrid grasped Cedro's chin. He moved his face closer. "I'll wear someone else's skin and you will walk for hundreds more days. Tell me what you know."

"Fuck yourself. Wear my skin. Wear it well. I hope it rots early, testicles first."

"You will regret this."

Cedro half-laughed, half-sobbed. "I won't survive this. And you'll continue with your existence and your big problems to solve."

The nerve had drained out of Kara. But Alec persisted, and she followed. They closed the distance, coming directly behind Indrid.

Alec grabbed one of Indrid's wrists. Kara grabbed the other. The skin had an unnatural give to it. Like a damp sponge. Moisture seemed to leech off his arms and cling to her hands. She implored herself to ignore it, as they strained to work his hands apart and away from Cedro.

Slowly, Indrid moved his face close to Kara's.

Drooping eyes holding hers, graying skin, sewer stench. Her throat closed in protest. She suppressed a gag and pressed her mouth closed. She ground her teeth with violence and met his stare, breathing slowly, shallowly.

"Forget you. I don't want to look at you," Indrid told her, turning to Alec. Indrid shoved them away, hard. The three of them ran for the doorway.

Quickly, Indrid rushed after them, grabbing Cedro by the back of his shirt. Alec and Kara stopped in their tracks.

"Why the fuck are you still here?" Cedro shouted at them. "Get out!"

"Why waste your breath?" Indrid's grin tightened. His mouth opened wide, as he held Cedro's wrists together.

"Not *you*," Cedro spat. "Kids! Leave! Run! You shouldn't be here!"

Cedro shoved his knee into Indrid's gut, trying to pry himself away. A short struggle, and Cedro's head crashed against the wooden threshold leading to the lobby, leaving a smear of blood, and both parties on the ground.

Cedro groaned, eyelids fluttering. He touched the back of his head, staring at his bloodied fingers. He looked around, disoriented.

Indrid pressed his body on top of Cedro, holding him down. Cedro shook his head, more alert now, and punched Indrid awkwardly in the face. Laughing, Indrid grabbed hold of Cedro's arms and pressed them against the ground.

"Fuck! Kids!" Cedro screamed out. "Why are you still here?"

Kara sobbed angrily. "We have to help you." Besides, they couldn't get past the threshold to the front door. They were blocked.

"There's nothing to be done. Use the door at the back," he instructed between panicked breaths. Then, he spoke in Italian. "Trova lo stand."

Kara didn't know the phrase. She didn't know any Italian, in fact. But she repeated it in her head, trying to memorize it.

"Come on," Alec whispered. His eyes were grave.

"No," Kara said quietly. She stood still in the dark workshop, doing nothing.

Alec pulled her hard by the arm. "Your dad," he said. His eyes bore into hers. "We have to keep on. Cedro is gone and he knows it."

Kara forced her feet to move. Followed Alec past the statues.

A growl came from behind them. Kara looked back. Indrid had unhinged his jaw, his mouth stretching wide, like a steel trap. It pulled at the flesh on his face until his cheeks tore. With the shriek of something wild and inhuman, Indrid closed his jaws over Cedro's shoulder.

Behind the howling played the song of Cedro's collarbone snapping.

Just like that, his body went quiet. Blood poured over him in fast rivulets. Puddles stretched across the floor.

"Is he drinking it?" Alec's whisper was deathly quiet.

Kara didn't respond.

The crunching stopped. Indrid sat back on his haunches and spit into the gaping wound. Immediately, the blood seemed to expand, or at least thicken and congeal.

"He's liquefying him from the inside."

The thick red oozed out from the wound. Out from Cedro's eye and mouth holes.

Alec and Kara broke into a run into the pitch black at the back of the warehouse, finding the dim red exit sign, and slammed the door open. A fire alarm pierced the night. Kara made sure it latched behind them, and the sound ceased. They didn't stop until they were inside the car.

Kara gunned the engine and sobbed. "I can't believe we're leaving him."

"Please just drive." Alec didn't cry, but his voice was very small. He just stared at the dash. "We'll go to my place. Call the police."

She drove. Looked behind her before turning out of the lot. Nobody was following them. "What will we tell them? Nothing makes sense."

"I guess just start with the fact that Cedro's been killed. We'll figure it out on the way. We have to say something. There's a—" he paused. "There's a body. His body. In there."

"Will there be, though?" Kara struggled to see the road, her face contorted with crying. She wiped a hand over her cheeks, smearing the tears. She took a deep breath and coughed, then shut her mouth tight and swallowed her spit. "I feel like I'm gonna throw up."

"I know."

"Do you think Indrid will come for us?"

"I have no idea. Hopefully he got everything he needed."

Kara reached a stoplight, looked at Alec. "Hey. Do you think you're in shock?"

Alec shrugged.

What the hell could she do about it? Besides distract him. "What was that thing Cedro said? Trova lo stand. Is that Italian?"

"Yeah. It means 'find the booth.' Which makes sense."

"How?"

"Remember when we were waiting at the door in the lobby, when we heard the footsteps on the roof?"

"Yeah."

"This is so crazy," Alec shook his head. "You know when you went to the bathroom? When he heard the toilet flush, he grabbed me by the wrist and looked at me all serious. He said, 'If anything happens to me, go to the antique mall.' I asked him why. He told me the booth number."

"What's the booth number?"

"I can't remember. Three hundred something."

"Three hundred *something*? Alec, he's dead now! That place is *gigantic*!"

"Fuck, I don't know! I wasn't thinking he'd be dead and we'd have to go there. I was trying to be positive. Three hundred forty . . . something."

"How sure are you?"

"*Almost* totally sure."

"Okay, well. First things first." She pulled into his building's parking lot, new sweat prickling over the old sweat growing cold on her face. She swiped the back of her hand over her cheek. "We're here, so we'd better get inside and call."

16

ANTIQUE MALL

Ten minutes after Kara called 911, there was a knock at the door. Two shiny-shoed twenty-something police officers introduced themselves. They smelled like leather and wore nervous polite grins. For the briefest moment, Kara wondered if they were exotic dancers in expensive costumes.

"Aren't you going to the workshop?" Kara blurted, then bit her lip. Her stomach soured. She'd been secretly hoping nobody would show up at their door.

The guy—Officer Garrett—quirked an eyebrow and cleared his throat. "We were sent here, and some others were sent to the workshop." He was the same height as Kara, and somehow it made his gaze feel more direct, which intimidated her. Garrett looked down at the woman, Officer Browning. She wore her wiry blond hair in a side ponytail.

"Dispatch told us this Cedro Testa was murdered by a strange man? Without the use of a weapon?" He kept his eyes on her as he fiddled with his radio, then crossed his arms.

"Yes," Alec piped in. "That's correct."

"Had you ever seen this man before?"

"Alec hadn't," Kara said. "But I have." Kara was warring with herself over giving the supernatural details. What could they really do to help with that part, besides catalog this death and discredit the supernatural happenings until another life was taken? She shuddered as she realized, again, the implications of what had happened. The panic kept washing over her at random moments.

"Where else did you see him, and when?"

"At the gas station on Broad Street and Main. I think around seven."

"Today?"

"Yes. Tonight."

"Did you know him? Know his name? Had you ever seen him before that?"

"No. He started talking to me, unprompted. Saying things that didn't make sense. Then ran after me. I jumped in the car and locked the door. He seemed like he wanted to get in. Or maybe was just messing with me. He said his name was Indrid Cold." She watched the cop's face for a reaction.

Nothing. Not even an eyebrow twitch. "What did he say at the gas station? Did he make any verbal threats?"

"No, none. He was talking nonsense, it seemed like. But I was terrified when he tried to get in my car."

"And did he know where you were going later?"

"No. *I* didn't even know where I was going later. Not at that time."

"Based on your interaction with him at the gas station, do you think he would have followed you to the workshop?"

Kara paused before answering. That was an apt question. They'd researched the workshop at her mom's, and gone there on their own. And then Indrid had ended up there. Was that a coincidence? Was she followed? Was it both?

Finally, she spoke. "Probably, right? Otherwise that's too much of a coincidence."

"And what were *you* doing at the workshop at that time of night?"

Kara opened her mouth but nothing came out. What reason could they give without getting into the weird paranormal research they'd been doing?

"Her dad just died," Alec said quietly. "Cedro was working on her dad's monument. It might seem informal and kind of random, but she's been really going through it lately. We went there to bring her some comfort, some peace of mind. She's been concerned about his resting place. Making sure everything's all right with it."

"Is this true?" Garret directed the question at Kara. She nodded, hoping she didn't seem too eager. Plus, it was sort of partly true.

Officer Garrett sighed and shifted his weight to the other foot. "So, then. Tell me what happened tonight."

"It was all very strange," Alec pressed his lips together, thinking. "Did you hear what happened to his partner?"

"No, I didn't," Garrett said. "Is it related to what happened tonight?"

"We watched Cedro die the same way Dino probably did. It's very hard to describe."

"Dino? Who is Dino?" Officer Garrett furrowed his brows.

"That place has a history," Alec said. "Cedro's partner died at that workshop thirty years ago."

Kara squeezed Alec's arm. "We would have been *five* when Dino died," she clarified. Just in case.

"Walk me through what happened," he instructed her.

She shook her head, trying to loosen up. To continue a normal conversation, while everything inside her was still curled up and terrified. "It's just a weird situation," she said, her voice shaking. "What we saw was *very* odd, and upsetting. And we don't know how to explain it."

"Give it a try," Garrett said.

"We heard footsteps on the roof," Alec's words were drawn out. Slow. Like he was giving himself time to say the rest. He took a deep breath. "The killer jumped down from the roof and ran inside. Grabbed hold of Cedro. There was a struggle, and he hit his head."

"Who hit whose head?"

"The killer. Hit Cedro's head."

"With what?"

"Against the doorway," Alec said.

Browning scribbled on her pad, her eyes wide, brows raised. Face pale.

"Then, Cedro was on the ground." Alec's voice wavered. "And he was still putting up a fight, but clearly not doing well."

"Did you offer assistance?"

"We were scared," Kara whispered. "Cedro kept telling us to get out. We really didn't feel like we could save him."

"Was he armed?"

Kara paused. "Not exactly."

"What do you mean not exactly? Is it a yes, or a no?"

Fuck, Kara thought. *He thinks I'm being cagey.* "Sorry. No. He didn't have a gun or anything."

"Did the other man threaten you during this interaction?"

Kara thought for a minute. "Yes."

"What did he say?"

"He told us if we came any closer to him, he would maim Cedro with the thorns of his jaw."

"*What?*" Garrett asked.

She mumbled the phrase again.

"Did he seem like he was on drugs, maybe?"

"I don't know. I don't think so," Kara shrugged, bracing for the most unbelievable part of the story.

"So what happened after that?"

"We ran, like Cedro told us to," Alec said, quietly. As we were heading for the back door of the warehouse, he bit Cedro."

"Bit him? How did you know he bit him if you were running away?"

"We could hear crunching."

"Crunching?"

"Then he spit on the wound, and Cedro started bleeding everywhere. Like everything inside him. Everything was coming out."

"That doesn't make any sense," Garrett said.

"I know," Alec hung his head, hands in his pockets.

"That doesn't make sense? Is that really what you're supposed to say in this situation?" Kara asked quietly. Her face was burning now.

Garrett ignored her. "Tell me what really happened. If you didn't see it happen, if you ran off, that's totally fine. But don't make things up. You've reported a death, here. And now you're talking about vampires or something."

"I never said that. We're not making anything up," Kara mumbled. Her eyes filled with tears. Someone had to be inspecting the body by now, right? They'd see how weird everything was.

"It's what happened," Alec said, his voice strong and somber. "Believe what you want. If you contact the officers at the warehouse they can confirm what we're telling you. What happened to Cedro tonight? That's nothing we're capable of doing."

Kara stared at Alec, eyes spilling over. Dabbing her tears with the heel of her hand, she realized that, despite everything, she hadn't felt like he believed her when she came to his house from the gas station. He'd been kind about it, but he hadn't confirmed he believed her. Despite all that had happened.

She didn't realize the distinction until he defended her just now. How good it felt when he backed her up. She took a deep breath in and a literal warmth enveloped her.

His reassurance was high on her list of needs. Especially now.

The cops' radios crackled simultaneously; Garrett and Browning stepped away down the hall to answer them. Kara could hear clipped discussion between Browning and whoever was on the radio. She and Alec waited, gazes shifting around the room, eyes occasionally meeting.

Finally, the scuff of shoes on carpet brought Browning back to their door.

"We're needed elsewhere," she said evenly, her eyes slowly meeting theirs. She produced her card between thumb and pointer. "If you think of anything else we should know, here's how to get in touch."

"Thank you," Kara said.

Browning turned as if to leave, then doubled back. "Maybe stay together tonight."

Kara nodded quickly. "Yeah."

"I'll talk to them about a patrol, okay? Someone to stay in front of the building."

"Okay."

Browning nodded in farewell. Her and her partner's muffled voices faded down the hallway until they were gone.

Something was twitching in Alec's jaw as he dressed up his couch to sleep on. "They could've thanked us or something," was basically all he said besides logistical offerings of an extra toothbrush and toothpaste, and changing the sheets on his bed. Kara took the other side and helped.

"*She* was kind, at least. And they didn't haul us off. That's something," she said. He was still frowning. "Do you wanna talk any more about it?"

Alec sighed. The lines in his face were set and shadowed. He almost looked ready to cry. "I'll be fine." He almost turned to go, then stopped. "Are *you* okay?"

Kara hugged herself. "I guess."

Alec stood there, watching her. That jaw was still twitching. "I'm not convinced."

"I mean, I'm *not* fine. No. But we both need rest. We can talk in the morning."

Alec rubbed his face. "You're right." He smiled sadly. "I just hope we can sleep."

"You look exhausted." Kara had felt a gush of fondness and worry as she said it, but it came out flat and unflattering.

Alec turned to go.

Kara's breath caught in her throat. "Wait."

Alec raised his eyebrows, his face barely changed, but his eyes glimmered amusement. "What's up?"

The prospect of being alone in any room in the dark was suddenly unbearable.

"Can I just sleep on the other couch by you?"

When Alec's smile returned, it lit up everything. "Okay, but you're getting the one with the sheets on it."

***

Kara knew she'd slept that night, but it couldn't have been for long. She'd woken up without the need for an alarm at 5:45, fully incapable of drifting back off. Her mom had texted. "Call me when you can," with no indication of what she wanted. She'd started to respond, but deleted it. She couldn't think of a good excuse why she'd text instead of calling. "Can't now, solving undead shit"? "I'm mad at you for trying to dig up my already undead dad"? She continued that train of thought for a few minutes until she was too disgusted. She settled for scrolling through the news on her phone, checking if anything popped up about last night while she waited for Alec to wake up. Nothing yet.

Naturally, she and Alec were at the antique mall the second it opened. From his drawn expression and vacant stare, she assumed he'd slept the same. The drive had been short but silent. Alec hadn't even chosen any music. She'd had to make that executive decision, leaving on some ungodly morning show and cringing the whole way. She couldn't think of any music she wanted to listen to, and instead endured what was already on.

They crossed the parking lot to the door of the antique mall: a series of four creaky, sprawling barns, connected by three-seasons hallways that required shoppers to keep their coats on for the duration of their visit on cold days like today.

"What do you think happened when the police went to the workshop?" Kara plunged her hands into her coat pockets.

Alec stumbled on the uneven ground. He shook his head. "God, I have no idea. I hope the inane shit in Dino's report from thirty years ago was reason enough to close the book on the whole thing."

They made their way inside, and Kara elbowed Alec. "I hate the way this place smells."

They passed the front desk and smiled politely at the twenty-something girl with the septum piercing. She gave them a forced smile, then turned her attention back to her phone.

Alec waited until they were around the corner to respond to Kara. "It smells like hundreds of people, depending on what area you're walking through."

They entered a booth, absently scanning the organized chaos that was booth 26.

"Exactly." Kara made a choking noise as she straightened the frilly white bonnet on a doll with cracked eyelids.

"To me, this place never gets old. I always notice something different when I come. Think of the lives all these different things have touched."

"Yeah, they're all just waiting for their human masters to return to rock their rocking chairs and play—Stocks and Bonds, The Game of Investments?" Kara said, reading off the board game that was placed sideways on the bookshelf in front of her. She and Alec picked their way through a narrow makeshift walkway designated by tall bookshelves.

"You've got to be kidding me. Stocks and Bonds? That's a real game?" Alec bent over, inspecting the box on a poorly painted brown particle board bookshelf.

"Like Battleship, but with money-torpedoes."

"Or Wall Street Monopoly, maybe." Alec laughed, then shrugged. "Find something different every time."

"All of this makes me feel awfully existential," Kara said under her breath. "All these personal items. Did they belong to someone's grandma? Or their grandma's grandma's grandma? How long have these people been dead? Will all my stuff be here before too long?"

"I hope not, Kara." Alec looked sideways at her.

Kara realized she'd been standing in a booth that smelled like bread for a few minutes now, not really moving. "I thought we were gonna die last night."

"Me too." Alec took a seat in a wicker rocking chair. "I hope we make it through this."

"We will," Kara said. "We have to." She lowered herself until she was sitting on the floor beside him.

"We have to," Alec said, nodding in agreement. His voice lowered. "I couldn't go a day without you." He ran his hands through his hair and stared at the floor, tapping his foot.

Kara's guts throbbed. "Me too. I mean, me either."

Alec smiled and shook his head. "Anyway. We should go ask about that booth. I think it's 347, but I'm not totally sure."

"They can help us, I'd assume?"

"Yeah, I think they have a record of whose booth is whose, at least."

Two barns and two cold hallways later, they approached an old lady behind a desk. She wore a pink sweater and cleared her throat a lot. The sweater looked hand-knit; a vape pen stuck out of the vest pocket. Her name tag said Doris.

"Hi Doris," Kara smiled. "We're looking for Cedro Testa's booth. We are pretty sure it's number 347."

"Yes . . ." Doris made a thinking sound like a motorboat and pulled out a clipboard.

She walked them down a long landing strip of worn blue carpeting.

Doris stopped and gestured at a booth area marked with red masking tape. "I'll leave ya to it," she croaked, and walked away.

Booth 347 was flanked by two vintage windows, painstakingly painted a bold light blue. It made the area feel more enclosed, a complete space unto itself.

Tentatively, Alec and Kara stepped inside.

A short hickory bench and a dark blue French Provincial loveseat were placed in back. Several 50s radios sat on glass shelving along the right. To the left, an assortment of table lamps sat on a makeshift table.

"I don't even know where to look first," Alec said quietly.

"I think I do," Kara said as she spotted a nightstand to the right of the loveseat. It had two drawers at the top, and a bottom shelf filled with books. Immediately, they headed over there together.

"Ho-ly shit," Alec said, and whistled quietly, placing his finger over a group of identical blue spines.

"*Our Heavenly Visitors*," Kara mumbled. Goosebumps covered her arms. "What's he got five copies for?"

"Maybe this was a big thing that got passed around back when it came out, since our town is featured in here?"

"Yeah, I'd imagine after that happening with Dino and Sammy, and then some author poking around asking questions? This had to be well known for that generation, right?"

"That makes a lot of sense."

They pulled the books out and started rifling through the pages. All five were clean copies; not one mark. Nothing stuffed in the pages.

"Geez, these are in mint condition. Looks like they've never been cracked open," Kara said. She put the three books she'd grabbed back on the shelf, straightened them, then pulled open the top drawer.

Empty.

The second drawer had some old instruction manuals for what looked like appliances from the 50s.

Refrigerator. Ice box. Washer and dryer. She picked them up and placed them next to the lamp on the nightstand.

In the corner of the drawer was a perfect sphere of Barre gray granite, a paperweight the size of a bocce ball. A thin receipt poked out from underneath. She hefted the paperweight, hoisted it two-handed over to Alec, then unfolded the receipt. The printer ink was almost completely faded. She flipped it over.

"Oh my god," she breathed. On the back, the tiny, hurried handwriting of Kara's father scrawled the words:

"The one with hair of gray and gold". And beneath that:

OnrefnI OUS

We, below, and she, above,
The summer rain, it licks her skin.
The World Tree's boughs, and branches, all,
completes the lie she lingers in.

Our Snake with the wings now shorn
Climbed the twisting storms of Hell.
Gazed on its majestic circles.
Dreamt the rings of the Tree Infernal
could carry her to the world above.

She won't return, we cannot join her,
We've been replaced with the freshly dead.
Each night we try to claim them,
they've up and left their earthly beds.

We earned our place in dreaded Gehinnom
And she belonged with us as well.
Higher still the lords of Hell,
Hear our cries and heed our prayer.
Our riverbanks to Sheol are bare.

We believe
She waits there still, for The Cold One.
The traveler with the flying machine
To drag her 'cross the dust of space
He: the bird, and She: the serpent.

"Okay, this is getting more and more insane," Kara mumbled. They sat together on the loveseat now, reading quietly.

Alec tapped the paper with the backs of his fingers. "What the hell does any of it mean?"

"Well, it's definitely *about* Hell, right?"

"Yeah, it has to be, I think," Alec leaned back, placing his thumb over his lips. "Snake with shorn wings? Snakes don't have wings. What is a snake with wings? A dragon?"

Somewhere in the distance, there was a metallic bang, followed by a loud hum. The heater must have kicked on. Kara's heart started pounding again. *Doesn't take much these days*, she thought.

Alec took a breath. Sat back up. "Could the World Tree be *our* Red Tree? Or, you know, all those things? The World Tree in Norse mythology has a dragon at its roots, called Nidhogg."

"I wonder how old Red Tree is," she said quietly.

"It does look crazy old," Alec agreed.

"And how come it's mostly English with some Hebrew?"

"Ah, those words are Hebrew? What do the Hebrew parts mean?"

"Well it's an English transliteration of course, but in Hebrew, Gehinnom means Valley of Hinnom. It's an actual historic valley surrounding Ancient Jerusalem from the west and southwest." She gestured vaguely. "But it has a dark past. As the story goes, some of the kings of Judah sacrificed their children by fire there."

"Holy shit. What are we supposed to do with that?"

"Well, that's only the practical geographical and bible stories part. Some refer to Gehinnom as the 'destination of the wicked.'"

"There's a Hell in Judaism?"

"Some say that, yeah."

"And what about that other word? Sheol? Is that Hebrew too?"

"Yes. That's just generally 'the abode of the dead.' So the Jewish version of an underworld."

"So what are we getting from this? That there is another realm below our own? A literal underworld, like so many religions would have us believe?"

Kara laughed. "Spoken like a true heretic."

"I can't even believe you're laughing." Alec laughed a little, too.

"I don't know. This really sounds like there are things living down there and they're mad that this dragon-snake lady is stealing dead people that are destined for the underworld. She's screwing them over somehow."

"But why?" Alec bugged his eyes at Kara.

She laughed. "I don't think I'm ready to believe in an underworld. Yet."

Alec bit his lip and nodded vaguely.

"I'll believe it when I see it." Kara crossed her arms. "And I don't wanna see it."

"Who's the Cold One?"

"I dunno. A really bad dead guy? And this title." Kara shook her head. "I'm never gonna get this title."

"OnrefnI OUS," he read slowly.

"See how the letter at the end is capitalized? Do we read this backwards then?" Alec asked. "I don't know *why* it'd be backwards but that makes sense."

"Inferno *definitely* works," Kara said. "But *OUS*?"

"Backwards, it's *suo*, which means 'his' in Italian. So 'his Inferno,' or her inferno, since the poem is about a woman."

"Well, aren't you fancy. But does this help us?"

"I don't think it solves anything other than—you know Dante Aligheri?"

"As in, Dante's *Inferno*?"

"Yep. That's what I'm thinking. Italian, that's his language, too. And the 'majestic circles' could be referring to the nine circles of Hell, like what's described in Dante's *Inferno*."

"So, demons read human lit?" Kara grinned.

"D'you think that's what the course would be called? Human lit?"

"Hah."

"I'm just glad I got a turn to translate too."

"I guess that's pretty cool. You always were a show-off."

"With you?" Alec flashed a grin. "Always."

Kara flushed. Alec was either way too cocky, or awful at flirting. For how well and how long she'd known him, why couldn't she tell the difference? He'd always joked with her like this. Was the part of her that awoke three days ago—that caused its own inferno within her—the part that looked closer at his joking advances and just wanted to see truth in them? Was he responding to some change in her demeanor? Or was this a new awakening for both of them?

She sighed. Willed herself to breathe, waited for her face to stop burning. "Hang on." She picked up her phone and punched "World Tree" into a search engine.

The results came up, and Alec leaned in. "Check this out! The World Tree! The uppermost branches touch the heavens, the roots go to the underworld, and the trunk is located in the terrestrial world, where we're at. This is Norse stuff. I love this stuff."

"That's right." She chewed her thumbnail, eyeing the Gjallarhorn tattoo on his bicep. "So, *our* red tree is tall, but it doesn't touch the sky."

"Remember what Charlie said about the tree, though? When Sammy chopped it with the ax, the sky started spinning, like the branches were scratching the sky. Maybe to us it doesn't look as tall as the sky, but I mean if there's an underworld, demons, magic bullshit flying all over, why can't a magical tree touch the sky?"

"And look—" Alec pointed to the picture of a giant tree with reaching roots and branches. "Down at the bottom of the tree, there's a snake, and up in the sky, there's a bird, just like the poem."

"What does that mean? If 'she' is the serpent, then is the Cold One the bird? So what does that represent? Literally a bird?"

"I don't know, it depends what the heavens are. Heaven? Space? What if it's like, an alien?"

Kara guffawed. "A bird represents a fucking alien?" Quickly, her smile melted. The blood drained from her face.

"Suspend that disbelief, Kara. It says 'a traveler with a flying machine.'"

"The Cold One. Is that Indrid Cold? Is he the alien?"

Alec thought for a minute. "I think you're onto something there."

"Fuck."

"Indeed." Alec rubbed his face, messing up his hair, his eyebrows. Her heart throbbed. "Do me a favor, Kare?"

"Yeah?"

"Promise me you won't take that ring off for anything."

"Yeah."

"Say you promise."

"I promise." Was this really possible? She couldn't think of any other explanation. The pieces were real, and they were coming together. Indrid was an alien. Like *The Mothman Prophecies* had insinuated. Like this poem confirmed. But what did that mean for Barre? Indrid had come for some new skin. But why was he here to begin with? On a planet where he needed to borrow skin? And what did that mean for her father?

Her poor father, unlucky enough to die in a place where the dead don't rest.

17

ALEC

Night fell, and Alec stood alone, in front of his parents' house. Just last night, being by himself had felt normal. Right before Kara had showed up, anyway.

Tonight, he was collecting some of his stuff from the shed so his dad could start a project; Kara had dropped him off and left with his old murder car. He'd asked her to stay. Tried to put it all under the pretense of him wanting to protect her. Honestly, thinking back a half hour ago, that was mainly the reason. But now that he stood here, dreading going into that shed alone, the memories hit him heavily.

He hesitated there for minutes, staring at the old white house with the dirty, dented siding. A lonely little home swallowed by the farmland around it.

He thought about his Mom and Dad. They were probably inside, sleeping in their separate beds, Mom in what used to be the guest room, though now they'd switched to just calling it Mom's room. His dad still loved her, and in return he got tolerance, at best. Alec figured if he ever unpacked how that had affected him growing up, he'd have to burn the whole damn suitcase.

And that shed.

The summer of junior year, Kara had gone in there to look for something of Alec's. A video game cartridge or a movie or something. Tyler had followed, then returned ten minutes later, acting really weird, claiming he didn't know where Kara was. Eventually, Tyler admitted he'd locked Kara in there. Alec had nearly killed him.

Tyler claimed she'd made a pass at him. She wouldn't take no for an answer, wouldn't get off him, so he'd locked her in there.

And she was in there, all right. Disheveled, and furious. Her eyes wild with rage. Alec had been sick to his stomach. His disgust when he'd looked at Tyler was nothing compared to his feelings when he looked at her that night. The utter helplessness and worry, when no matter how he pushed, she wouldn't tell him anything. Not only the panic of not knowing, but also the idea that something was so upsetting she couldn't open up, couldn't bring herself to talk to him about it.

Fear had owned him fully that night, caving his chest in, squeezing his heart. He hadn't believed Tyler, of course, and had asked her to tell him it wasn't true.

She'd said yes, she'd made a pass at Tyler. He told himself she was being sarcastic, but she wouldn't budge any further. Her eyes were teary, but hardened. She'd stared at him, unblinking. So she must have meant it. His fear melted, dissolved, and in the cavity it left behind, jealousy wrapped its vines in his guts.

Stomach twisted, eyes burning, he'd tried to ignore that feeling like something was lodged in his throat. Tried to get her to come back in the house, but she had refused. Said she'd walk home. She had walked the twenty minutes home and he'd gone with her in an unseasonable forty-five degrees, blasted with icy biting wind the whole way.

That night, he'd given Tyler bus fare and kicked him out. Afterward, he regretted giving him the bus fare. Alec called Tennyson, told her everything he knew. She promised she'd keep an eye on Kara. Be there if she needed anything.

Kara clearly wanted to be left alone, so he obliged. Alec didn't see her again until school was back on, and by then, all traces of that night had melted from her face.

When he saw her again in the hall, her relieved smile at seeing him made the past few weeks soften immediately. She'd updated him on what she'd been up to, their friendship as strong as ever. He was mostly relieved, though he still looked at her sideways for months, worrying about the weirdness around her being locked in the shed. Was she really okay now, even late at night, when both he and Ten couldn't be there?

And slowly, slowly, as the worry floated away at the edges, any attempt to ignore the *other thing* was nothing but an act.

That warm, burning ache for her—before, a sleeping monster—was now settled heavily within him.

And the sickest part, the part he most wanted to forget was, from day one, his fantasies revolved around her approaching *him*, instead of Tyler, in the shed.

The ache Alec felt at this memory warmed him unexpectedly. He shuffled cautiously into the dark of the shed and promptly stubbed his toe on a large rubber mallet. Heart rate ratcheting, he heaved the thing aside. He stepped further into the dark, leaning toward an old Tiffany lamp sitting on a worktable, and clicked it on.

The dim yellow light revealed a stack of old produce boxes his parents had probably picked up at the grocery store. Some of his books had been stacked down there with the boxes, on the gritty floor of the shed. The rest of his stuff was slumped over on the shelves, as if someone had started the job for him but gotten distracted.

Alec kicked at the grit on the floor: years' worth of dirt, oil, sawdust, and metal shavings. He crouched down, tried wiping the floor with his hand so he could sit.

Gross. Sighing loudly, he ripped open an empty box labeled CLEMENTINES, then maneuvered it until it laid flat on the floor, and sat down on it.

One of the neighbor's horses whinnied loudly outside, making him jump. Immediately after, Alec heard galloping, something running right past the shed, and away.

That's odd, he thought. At ten at night? And this close to his parents' property, too. The fencing of Frank's farm butted up against theirs, but that property was 300-odd acres, with the house and stable smack in the middle of it. A good ways away.

He lifted a stack of books in one hand and turned them over, swatting more workshop grit off the cover. He wiped the spines off on his pants, dragged another box toward him, and started placing the books neatly inside.

He finished with the books on the floor and stood up. Brushed himself off, and reached up higher, for the CD's. Wondered vaguely if he'd ever use them. He didn't even own a CD player anymore.

From the corner of his eye, he saw two dark shapes rush past the small metal-framed window. Those shapes were darker than the night outside. He paused, standing perfectly still for a minute or two.

At first, all was quiet.

Then a high-pitched laugh—like a hyena—rang out, just past the shed.

Alec's breath locked in his throat, his heart rattling wildly in his chest. Swiftly, he moved to the lamp, turning the knob slowly and quietly to the off position.

Another shape passed the window, this one moving slow. Alec shrank back from the window and moved toward the bookshelf.

The thing outside slowed to a stop, and turned. A silhouette cut itself from the night sky. Its face wasn't human: no distinct nose or mouth, but rather a short, ugly snout. The silhouette softened.

It turned its gaze to look at him, dead on.

Barely, just barely, its eyes held the moonlight. They were set back but protruding above the snout.

Those eyes are on me.

He knew it, even in the near dark. Its gaze was alive. Visceral. Boring into him.

Dog person. The thought hit him like an ice pick to the brain, fear grabbing him by the guts. He stumbled, wild and quiet, to the shed door, scared to touch the handles and make noise, but even more scared not to secure them. He held the doors shut with all his strength, his arms straining as he struggled to quiet his ragged breathing. To tune in to the sounds outside.

Galloping hooves pinpointed the horse's location. It was somewhere near the fence that separated Frank's property from theirs. As quickly as the running started, that sound was cut short. A panicked grunt and a loud whinny followed.

A strange, high-pitched scream started up. This wasn't the horse. It sounded like a human howling in agony. First one, then two, then three or more.

Chaos battered the dirt. Quiet followed.

Two minutes passed. Nothing. Then, a loud grumble bubbled up. Another whinny, but low, distressed, unsure. The sound went on for what felt like a half-minute. Then more of that dirt shuffling sound. It sounded like a pack of horses all clustered together.

But Frank only had one horse.

The grumble came back, coupled with the same wild violent shuffling. It grew louder, more frantic. Seconds later, it was joined by another bedlam of frenzied screaming.

Shaking, Alec ran back to the window. The field was dark, but his eye caught movement picked up by the moonlight, not ten yards away, just past the fence, and into Frank's property. Multiple dog people were attacking Frank's horse, much like any known pack of predators on the back of a larger animal. The horse groaned again, the sound starting slow and low, and reaching a hellish, high pitch.

Alec felt sick. He breathed in deep, held it, then made his decision. He rolled one of the shed door panels open just enough to fit through, as quietly as possible. He ran around the side of the shed and up to the fence, breath short, heart hammering. He lifted one foot to rest on the lowest rung of the wooden three-rail fence, hoisting himself up.

The familiar clunk of his parents' backyard light clicked on, and the scene was illuminated.

Five dog people hung off the horse, a gang of predators locked on their prey. One had its teeth buried deep in the horse's throat, its jaws locked tight. The horse's colossal muscles trembled and twitched as it tried in vain to throw the creature off. A second dog person climbed up on the horse's side, trying to get a good mouthful of its shoulder. The other three tore at its back. One of them seemed to be heaving itself roughly against its hind quarters making some wild chattering sound, like a stuttering bark, or laughter.

None of them had reacted to the backyard light whatsoever. They were like mosquitos mid-feed, desperate and drunk on blood.

"Oh fuck," Alec whispered, his dinner rising like acid in his throat. He shut his mouth tight and clamped a hand over his mouth. Everything in him had tightened, frozen in fear and disgust. He tried to swallow but his throat was paralyzed.

The door on the back porch slid open.

"No!" he whispered, emphatic. He ran, hard as he could, around the back of the shed. The kitchen was lit up bright, all its homey clutter on full display, a free show for anything that lived in the dark to come and watch. To come and join.

Alec tripped up the deck steps, grabbing the railing hard, jamming three of his fingers. His dad stood there, mouth half open in alarm, looking half asleep in his scruffy half-beard. Alec shoved past his dad and yanked the sliding glass door shut, locking it.

"Alec?"

Alec clicked off the kitchen light, sat with his hands on his knees, heaving for breath, his mind reeling and scrambling for purchase.

"Al." His dad's voice had quickly gone from shrill to sober. "What's going on? Did you hear that noise?"

"Heard, yeah. And saw," was all Alec could manage for a good few seconds. All he could think about was Kara, alone. His mind searched wildly for what to do, and settled quickly.

"What happened?" His dad's words were sharp and tightly wound.

"Something happened to Frank's horse outside. Some wild animals. Call the police. I need to check on Kara."

18

YARTZEIT

Kara pulled Alec's car into the parking lot at her place. When he'd asked her to come with to his house, she'd declined. She wasn't in the mood to talk to anybody after what they'd found. She needed some time to process everything.

Shivers ran through her as she exited the car, so she tried wiggling deeper into her black jacket. She'd left her dad's green one at her mom's, she was almost sure. That plus Alec going back to his parents' house had made her miss her dad again. Maybe Alec's shit was all dusty and moldy, and kept in a shed, but at least his dad wasn't dead.

The thought made her throat tighten, resisting the unwanted thought. Shaking her head, she cleared her throat. What a shitty thought. What did any of the shed stuff have to do with anything? She didn't want Alec to lose anyone he cared about, so why think that way? Guilt flooded over her, souring her stomach.

A sigh leaked out of her as she tucked Alec's key in her coat pocket, then fumbled for her own building key.

She thought about the times she'd spent too long in the hospital cafeteria when she should have been sitting with her dad. His life had been cut short, and she was scrolling through her damn phone looking at stupid videos. She knew she wasn't being fair with herself, but her mind was a train with no brakes sometimes.

She'd seen a therapist a while ago. The instructions were getting fuzzy, but the therapist had said to focus on something you *can* do. Even something small. Even something that won't fix anything. Literally anything, so you can turn on the useful part of your brain. Remind yourself there are other parts of you.

That's when she remembered the Yartzeit candle: to light it in remembrance of her dad. Her mom had mentioned back at the house that they'd never lit it.

They got a reminder every year from her grandparents' synagogue to burn it on the anniversary of her grandfather's death, too, to honor his memory.

The first night they had lit the candle for her grandfather, Kara had heard someone whispering her name from the hallway. Her mom heard *her* name whispered, too. It was like Grandpa had been allotted one last goodbye. Like magic.

Kara smiled wistfully. At the time, instead of being frightened, it made her picture her grandfather hanging out there, spending just a little more time with them. Like the light from the flame was their candle in the window, helping him find his way back one last time.

It wasn't a traditional Jewish belief. Just kind of a secular thing with the Yartzeit thrown in as a little spiritual bonus. The Talmud was full of ghosts as it was. So, far from taboo in Judaism, at least.

Alec had been skeptical that Kara was truly going to go home and rest. He'd pushed for her to come with him.

"You've been on this 'find everything supernatural going on in our town' bent for days now," he'd said. "And now you want to just go home and chill?"

Kara had smiled, then shrugged. "Hey, I can feel when I'm burning out and need to take a break."

"No, you can't. You have no radar for that at all."

"Maybe it's a new me," she'd said.

Kara closed her eyes and pictured the look he'd given her. His eyes had been so soft and open. Like an offered hand. Her guts had melted like chocolate. She'd bitten her lip, physically holding back something she wanted to unleash. To reach back, to literally touch him. To go with him to his parents. To stay on the same page.

"Shit," she'd said to no one, alone in the lobby. The minute she hit the elevator button, she realized how right Alec had been. She was going to go get a Yartzeit candle, take her dad's ring off, and see what happened.

And she was gonna do it tonight.

***

"I'm home!" Kara set her purse, a half-filled grocery bag, and her waitress book on the front hall table.

Ten greeted her from the kitchen. She was leaning against the counter, eating a plain flour tortilla. Kara walked over, rubbing her face.

"Whatcha doin'?" Kara leaned against the threshold to the kitchen.

"Just eating something with my vitamins. Your mom texted me. She's looking for you."

That bothered Kara. "Seriously?"

"Yeah. What's going on with you guys?"

"Nothing serious. She said some weird shit. I didn't like it, and now she wants to 'talk,' but who knows about what. She didn't text me that long ago. She can wait."

Ten swallowed her food and stopped eating. "So you don't wanna talk about that. Can I trust you to call her soon? I'm gonna tell her I talked to you. Like a good best friend."

"I'll try. There's a lot going on right now."

"Fair." Graciously, Ten changed the subject. "What's that you brought home?"

"Yeah. I bought a Yartzeit candle to burn for my dad. My mom never did it. Wanna sit with me while I light it?"

"Is this another instance of you looking for puzzle pieces?"

"Possibly."

"Were you afraid to come out and tell me that because you were worried I'd say no?"

Kara laughed quietly. "I'll tell you what wasn't in my plan: you figuring out what I was trying to do before I told you."

"What do you think I'm going to say?"

"I don't know? I sort of thought you were going to say, 'slow down' and 'stop throwing yourself against a brick wall' or something much more tactful and wise."

"It's funny, because now that I know this is all happening, I think the best thing is to explore all this."

"You aren't worried I'm going to get myself—get us, killed?"

"I guess there's a risk? But you're not going to be able to live with giving up and not helping your dad to his final rest. Isn't that what the whole funeral was supposed to set in motion? And now the big concern is that's not happening."

"Yep. I don't think anybody else is going to do it."

"Probably not." Ten smiled sadly. "So, what's the plan?"

"Honestly? Take off my necklace so I can see shit again. Then, light the candle and wait. See if anything happens."

"Okay. That feels more low risk than what I thought."

"Really. You think that's low risk with the bees' nests we've been playing catch with?"

"Good point, I guess. But you think your dad will just automatically haunt the candle like what happened with your grandpa?"

"We'll see, I guess." Kara rubbed her hands together.

"Are you worried it could draw someone else's attention?"

"Definitely. But you know what, let's be optimistic tonight and ignore the maybes. Finish up that tortilla, we're about to see some shit!"

"I'm not hungry anymore." Ten tossed the half-eaten thing in the trash. "But yeah, let's go see some shit."

They set the candle on the coffee table in the living room and Kara lit it with a gun lighter. They sat cross-legged on the floor next to each other and waited.

Ten checked her phone. Rain started to tap high-pitched against the windows outside.

"Is it supposed to be cold tonight?" Kara asked.

"I don't know."

Stretching her arms and back, she sighed.

"I guess this might take a while, right? My grandpa didn't visit until we were sleeping. He woke us from a dead sleep."

"I didn't think that far ahead but damn, this gets creepier, doesn't it?"

"It sure does. Will you sleep in here with me?" Kara grinned at Ten. "The couches are almost comfier than the beds!"

"Yeah, sure. You keep telling yourself that, chirpy."

"Chirpy, huh?"

"Yeah, that's how you sound when you try to convince me of something. Chirpy."

"Well I'll just assume it's a compliment."

"You do that." Yawning, Ten kicked her with a slippered foot.

***

Sometime in the night, Kara woke, shivering, to a dark figure with Tennyson's voice. Ten was mumbling something in a tone that lilted up like a question. Kara mumbled back about extra blankets in the linen closet, hoping that was what Ten needed. The candle's orange light glowed across her face, but didn't reach the shadows under her eyes. Ten stared at Kara like she was processing the answer, then turned in the direction of the closet.

"Shit." Kara realized in all the attention she'd paid to setting up her sleeping spot on the couch, she hadn't taken the necklace off. She set it in the little alcove in the back corner where the couch cushions met, and let the chain slowly drop from between her fingers.

19

NIDH AND COLD

Thousands of years before humans settled in the land they named Barre, Hel, Earth, and Sky were as they should be. The World Tree touched all three realms, and nothing in the terrestrial world dared disturb it. Insects wouldn't land upon its branches. The instinct to avoid the tree was inherited. As automatic as feeding.

The World Tree's roots were the most revered, as many thousands of leagues of them were hugged, sanctified, by the earth, in loving protection. Deeper still, the inhabitants of Hel were sentient, with supernatural understanding, and knew of the balance it offered to the realms.

In those times, those Long Ago times, Indrid Cold visited Earth, and breached the ceiling of Hel.

Nidhogg was alone, in the deepest tunnels of Hel, when Cold's entry caused the tremors.

At the time, Nidh's employ, the Dessicated, had paused in their digging for their allotted rest. She'd been inspecting their work; the integrity of the earth they'd packed five hundred heads high; ready for the Blackstone ceilings and columns to be carved and

202

fitted. The finished halls above her were so smooth they gave the appearance of being endless. A chasm with no edges. A sky with no stars.

The shaking alarmed her. The halls she occupied had not been fortified with Blackstone, and the integrity of the ceiling was tentative. And this time, the trembling resounded from within herself as well as underneath her taloned feet. The movement inside her carried a rhythm, like too much blood chugging through her veins.

When the integrity of these tunnels was compromised, the rumbling could mean—not doom, perhaps, but long periods of darkness. The workers' first priority was to locate Nidh, their superior, and ensure she was not trapped. Those who managed to avoid cave-ins would wait for the rumblings to settle, then continue their work. The rest would need to be dug out.

The surrounding area grew hotter beneath the pads of her feet. Embers glowed red-black, like coals in the dirt. Quickly, they cooled and whitened. Small pieces of glimmering rock fell slowly from the concave dirt ceilings like snow. They shone, borrowing light from nothing as they floated down.

Nidh watched in awe, as she issued a series of shrill, quick cries, alerting her creatures to her location. She started her ascent, to meet her employ at higher ground, where they could avoid being trapped, and wait out the tremors.

Coming down from her warning call, she felt Cold. His spirit licked her psyche from deep within the central tunnel. A new fire burst in her skull, a fire that smelled sharp and clean, a bright, living green. He'd trickled down from a door in the floor of the nearest lake. And he was headed this way.

"He *must* be lost," she said to herself.

By the time Cold reached her, heat wavered in a curtain before him. Nidh wondered if he was a mirage. It had been thousands of years since she had longed to leave her station, and his presence gouged at the bindings of that feeling.

When he approached, she noted he had no skin. His form was bare muscle. Red striations raced up and down his arms. Most who traveled from another realm did not possess much of a body upon entry, as any corporeal form could not survive in its same form from one realm to the next. She struggled to make out his form; it was especially difficult in the near-darkness. Two glowing white eyes, marbled with black, appeared where his face would be, which was helpful. At least there was somewhere specific to look while they communicated.

"You have traveled a far way."

His voice was like the growl of a lion. "That is an understatement."

Not one for formalities, apparently. Or perhaps just uninterested in grinning through the pain that his entry must have brought him. "I don't receive new blood here," she tried. "This place has no visitors. Why have you come?"

"I am Indrid Cold. Here from the planet called Lanulos. I've come seeking your assistance."

"My assistance? Who do you need to find?"

"You."

This was the last thing she could have anticipated hearing. She believed she'd seen all, and this assertion left her without speech. "Me," she said, dumbly. She had to make sure. Something burned inside her. A geyser of hope. But she was wary. This being she'd never seen before, looking for her.

Nobody looked for her.

"Unfortunately," he continued, "I am in need of your help."

She scoffed. "Unfortunately?" A most diplomatic beginning.

"You are Nidhogg, yes? The serpent with shorn wings at the roots of the World Tree?"

"I've been described that way, yes."

"Most of our forests have adapted to underground life by what we think of as 'ungrowing.' But what actually happened was they regrew below the surface. The majority of our forests are subterranean. Most of our trees hang upside-down in the ceilings of the underworld. Recently, our world tree joined the others. This has been catastrophic for our planet. We need the trees to be able to thrive."

"That's a very interesting problem." She waited for him to explain where she came in.

"You were not easy to find. When were you moved here? Do you still perform the same function from when you relocated?"

So, he didn't know.

"I was moved here some thousands of years ago. The Dessicated serve me. I guide them, try to keep their bodies in one piece, I suppose. They serve as the teeth of the tunnels of Hel. They dig and get

205

sustenance from the richer deposits of soil. It keeps them from . . ."

"From what?"

She shrugged. "Disintegrating."

"I see. Do they expire at that point?"

"No. They continue to exist. If they break down fully, they lose their form and become liquid. Sentient sludge, we call it here."

"Can it be reversed?"

"Not that I've experienced."

"That is quite a punishment."

Nidh poked at a gathering of white flakes with her talon. "Agreed. Which is why I do what I can to help them avoid that fate."

"Fair enough."

Nidh bristled. Had she made the rules? No. Had she signed up to have this stranger critique her performance? Also, no. "I have not heard of Lanulos. I suppose you've traveled far, yes? I am almost sure I cannot actually be who you are looking for. Might I assist you in moving on to wherever it is you need to be?"

"Ah, yes. Not one for pleasantries, are you?"

"I am, when they are pleasant."

Nidh saw the beginnings of a smile threatening to insinuate itself on Cold's face, but he pressed it back with his garishly red lower lip. "Is this the *center-most* circle of your hell?" As he spoke, the smile became more prominent.

"No. It can be worse than this, but that is not my specialty."

Cold laughed. A short, rattling thing that resembled a human dying. "Regardless, your station sounds agonizing."

"Grueling physical labor without the help of tools? Panic inspired by the threat of eternal darkness? It's *definitely* agonizing."

He laughed again. "Am I close, though?"

"You are two stations away from the center-most circle, yes." The snow-like material was still falling. She extended her forked tongue and caught the flakes, tasting them, feeling them. "This is not cold. What is it?"

"Stone."

"Is the dust of stone not finer than this?"

"It appears in a finer form when it is cut by tools, but I produce stone. Where I come from, this is my purpose. It's what I'm good for."

"Only those most esteemed here are permitted to cut stone. It is a holy calling. What do you do with this ability? Do you construct shelter?"

"Some like me do."

"Not you?"

Cold made a short growling sound, like he was displeased with where the conversation was headed. He didn't respond.

Nidh decided to wait him out. Cold could decide what would happen next. After all, hadn't he just demanded too much information from her, and then judged her?

When Cold eventually responded, he dodged the question. Of course. "Why is this your position?"

Nobody had ever asked her this question. She'd not spoken of it in thousands of years. She'd had plenty of practice in not thinking about it. However, no matter how many times she relived it, her regret was only that she hadn't skirted the punishment. The very public amputation of her wings, and being appointed here for what remained of eternity.

Now, though, she'd resigned herself to it. She'd kept her head down and kept out of trouble.

"I disemboweled a superior."

Indrid's glowing white eyes widened. "You are serious." He almost stated it, like he knew but couldn't quite grasp it.

"I am."

"Do functioning parts . . . grow back . . . here?"

"Would it upset you greatly if I told you they do not?"

"Upset me, no. It would surprise me, though, that you'd do something that is irreversible."

"Are you often surprised by strangers whose reputations you do not know? They can regenerate, yes. For his kind. Though it is a lengthy process. And very uncomfortable."

"You are far more interesting than most."

Nidh's flesh flooded with heat. "I see."

"Why did you eviscerate this creature?"

"I refused to continue my job of eating the flesh of the dead. They attempted to force me. And I would not be forced."

"In Hel, somebody betrayed you." Cold smiled again.

"As you can imagine, it's quite common here. However, despite everything, I've grown here. I now realize the emptiness of blind ambition. You climb only to want more. It does not stop. This place is filled with those who are incapable of learning this. I help those who have no hope of ascending."

"I've heard about your abilities. You can control others. Lull your lessers into subservience."

"I take a hopeless situation and shave the edges of the unbridled fear and rage that they feel at their station. I keep a horde of miscreants from spiraling into insanity or allowing themselves to become a sentient puddle of mud."

"So you say."

"So I say. And might I mention I find it amusing you haven't yet said what exactly your responsibilities are back on whatever dusty old rock you hail from."

Cold smiled and looked down. A tiny shuffling sound followed as the flakes of stone vibrated against the dirt. Nidh realized that Cold's emotional reaction caused the flakes to do this. "My position is not to build with stone. It is to conceal," he admitted.

"You cover things with stone?"

"Yes."

"Ah. Well, that's very interesting. Covering things seems a dishonest trade, regardless of whatever details you seem to have left out."

"Now I know how you felt when I judged your position."

"I find it odd, that you are so open to admit your position and then note how your actions would be perceived."

"I have been called odd before. Both myself, and my actions."

"Might I respectfully repeat my question regarding why you came, and why you remain here, speaking with me?"

Cold's eyes flitted back and forth, as though he were considering something. "Come back with me."

"Why do you respond to all my questions with irrelevant statements? Are they too direct? Must I coax everything patiently out of you like a larynx from the throat of a mummified corpse?"

"You should come back with me, and work with me."

"Are you out of your soft fucking skull," Nidh stated, staring hard at Cold. Daring him to wiggle out of this. To craft a perfect convincing pitch that would lure her to his invisible mystery island of a planet.

"Your dedication is unmatched. You do not accept anything I say and implore me with great force to remain honest. This is why you are perfect to me."

"Perfect to you, or perfect for this job?"

"Just perfect."

"Hm."

"I have made a mistake. My job is, how do you say, to complete one project at a time with various clients. There have been times I've used my ability for things I shouldn't have. To cover over something that should not be concealed. I, same as you, have done things I now regret."

"What is it you have done?"

"I have covered up important resources. Water-giving resources."

"Why?"

"No reason, other than that was the job I took."

"So how am *I* to assist you? I cannot manipulate stone."

"I've heard the world tree on your planet responds to you, and only you. My request, should you honor it, would be to speak to my planet's world tree. Spend time with it. Convince it I can help restore order above ground."

"And what would become of these creatures under my employ?"

"I can have a ship ready that will transport all of you. You can control their fear. Control their emotions. You can control *them.* Prevent them from revolting."

"Indrid," Nidh growled, "I have been on this job for many thousands of years. Yes. I most certainly can do that. However, you have proven yourself dishonest, and you have created a mess for yourself that I have no stake nor involvement in. To leave my station. To leave my *planet* to come help you is far from appealing. You do realize this, do you not?"

"I'm sorry. I cannot leave without you."

"You have no choice. I am not going."

"You are wanting to remain here, then?"

"For Satan's sake, yes. Are you daft?"

"Where I come from, to not follow one's own desired path is equivalent to building your own coffin and securing it shut from the inside."

"Where I come from, we do not die."

"Immortality is not a reason to throw away your lived experience. You have infinite time, yet you are still affected by what you do with that time."

"I don't have a choice. I have been forced here for—"

"I am right here, right now. And I am *offering* you a choice."

"I do not, nor will I ever, trust you. I do not have a way to leave without risking lowering my station even further, and eternally."

"I've said what I came to say. And you may not admit it now, but I believe you may change your mind if I afford you the time to think it over. I can have a way for you to leave upon the next full moon. The world tree can be fed your flesh, and if you devour its bark, it will grant you access to the terrestrial world. It will pull you up by its roots."

"I am forbidden from using tree roots to ascend. My station no longer permits it."

"I am aware. Please know I am risking all to offer you this. And I am taking a risk in admitting to you that I came here precisely to ask you to join me."

Nidh's soul twisted. She sighed. "At this point, you are incapable of surprising me any further."

It was she who lied, now.

"I believe it," replied Cold. "I will have a vehicle that can transport you and your employ once you ascend. We can access the vehicle, then use my technology to bring your others into being on board."

"Is that so?" She decided to let him continue.

"If I do not return for you, come find me at the surface of this place after ninety revolutions."

"How will I find you?"

"Travel South from this place. When you are growing near, you will find a large symbol I will create by parting the tall grasses. Continue walking through the parted grass, and you'll find a lake filled with creatures of the oceans. Within the lake I'll conceal the ship that will take us away."

"Ocean creatures in a lake? That is unusual. What is the symbol?"

"I will choose a symbol that reminds me of you. Are you familiar with Ammit, devourer of the dead?"

Nidh grinned. "I delight in stories of her."

"She reminds me of you," said Cold.

Nidh's skin grew hot. Her insides smoldered. "Ah, is she real?"

He chuckled. "I feel like she is when I look at you."

20

HEL

The tunnels had warmed and cooled sixty times before Nidh learned anything at all. Anticipation grew until it usurped her gut, the kind that arrests one covertly, and fully.

Her existence since she'd taken this station had been hectic and trying, but this restlessness, this desperation, was a new, deepening ache. The possibility had been dangled in front of her and now it haunted her skull, making every moment feel like an insurmountable challenge.

Obsessively focused on this new, worsening despair, it took Nidh a while to realize that something was watching her.

The roots of the world tree were sentient. That, she already knew. The Old One had been there longer than all. As long as this world. Perhaps longer.

All the same, the roots extended lower than normal in the upper tunnels now. They caressed Nidhogg as she passed through.

For a time, she tried to ignore it, to treat it as an annoyance. Ignoring the possibility that it could be touching her purposefully. She would never risk injuring them, though she entertained the idea. She tried to conduct business in a way that brought her near the world tree less often. She delegated. Sent others up on her behalf.

When she was finally forced to return, the red embers that lit the place had dimmed to almost nothing, even when the earth was warmed by its proximity to the sun.

Something up there cried quietly in the blackness.

"Who is that?" Nidh felt her way cautiously down the tunnel. She called out the names of her employ to gain a response, but no voice returned her query. She remained at a distance. Any more sudden sounds, and she could still retreat back down from where she came.

"I cannot speak," the voice was tiny and choked. Frightened. After that came a gasp. A long pause. "I *can*."

The crying continued.

"Are you the world tree? You are capable of these sounds?"

"You can hear me?" the tree replied. "Understand?"

"Yes, I understand." Nidh was still poised and ready to run.

"Do not have fear. You are safe with me."

"I don't like you touching me when I pass. Was that intentional?"

"I feel your pain more directly when I touch you. You wish to be where the sun can wash your skin. Where my body resides."

"Please be cautious when you speak of this. I—"

"Nobody is here. If anyone is near, I will feel it. My fingers are many. They reach further than your imagination would advise."

"Your fingers. That means your lower . . . extremities? Your roots?"

"Yes."

"And what of your branches?"

More sobbing. "They penetrate the heavens. Much like you wish to do. I am sorry."

Nidh's throat tightened. Threatening emotion. "This is not your doing. And so you needn't be sorry." She worried why this world tree would care so. It seemed the tree had never spoken words in all existence. Why would it speak now? And to her? Nidh tried to ignore the gravity of this realization. Instead, she'd focus on this differently. Tried to frame it instead as having a friend down here in the tunnels.

No, this did not seem ideal at all, actually. Too much responsibility. However, there could be opportunities. Benefits to such an alliance.

Her heart kicked up suddenly when an idea materialized. "You say the sun can touch your body, and you can see what occurs in these tunnels. Are you able to help me?"

"How?" The tree sounded small and tired, despite its staggering breadth and importance.

"Can you see up there in the same way you do down here?"

"If my roots can reach the place, yes."

"And you can just tune in at will?"

"It taxes me, but yes."

"How much do you know about what upsets me?"

"I can feel your sadness and despair, and I remember when the extraterrestrial was here. He wanted you to go with him. I felt your spirits marry. This is quite rare, and I was fortunate to witness it."

"Our spirits married?"

"Yes, it occurs, albeit occasionally."

"I see. What does this mean?"

"It is a pairing. When two beings are destined to be together, and can come to serve some higher purpose. It occurs in times of great need."

"Great need. Can you elaborate?"

"I do not know more."

"Might you tell me if you can locate him?"

"I will try, but I will be silent for some time as I search."

"For how long?"

"I am not sure. However, it will probably be a length of time that will cause you to question if I will return to you."

"I will just have to wait, then."

And so it was. And Nidh stole off each time when late gave way to early, when the earth was still cold, affixing an anglerfish lantern to her head to see better. The lanterns were normally reserved for times when the tunnels threatened to crumble as they slept. For emergencies. Only the workers were to use them. She hoped nobody would see, but the agony inside her shoved her old cares away.

Each morning she would sit with the roots and the dead embers, and wait for any sound or movement from the tree. She'd imagine Indrid Cold's return being earlier than he'd promised. *What if it was today,* she thought each morning. How surprised she'd be. What would she say? She practiced the words in her mind. Turned them over and over until they were smooth and slick. She pictured his smile, large and loud and garish. The ribboned red meat of his cheeks, rising. His eyes, glowing in welcome.

As the visits mounted and she was met with nothing again and again, the concern leeched in. She had spent so little time with him. How well did she know him? It didn't matter, she insisted, batting away that tight feeling in her guts. Sidestepping the subject to allow those brighter feelings to return. There would be time for that.

As Nidh worried, she noticed the roots of the world tree were growing. Bigger, stronger, and faster. Instead of lazy tendrils, they were gnarled, thick, and dark brown. At times they paled to the color of a jellyfish and shivered when she spoke to them. Sometimes the sound of crying echoed around her, causing her to think the tree's consciousness had returned. But when she spoke, no answer came.

Finally, the words surfaced. Murmured whispers from the world tree offered little.

Scouts found Indrid. Questioning Indrid.

Hearts beating fast, she massaged the hard, twisted roots. Sending a message of her own: *I'm here. I'm listening. Please say more.* But the words had dried up and nothing more came. Nidh's blood bristled thick with fear. When the scouts of Hel caught wind of an act of defiance, questioning was not a verbal exchange. It meant identifying and accessing a being's information center, extracting all, and locating what items they required. She tried to hope that because Indrid was not of this planet, they would have trouble.

Trouble, though? Trouble would only mean more turmoil for the subject until the objective was met. For those who interfered with the terrestrial or extraterrestrial kind for their own entertainment, difficulty of overcoming a subject could be somewhat of a sport.

Some excelled and took great pleasure in it.

But the scouts' livelihoods depended on it. Their intentions would come to fruition no matter the cost. There was no option of returning without procuring what they were sent to find.

Nidh found herself completely unable to focus beyond her intense worrying over Indrid. Was he still living? The agony of not knowing consumed her mentally and physically. A smoldering fire stealing away all her other cares. All of it, now, was for Indrid. The earth shook and fell. She lost three souls and hardly directed her team on where to search. The hopelessness and fear hardened to determination. The tree was not trying hard enough. The thing that made her feel, made her anything at all was out of reach and the only thing between herself and Indrid Cold was the world tree. Slowly, the need that coursed through her created a new initiative. The tree would not be allowed to leave again without reuniting her with Indrid.

It took ten more cycles before undulating clouds of brown usurped the white of the roots. They swirled, then languished, the colors fluid and free, like an octopus shifting its colors. Each day she had to convince herself the color was growing healthier. The change was painfully gradual.

By day eight of the change, Nidh started begging. Her tears dropped in the earthen tunnels.

Briefly, she thought the ground beneath her feet trembled slightly. She looked down but saw nothing. No loose dirt moving, nothing shaking. Just the muscles of her feet inventing falsities. Betraying the truth.

"Almost." The word touched Nidh physically, warm and acrid, like a breeze winding itself through a crypt, silt and dust caressing her, settling in a film against her skin.

She closed her eyes. Feeling it, receiving it.

Nidh touched the roots. They paled again, as though it had taxed the tree to speak. She ran her claws against the wood.

"I cannot wait anymore. Return to your body. Tell me what they've done with him," she commanded.

"Almost," the tree repeated.

Her anger boiled over. "Now," Nidh shouted.

The ground truly trembled now. Accompanied by rumblings. Then, a sound like stone splitting. Earth rained down from the ceilings.

"I'm here," the tree thundered. Roots straightened. Shot to the ground like feet setting themselves down to walk.

Nidh's mouth had become dry. "Tell me what you've found of Indrid."

"I warned you this would take time."

"I know." Her eyes stung. "I couldn't wait any longer."

She seemed to rethink. "Stop, please, I can feel your feelings. It hurts."

"I needn't tell you, then."

Her voice was quieter now. "No, you needn't."

Nidh lowered hers to match. "Please tell me." Her throat hardly carried any sound.

"He has betrayed you, Nidh."

Nidh's soul dropped. She felt gutted. "No."

"He was hardly questioned. He took an offering from them, immediately."

"This is against what was agreed. Against *everything.*" Nidh's throat closed. "I can't stay here," she shouted. "I have to get out of here. I have to confront him."

"That is not possible. And you don't need me to tell you that."

Nidh sneered. "Not possible, or never done?"

"What do you mean?"

"You will take me to the surface, like the travelers who come up to claim the dead and bring them down here."

"No. They can only do so because they are tasked to do so. They can only travel using the roots of dead trees and their ancient magic."

"Do not lecture me about how this realm operates. I know very well," Nidh growled.

"I am the world tree. That is not my function."

Anger, determination boiled within Nidh. She felt emboldened. Nothing else mattered except this objective. "Do not underestimate yourself. You will do this."

"You cannot force me."

"I can." Nidh's stomach cried out as though it had stood empty for decades. She doubled over, clutching herself. "I'm starving," she squeezed her eyes shut. "I'm craving—" she cut herself off. Such a thing did not make sense.

More tremors. A loud crack sounded as more dirt shook loose from the ceiling of the tunnel. The tree wrenched a root free. The tree lifted her appendage, old as the earth itself, one of an infinite many, in front of Nidh. A gesture of comfort.

Nidh shouted out in agony. Her heart reeled, wild, roving and desperate. She bit down hard on the root. The pain hit her like a stone. Short, sharp breaths were all she could grasp with her lungs. She doubled over again. Covered her face. Held a claw over her lips.

Instead of dissipating gradually, the throbbing grew stronger and stronger. She bit down on her lip to keep from crying out. As unbearable as the pain may have been, worse still would be her fate if her employ found her like this. They would alert someone else. They would take her away. Her stomach would eat itself.

As Nidh bit down, her gums rebelled. "What?" she breathed. Her teeth pressed forward, fighting their station. Ripping her flesh. She dug her fists into her forehead, forcing more small breaths.

Something was happening. In a place where nothing changed, Nidh was changing. She'd heard whisperings from other realms, other worlds, that sheer will and want, if it were strong enough, could lead to physical change or manifestation.

But what was this change for?

Sharp pains now, from deep within her jaw and the top of her mouth. Something was emerging. "New teeth?" she tried to speak, but instead her lips met around her old mangled ones. She spat blood.

Her old teeth dangled loose on her tongue, one stuck to her inner lip.

Nidh cried out as sharp pain racked her gums.

They had formed a double rainbow, the old teeth and the new, practically touching each other.

She felt her mouth gently.

"I see you now," the tree sounded hesitant. "Your new teeth are sharper. They are meant to penetrate."

"My lord?" a voice came from the dark of the tunnel opening. Krill, one of her employ, was conscious and ready to begin his day's work.

Nidh didn't reply. "No," she whispered to the tree. "We must go. We must hurry."

She felt her new teeth. They were jagged little lightning bolts fashioned from bone. She spit out more blood. Her jaws ached.

Krill spoke again. "Please, my lord. Respond. I must come to assess any damage. To make sure you are safe. We heard a commotion."

"I want to be left alone. I am fine," Nidh growled. She turned to the tree. "It wants symmetry," she said quietly. She stretched her mouth open wider, wider, a million popping sounds, short and severe, like the splintering of a tree as it fell. She moaned loudly as her jaw cracked into a million tiny pieces. Until the two half-circles joined in one flat, perfect circle.

Footsteps drew close to the mouth of the cave. The sound of someone climbing into the tunnel.

Nidh couldn't speak. There was no flesh to close around the sounds her throat made. Her stomach cramped again. She ran her hands over herself. Her green, iridescent, fine leathery scales remained. She felt her legs. Her feet. Her tail. Her thick serpentine shape remained.

But she might not keep this body for long. It was time to go, now. To leave this place. There was no telling what her body would consist of when her journey was complete.

Mouth gaping, she pointed to the branch. Time to try again.

Take me up, Nidh thought with all her will. She placed the branch within the opening and tightened her new orifice. Her teeth pressed down, and in. The pain was replaced now with a satisfying pressure. Better than scratching an itch. The hunger pangs quieted.

"What will this do?" the tree asked her. "You cannot pass through miles of solid earth."

You can, though.

"You are suggesting I can pull you up?"

Not suggesting.

The tree could read Nidh's thoughts now. Suddenly, her hunger pangs returned, stronger than before. The bark smelled unremarkable to her. But she inhaled a fresh, sharp, green smell and her spit melted like heated molasses. Coated her mouth, her throat.

She began to drink the blood of the tree, and as she did, she felt her own blood leaving her mouth, mixing with the tree's own blood. An exchange of life elixirs.

"You know very well you may never return."

Nidh nodded. Her feet left the ground and her neck tightened with the weight of her body. In her peripheral, she could see Krill running toward her. A silent laugh rattled within her as she imagined what he must see.

The flesh of her mouth and every fleshy inner surface rolled with pleasure, from her tongue to her feet.

The dirt opened as she rose, swallowing her completely.

*****

Nidh couldn't breathe, yet the flavor of spring languished in her throat. That sharp earthy tang of late snow saturated the dirt to become pre-spring mud.

She remained latched on with her mouth as she and the tree climbed and climbed. Her muscles howled for mercy. The vertebrae in her neck and back groaned, popped, threatened to crack.

The mud clung to her in streaks. It stung her face, burning outside and smoldering within, fierce like the paint of war.

She was still, slow like the mud wraiths she passed, the world tree's roots ripped at her wrists, moving her up, up, up until she was borne, violently, into the world above.

She unlatched from the root, her mouth folding stiffly, having more bends than corners now due to its new shape. Her skin peeled thick down her fingers, rolling all the way down to the V's between her fingers. Discarded sheaths of skin revealed the true substance underneath. The wind stroked this raw redness, bringing a sharp, brilliant pain.

The sun rode high in a muted white sky. She tried to regard it, but it shouted her eyes down. Even when she lowered her gaze, a yellow after-image persisted.

"This is madness. Do you not suffer from experiencing this daily?" she asked the tree.

"Nidh, I do not have eyes."

A scrambling sound came from behind, from the opening her body had left in the dirt.

"No," she whispered. *No, he cannot have followed.* Without thinking, she shouted, "Close the opening. Cover it with dirt."

"Do you know what you're saying?" the tree asked, but it was too late. An arm hooked itself over the opening, grasping at the flattened grass.

As soon as his face crested the opening, she knew it was Krill. His face was slack on the left side. In life, he'd been a petty thief. In death, he grew lost in the tunnels on his first cycle. Tried to escape them. A renegade demon had trapped him for a half-century, and when she caught wind of that fact, she'd sent another to seek him out. He'd gone so long without sustenance he'd begun to melt. That malady had never healed, and he'd kept within close proximity to her ever since that time.

Krill shifted his weight to one forearm. Gritting his long, sharp, teeth, he leaned forward, struggling to grab on to the tree's branch that lay near the opening. One eye squinted. The other—the one on the ruined side of his face—stared blank and bug-like, no longer functional. Its lid was a curled, dead insect, pilled and leathered by time.

The tree moved her branch away, as if disgusted.

Krill held himself up with trembling arms. His biceps quivered beneath his weight. "I did not know you were leaving."

Nidh walked over, reached her hands toward him. He took them, and she cried out in pain, pulling with all her might. Eventually Krill was able to crawl on his belly and emerge from the opening. "I did not intend for you to know," she chose her words carefully. Could she get him to leave? To go back down? Or convince him not to follow her? She couldn't see how. Nidh did not know what to tell him. "How could he have followed?" she asked the tree.

"He remains intact while your skin sheds. Your sacrifice was his easy passage," the tree replied. "He must have followed directly underneath you."

"The world tree!" Krill shouted. "It speaks to you?"

Nidh didn't respond. She narrowed her eyes.

He stared at her. "Your skin, it is coming off."

Nidh's face stung. She touched it, and the stinging intensified. Just like her fingers, she could feel only muscle. She imagined she must look like Indrid, now.

"This place is so bright," he gasped, looking around. "How that star shines."

"Yes. Indeed it does." She awaited more inquiry, trying to ready herself.

"Why did you not ask me to join you? The passage was dangerous. You could have used my help."

"This is something I must do alone."

"Who will lead things during your absence?"

"It remains to be seen."

"This must be a fast trip, then. Perhaps nobody was needed?"

"Perhaps," she lied. How could she get him to leave? To go back down? And if he returned quickly enough, if he alerted others, she feared she could be located. All the same, he could not come with her. "You must go back the way you came. You should not have followed me."

"When will you return?"

"I do not know. I have things I must do."

"How will you return?" He pointed to the opening they had just used. "It was not safe to travel this way, and it will not be safe to travel back. We must find another way."

"There is no other way," she said sharply. She'd tried patience, but oh, how it waned.

The ground shook around them. Krill stumbled. The earth was closing up again.

"Hurry!" he whined, though he did not move toward the opening. His good eye widened, and his breath quickened. Panic was taking hold. His way back was disappearing. She felt for him, but she feared his reaction more. "You aren't going back, are you?" he asked.

"I do not know what to tell you. I have things I must attend to."

He stared at her for a few moments. Long enough for discomfort to set in. His eye narrowed. "You are not returning. Only by chance did I learn that you left. And you would leave us to rot." Krill's voice was low and dangerous. When his temper flared, she could see the yellows of both eye sockets.

It was not flattering.

Krill shook his head. "This is ridiculous. We have to go now. Come with me. We will find scouts up here. They'll find a passage back down." His tone was condescending. He reached for Nidh.

She slapped his hand away. "Do not touch me. And do not follow." She moved to walk away.

Krill lurched forward, closing the distance between them. He caught her by her two outside fingers and squeezed, drawing her closer to him. Nidh shouted, Krill's oil-dirt skin upsetting her exposed muscle. He crushed her fingers so hard, the bones creaked. Every inch of her rattled wildly in silent alarm.

"If you do not come willingly, I will bring you to the scouts. They will not be pleased to learn what you've done," he growled.

"I did not ask you to follow me. You do not belong here. Release me, and leave me be." She gritted her teeth. In Hel, he was constantly at her heels. The risk of losing everything must have broken something within him.

"You are in poor shape. That is no condition to decide things, my lord," Krill said. The last words were volcanic. They burned sour in Nidh's nose.

She struggled against Krill but he'd grabbed both hands now, tightening his grip even further. She tried to shift her weight, to pull away without injuring herself further. She was coming apart now. The skin on her arms, her shoulders. In the struggle, all of it was loosening.

This is wrong, she thought. *All wrong.* A beating of drums sounded around them, now. Coming from Krill's chest.

His heart. It was beating faster, louder. Before, she couldn't hear it. But now, it reached her. Made her skull ache.

"Too loud," she responded.

"What do you mean?"

"Let go of me," she whispered. His grip tightened and the pain wound around her fingers, shooting up her arms.

The pounding sound grew. She wanted it to be gone. To be quiet. Two red blotches formed on the insides of her eyelids. Seared like blooded suns in her skull. She wanted to make it disappear.

"Take it," the tree growled. "He threatens you. Take his heart."

Nidh glared at Krill's chest, then closed her eyes again. Focused on the two red dots behind her eyelids. She pictured Krill's heart in her mind, and pulled it forward. Toward the red dots.

Inhaling slowly, she opened her mouth wide. Felt the heart disappear from Krill's ribcage, and within her maw.

Krill collapsed. Nidh swallowed the heart down, grinning her new folded-oval grin.

Finally, she was sated.

***

The trip up had weakened Nidh. But she would forge ahead, terror her constant companion at the horror she had just committed.

The heart of her employ lay digesting in her gut, and she set forth convincing herself the action was truly needed. Would he have carried out his threat? Why else would he have followed her up? Krill had needed Nidh in order to exist. If he had been allowed to live, he would no doubt have followed through on his threat.

But she could have trapped him somehow, Nidh argued to herself, created some advantage so compelling that he'd be forced to keep her secret.

And that's when the obvious hit her. She could have tried to use her abilities to influence him to stay and help her above ground.

She didn't know if it would have worked.

But she could have tried.

Fuck, she growled to herself. Krill's heart turned in her gut, writhing like some half-rotted worm. Was there any version of this story that did not make her the monster?

The tree. The tree was the monster. It had been the one who taught Nidh that she could take his heart.

Nidh quickened her pace, growing the space between her and the tree. All the while knowing she had no protection when she left its presence. The tree had told her so.

Could it be trusted, though? Nidh scowled. The tree had gotten her here. She was somewhere new now. Unfamiliar. It had helped her, but it had complicated things further with Krill's murder. Made her do something that caused her to fear herself.

This area above her realm was heavily populated with brothers and sisters of the world tree. She envisioned the canopy of the trees as the walls of her native tunnels. The shade they offered from the glaring sun helped to calm her.

Nidh traveled South as she'd been advised. She knew at some point the cover of the trees would break, that she would reach an area uncovered and unprotected. She did not know where Indrid was now, nor if the scouts had left him, nor what had become of the vehicle he'd promised her.

The atmosphere was staggering. To be in the open, nothing but sky and space above. There was space to stretch, to arch, to be. She was afraid, and she was hurried, but a disbelieving awe, a passion, had encompassed her. Something she felt she would struggle to come down from. If the scouts found her, how would she survive? How could she bear the punishment they would put upon her? How could she go back down there? The place she'd always been, and that she hoped never to see again?

Nidh stepped into deep mud, and stooped to scrape it off. When she lifted her head, she saw it:

Nidh had arrived at the place where the woods emptied into the open water, and her hearts soared. This was the place Indrid had led her to. She hoped again that perhaps the world tree had been mistaken. That Indrid would be waiting here, with no scouts aware of his plan.

They would descend into the lake that resembled a small ocean, and then ascend together. She would hold her planet in her hand, then discard it as they sailed through the heavens, to where the blue gives way to black and faraway stars. And the tunnels of Hel, and the Dessicated inside those tunnels would shrink. Would be so small to her that its size rivaled nothingness.

Her dreams and the hopes folded within them soared, but didn't land. Her feet refused to take her beyond the shelter of trees.

The lake stretched out, stopping just before the skyline, half-concealed by ice. Birds chattered, dove, and then climbed, but otherwise, all was quiet.

But something was wrong.

The air was warm. If the warmth was recent, that could explain why half the lake was still iced over. But the ice looked all wrong. Not the solid milky cataract-white of Hel she was accustomed to.

Nidh stepped closer. The ice—or whatever it was—was speckled, black and white like stone.

She moved closer to the water. Myriad fish roiled at the water's edge, lidless eyes staring at nothing and everything. Nidh was used to devastation, decay, torture. But this place held hope, the animals a peace she had never witnessed before. She recognized the elements of her prior existence, but here they were dressed in different clothing and thrashing at her feet, welcoming her back already to what she knew.

Familiar, and devastating all the same.

"Hello, my love." Indrid's voice came cold and sudden from next to her.

21

Don't speak.

She'll find you.

Do you feel me down here, Death Twin? In the cramped underground space, while you sleep upstairs? Folding up your troubles and playing with them in abstract. Your survival is a burden, as is my own.

I thought I felt you the other night as I observed the dead miners of Barre working. When they sleep in day, they are your people. But when they wake at night, they are mine.

They are so many, now. My adoring teeth. The stone Indrid grew, it eats their lungs from the inside, killing so many. But, in life, as long as they breathed anything at all, they continued their cutting. Some are more careful. Sometimes they wear masks. And sometimes, that is not enough. Now they no longer breathe, nor do they feel pain. And so, their work continues, until I reach the ship that Indrid has buried in the stone.

Maybe you can't feel me down here, Death Twin. Maybe your stomach turns softly as you sleep. Or perhaps a dark film has blanketed your dreams. Consider that my trauma, pressing against yours.

Either way, the cold steel of your father's ring sings to me from behind the anniversary flame you lit tonight. Perhaps I can't walk through your door; but from dirt, from where there is murdered wood, I will ascend.

Once we have met, you will wish I'd never found this room seated within the ground, beneath your house. The place where ugly things are hidden and forgotten.

I will find the ring. I will find what you already know.

You will not unlock the tunnels of the underworld, nor will you take my loyal dead to their eternal rest.

***

The light felt blue that night. It sank through Kara's eyelids and spilled into her dreams. A vague, puzzling terror popped and buzzed in her skull. Bleary dark shapes the size of people— fifteen or so—moved unnaturally quickly around and past her. All different sizes, most taller and wider than her, others just her height. They turned to acknowledge her as they passed.

Their eyes were blurry and black, and their demeanor conveyed one silent message: *Leave.* She tried to reply but her mouth felt glued shut, and a loud hum rattled her skull, her own voice foreign to her. Frightened, and frightening.

Her hum rattled against the blue walls. She could make out the ceiling lines, now. The lines stretched up and around her, and yes, the corners bled down from above, the lines darkening as she observed them. One of the figures shuddered to the front, and the others seemed to melt away, fading to a milky blue, then white, finally running lazily like a swirl of oil escaping a puddle.

The shuddering one came closer, climbed into focus. She screamed once more, and his face was as clear as the day he'd left her.

Dad.

His eyes were closed. Arms folded over his chest. A warm flickering sputtered suddenly behind her. She turned and saw nothing but a dark room. Her living room. She remembered his Yartzeit candle she'd lit.

"Dad," she whispered. "Can you see me?"

He squinted, harder and harder, until the squinting became a grimace. Slowly, he lifted a hand, index finger first, to his lips to quiet her. Then he held the heel of his hand to his collarbone and was still again.

"Dad," she whispered again. Hesitated. "What happens to you at night?"

His eyes shot open, eyes that held orange flames, like the candle. "The flame wasn't burning before, but now it is."

Kara's eyes stung. "I'm so sorry, Daddy. Mom forgot."

"Thank you. You burned it late, but the important thing is you burned it. I can get to the river, now. You'll come for me, but when the river washes your face like tears, you'll know I'm where I'm supposed to be."

"What river?"

"Don't speak. She'll find you."

"Who? The one at the quarry?"

"Nidhogg. Yes." He looked to the ground, as though expecting something.

A loud metallic crashing. Scraping and sliding, then another crash, and a clatter.

"Go," her dad said, his voice low and grave. "Wake up. Get yourself away."

"No, Dad. I can't leave you."

"I've left you already. Protect the ring I made. It's yours, now. You have to keep it with you."

Kara let out a sob.

"Go."

She looked everywhere, weaving around the figures that did not move. They weren't the ones causing the din, but she couldn't find the source. It felt high above. Or maybe far below.

The metallic sound suddenly cleaved Kara from sleep. She opened her eyes to darkness. Her chest roared with a fresh, searing pain.

Dad. She'd really seen him in that dream, hadn't she?

That noise. Was it only in her dream? Or did something in the room make that sound? Blinking, she lifted her head and looked around the room. The TV, the window, everything was still. Ten breathed quietly. Kara scanned the room again.

Something was standing there.

To the left, a figure. Something giant and robotic-looking—a shiny off-white upholstery pulled smooth over its hard metal skeleton—leaned against the wall, not five yards away from where she lay. It had a large, wide torso, and long narrow legs with hard joints. Like huge pistons encased into valves.

It was stooped down just to fit in the room, its strange oblong head tilted down as though it were a living thing, purposely avoiding the ceiling. Kara remembered she'd dreamed about this thing before, just as its head moved. It turned its body, smooth and quick, as if on a swivel.

It pinned her with its eyeless gaze.

The darkness shook in lines like black waves of heat, refusing to hold still. Kara looked at the candle. It seemed to fight with the dark room. She squinted, trying to force her vision to sharpen, tell her what was happening.

Please don't move again, she begged the robotic thing silently.

Afraid to move herself, she reached for the ground next to the couch, her fingers fumbling for purchase. "Ten," she whispered so quietly she wasn't sure a dog could hear her. "Hey!" she rasped a little louder. "Tennyson."

Kara felt in the dark for a bare arm, then a t-shirt sleeve, and tapped Ten gently. Then harder, and harder.

The sound of scraping metal formed words:

"She will not wake."

Kara shouted out, falling on top of Ten, and scrambled backwards to the easy chair.

"No, no, no," she managed before her voice failed her and she was just mouthing the words. Sweat sprang to her forehead and nausea crawled over her. "What did you do to her," she whispered helplessly.

"She has been placed under."

"Under *what?*"

"Between the land of the living and the dead. There they will remain until they reach the sun again."

"What? Why?" Kara's voice returned, shrill and stumbling over itself. She could move to the door. She could run. Right?

Slowly, Kara moved to stand.

Slowly, the hulking form leaned forward.

Panic gripped Kara by the throat. She dropped to all fours and shuffled behind the big armchair. Grabbed the big steel flashlight they kept underneath it.

A metallic creaking sounded, and the ground shook with a deadened thump. A rapid dragging now; two very large calves and scrabbling metal palms, the whole horrible mechanism, climbed the vertical carpeted landscape toward her. Any second now. Any second, and the strange staring face with no eyes would crest beyond the spot where she hid herself.

What could she do? What? She couldn't leave Ten alone in the apartment. But she could hit the thing with the flashlight. Get herself to Ten's room. The twin dragging sound grew louder, ascending along the coffee table to the other side of the chair that hid her.

The thing was close now. So close. She had to do it *right now*. She could make it. She had to.

The metallic thing scraped along the carpet. There was its head, moving past the side of the big chair, the back of its head narrow and pointed, forming a tail at the base of the skull. The lines were smooth, the surface glossy. Kara's heart flipped, but she was stuck fast there.

Quickly, quietly, she crawled toward Ten's bedroom door.

Her eyes were locked on the being's featureless face. She held the flashlight like a bat and swung, clocking it in the chin.

Its head didn't move an inch. The impact rattled her palms, stung her bones. A low metallic groan sent fingers down her spine. "You will not get far, my child." The thing shot an arm out, grabbing for Kara with its long, thin fingers.

She threw the flashlight at it. Ran to Ten's room, her legs completely numb.

Kara crossed the threshold just as the thing rounded the corner behind her. It walked like a faun: two monstrous legs bent backwards, blue moonlight careening off its smooth, cream-colored upholstery.

Amid a headlong sprint, Kara's foot caught the pile of laundry in the doorway. She pitched full tilt to the ground, hit her head on the corner of the dresser.

Please. No. For a moment, she was blind. She held her head with one hand and felt wildly for the door with her other. Her head spun and she pitched sideways, smacking her hip against the dresser, folding over it, clunking into the wall. *No.* It was too late, now. Far too late.

Do it anyway. If the dresser was at her left hip, the open door was just ahead. She grabbed it and shoved.

Something soft stopped it. The clothes. "God!" she cried out.

The blinding white light faded and her vision returned; the black of the room greeted her. She moved to kick the pile of laundry out of the way.

Cool, hard fingers gripped her ankle and pulled.

Her whole body reoriented and bowed violently backwards to gravity, the back of her battered head bashing against the thinly carpeted wood floor.

"Do not toy with me." The voice groaned high, the thing's fingers clinging to Kara's skull. "I can feel you're luring me away from it."

"Away?" Kara choked as she lay there in the dark. "From what?"

"The ring. The trinket of your father's." A strange crackling registered as laughter. "The ring is the moth, and your stupid candle is the flame. You've removed the ring. Led me right to it."

Her mind reeled. The ring. She wore it, and it did things for her. Others knew.

"You want my ring. So did . . . Mothman. He came for it, too."

"I sent him. He failed. Now that you removed it again, here I am."

What name had her father given? "Nidh?" she asked.

The dragging continued. It was on its knees again. "Yes."

"What are you?"

"I am something that has lived here much, much longer than you—"

Kara moaned. She tipped her head up, trying to lift herself by the elbows, falling back again. Her aching head swam.

"And I am someone who will remain, long after you have died."

Kara's eyes stung with wild anger; tears of acid. "What are you doing to my father? He's supposed to be dead."

"Stupid flesh being; that is not important."

Kara grit her teeth. "Why are you here? Why are you hurting my friends? Why are you using my father? I *said* he's *supposed* to be dead." Her head whooshed with pain and felt like it was stuffed with cotton all at once. She was going to die tonight, she knew it.

"I owe you nothing. I've told you. I'm here to take back my god damned ring, cretin. You will show me where you've hidden it."

Kara spit. "Fuck you."

Fingers grabbed her by the jaw, knocked her head back into the floor. It all went white again. She gasped, grabbed at Nidh's wrists. They felt like they looked: like pleather upholstery over a metal skeleton. Her own fingers clawed fruitlessly, slipping, barely holding on. This was all impossible. Impossible. She fought to stay conscious.

"You were at the workshop last night. Why?" The voice scraped at Kara, rattling her nerves.

"No." She squeezed her eyes shut.

"You did not understand me, filthy child. You will answer me. Tell me why you were there. Where is the one who carves the stone?"

Kara struggled, groaned. "He's gone, now." She tried desperately to wrench her neck, move her head. The fingers dug in deeper. "Indrid Cold killed him. Took his skin."

"What!" It threw her angrily against the desk, the side of her head clunking, loud and painful, against the edge.

Kara bent over, cupping the side of her head in her palm. She heard it pacing the room. "He is here," the horrible metallic voice muttered. "Has he returned or has he been here all along?"

"I don't know," Kara whispered, pulling herself slowly, quietly up to look across the desk. Her ruined head swooned, and white stars prickled her eyes.

"Are you really *so* useless to me or are you just spewing shit lies?"

The Barre-grey granite paperweight sat there on Tennyson's desk. Had Ten moved it there?

Kara's head throbbed. She knew she couldn't lift the paperweight. Instead, she placed her palms against the crevassed back of the stone thing and dragged it toward her, over the edge of the desk.

She landed with legs folded, the smooth stone trailing immediately after, dropping heavily into her lap with a soft thud.

"Human, what are you doing?" The heavy footfall shook the ground behind Kara, and those perilous fingers grabbed the base of her skull, took hold of her hair, and pulled her head back.

Kara cried out. Leaning back, she shifted her weight quickly and urgently to her hands. She lifted herself up. The paperweight rolled off her, dropping like a small explosion.

In response, Nidh yanked, quick and hard. Kara screamed as a sizeable clump of hair ripped clean out from the back of her skull. She landed on her side, palms spread. Gritting her teeth, groaning quietly.

She crawled, crooked and drunk with contusions, fast as she could, toward the door, but Nidh rushed to the space between Kara and the only way out.

Kara redirected then, dragging herself back toward the stone. Nidh would surely follow. Kara would just have to heave this fucking thing with whatever she had left.

The deathly fingers wrapped, tightening around her bicep like a vice. "Enough of this. I will bring you to the other room, and you will show me the ring." It yanked Kara violently upwards. Her legs would not support her, so she slumped down again. Kara lashed a hand out toward the stone, dragging it up her body. She hardly had any use of her good arm, so she just heaved the paperweight as best she could, like a bowling ball down a very short lane. Her soul sunk even before the thing connected; she could see it was barely going to graze Nidh's calf. This was the last thing up Kara's sleeve, and though she'd known it was less than nothing to begin with, it was the last thing all the same.

In hindsight, Kara would guess her arm was freed up before the screaming started. And suddenly everything was as good as it was frightening, as triumphant as it was horrible.

Kara was back on the ground, head reeling. The stone was at Nidh's feet. Something dark, red and sinewy was climbing out the back of the metallic suit, curving away from the paperweight on the floor, the suit slumping over, long arms going limp.

Kara shoved herself to her feet, then got woozy and fell to her knees. She picked up the stone and staggered toward the strange chaotic loops of muscle. They shrieked again. Kara dropped the paperweight right over the largest grouping of sinew.

Right before the stone landed, the muscles parted, dodging. They shrieked again, more and more of the stuff pouring out the back of the suit, the mass of muscles growing to roughly half the size of the suit. It towered over Kara.

***

Her head rang. Weakness washed over her, the edges of her vision threatening to go white again. Kara picked up the stone and held it in her lap. Shaking her head ever so slightly, waking her brain back up. She stared at the red mass, daring it to move.

Quickly, it created hook-like arms out of itself that wrapped around the shoulders of the suit, dragging it out the door.

22

THE BIRTH OF THE STONE

"Hello, my love." It was Indrid's voice, but when she turned, nobody was there. He was far away, she knew. But he'd come soon.

Nidhogg stood at the edge of the water that held the sky. A sky so bright it hurt her eyes. She looked down, watched the water ripples lick at the chaste white clouds. Sky and lake were leagues apart, but they touched each other all the same, in their own way.

Her eyes traveled down to the water's edge, where the land surrendered, to her reflection. Her skin had flaked for what looked like the last time. She touched her face gingerly. It crunched, like half-spent leaves under bare feet. When she'd lived underground, it would molt, and she would welcome her fresh skin underneath. But it was not to be on this terrestrial plane. Nidh blinked. Two small, cloudy blue eyes that had always been hers; but she'd never seen them this way above ground. They'd looked fetching, she knew, against her blue-green scales, but underneath this final sloughing was something deep red and raw; just muscle. The cold touched it in a way that was deep, and sharp, and whole.

Was she dying? No, no. She was immortal still, yes? Down there, she'd been immortal. What would this new life bring? Why had she come here? This was not natural. But no, it had to be done. She couldn't have continued in the old way.

Something large, cream-white and smooth, shaped like a living figure, rose to the surface of the water. A dead thing, perhaps.

She took a step toward the water, and the moment she lifted her foot, something from deep within her calf shifted. She froze in place, frightened, crying out. The muscles continued to stretch all on their own, making her groan and grit her teeth.

There was no mercy. The stretching was unrelenting. Her leg must be growing, she thought. As she looked down, she felt the muscles pop, one by one. She screamed in anguish, searing pain shooting up her calf.

Nidh dropped to all fours, breathing hard, testing her lungs. Her body felt like it was rioting, protesting its shape. Everything inside ached, and everything outside stung as her skin stretched, hundreds of small rips forming across her entire body.

Her muscles, a series of taut ribbons once tucked tightly against each other, teeming with purpose, every section in its right place, her defining shape, now wrestled loose from the sheath her skin had been.

She was coming undone.

Her hands broke free first. The skin of her fingers split, and her red ribbons twisted and teemed together slowly. Nidh screamed. Surely, this was the end. This matter would spill out of her and she'd become nothing but a mess in the ruined grass. Any moment now, her consciousness would cease, swallowed by nothingness.

She stared, mesmerized at the undulating streaks of red. The skin of her hands peeled gradually down to her elbows, but gravity was not claiming these rogue muscles. They were shifting almost rhythmically, winding around each other, caressing each other. She tried to move them, groaning as the muscles ripped open the surface of her bicep. Her hearts raced, her mind flipped, turning, racing, delirium and realization side by side, pumping through her. She still had control of her muscles, but now there were no limits to the direction in which they could move.

She repeated the command with her right arm, her torso, her legs. The tearing of her skin still brought her searing pain, but the moment it separated from her insides, it was dead. No longer a part of her. Now, the muscles were what made her. The wind on her raw surfaces made her mind squeal.

She stepped out of the pelt, looking down at what her mind understood to be her new arms. Flexing them, changing them, making them round, making them long, reaching out, touching the grass.

Hearts still racing, Nidh looked back to the water. The big, cream-white shape had crested the surface. Something with a torso, arms, legs, that had never lived. Something that perhaps had drifted out of Indrid's flying machine that waited beneath the water.

Slowly, she waded in, the water biting pain into her every surface. She needed some kind of protective sheath. Something to replace her skin. She turned back to her discarded skin, stiff and drying in the sun. That would no longer do.

She came closer to the white thing in the water, touched the back of it. For a split second, she felt nothing. Then, a slight vibration kicked on, responding to her touch. It hummed silently. Her body began to mimic the vibration. It was calling to her.

This was a suit. A suit she could wear, perhaps. A tool.

The Cold One's voice came from far away.

He will be back, she thought.

The wind roared across the stony water as Nidhogg climbed inside the mechanical body.

A pairing is a touch of the skin, turned magical. A marrying of souls. The universe blessing a union, and breaking something else.

***

Now

"Oh, god."

Kara sat bolt upright in a hospital room with off-white walls and no windows. Her head seared with pain, and her right eye showed her only darkness. She dropped back against the pillows, blinking rapidly. She covered her eye, uncovered it again.

Nothing.

The dream she'd had. Wild, but possibly real? She could see things now, couldn't she? And she'd dreamed about this creature before. Right after visiting the cemetery. The thing in her dream was the same as the one that had attacked her. It had a name.

Nidhogg.

Next to the small flat screen TV was a white board. "What's your pain level?" it read, with a succession of increasingly agitated faces, positioned under numbers one through ten. A huge question mark was drawn between five and six with a red marker.

She winked her left eye closed, leaving her right open, and saw nothing.

Damn, damn, damn.

"Kara! How are you feeling?" Alec's subdued voice sounded to her right, followed by a sniffling, like he was just waking up.

She turned and screamed, scrabbling backwards until she fell out of bed. A skeleton in a black hoodie. "Alec!"

"Kara, no, shit. Sorry!" He put a palm out in front of him, fingers spread, then covered his face with both hands. Pulled the hood over his head, and looked down at his lap to speak. "What happened?"

"I—"

"I found you on the floor in Ten's room. Called 911. You were *completely* out. Your face is all bruised up, and your ring is gone."

Kara gasped. "Where's Ten? Is she okay?"

"She is totally fine. Really fatigued, but fine. She's up in the cafeteria getting coffee."

Kara let out a big breath. But then remembered. "Shit. My ring!" Her heart sped up, and her headache intensified. She shut her eyes tight, thinking. "She might not have found it, though!"

"Who?

"Nidh. The one from the poem. The one at the quarry last night. She was in that big, white suit. She wants the ring, and—" she choked up. "She has my dad," she managed.

"That's who did this to you." Alec's voice was low and quiet. "There was no sign of break-in. Only the floor vent cover and the floor around it was busted to hell."

"Yeah. I didn't have the ring on me. I wouldn't tell her where it was. She got so mad. Kept hitting my head against the floor." Kara pointed. "Alec, I can't see out this eye."

"The doctor said . . ." He paused. "Wait, you didn't have the ring on you?"

"I—no. I think it's in the couch. Either she found it there and she has it with her, or it's still under the couch cushions."

"Why would it be there." A statement, not a question.

Shit. "I think it came off while I was sleeping. Lucky thing it did too—"

"The necklace fell off you while you slept? Are you telling the truth?"

Kara bit her lip. Took a deep breath. "No."

"I can't believe you took it off." His voice was low and icy. "We talked about this."

She shrugged. "I had to figure this all out, with or without you."

"Mm," was all she got out of him.

"I'm sorry," she whispered.

"You have lots of bruising around your eye, and your eye is red with blood." The cold voice continued, face down, arms crossed. "It looks really bad. He said you have Acute Hyphema. Bleeding in the space

251

between the cornea and the iris. The doctor says it's likely you'll regain your vision as it starts to heal, but it's still a wait-and-see thing."

"That's good," Kara said quietly. "I hope."

"Kara, when you don't tell me stuff like this, it scares me. I can't help you when I don't know what's going on. And honestly, I hate admitting this, but it makes me think of that summer with Tyler."

She squeezed her eyes shut. "God, I hate that guy."

"It makes me feel so helpless. Like, you're hurting so much. Your whole world's flipped inside out, and there is absolutely nothing I can do. I'm *literally* powerless to help you."

Tyler. That piece of shit. She hated that some part of Alec was still holding onto that. She wished she hadn't fucked up so badly with the necklace. They were supposed to be a team. They did everything together. She'd been so focused on figuring all this out that she'd forgotten. Even after the talk they'd just had.

If Alec had known, he'd have been there. And he wouldn't be angry and hurt and needing to hide his face.

And with that thought, just like before, the intense feeling of needing to see his face. Needing him to know she wanted *him* all along. *Not* Tyler, but just didn't know it. All of it smacked her like a ton of bricks. Something inside her ached, deeper and heavier than her head. She scrunched her face painfully, which of course made her head ache even worse.

The sobs poured out of her. Desperation and hurt. Everything was shattered. "Fuck. I'm so sorry," she cried, covering her face.

"Can I come over there?" His voice was softer now.

"Yeah," she said weakly, between sobs.

He sat close to her on the small bed, shoes and all, his side warm against hers. His soft hair tickled her face, and then his cheek was up against her own. For a second she was glad her right eye had gone blind. She let her mind see the *real* him. She inhaled big, and she heard him do the same. His hair smelled like sage and cedarwood.

"No offense, but it makes me feel better that you're crying."

A short laugh burst through her tears. "Thanks."

"Well, like, finding you like that? And learning you just threw all caution to the wind and then lied to me about it?"

"Yeah," she sighed heavily.

"I'd do anything for you, Kara. I just needed to feel like you cared, too."

"I do. So much."

"We're a team, yeah?" His voice sounded good this way. Muffled, the vibration of his honeyed voice in her skull. Heads together, bone against bone.

"Yeah," she said.

"We're in this together, okay?"

"Absolutely."

"I promise I'll help you now. I'll do whatever. If you swear you'll tell me what's going on. Keep me in the loop, okay?"

"I swear." She held him close. "I can't lose you," she whispered.

Alec turned so his head was buried against her neck.

Her blood surged, her breath catching in her throat. Everything that made this too complicated started to melt away. The only thing stopping her from turning toward him, touching his face, pressing her mouth against his, completely melting against him, was his face. The full gravity of what they were going through, right there.

It had something to do with what all was happening. But what? What had happened had marked just the two of them? It happened right after they held hands at the cemetery. And now she could see things, and Alec could apparently move through space, with nothing more than a desire to go somewhere. Liquefying time and space, and just slicing through it. These had to be for something. To serve some purpose.

They stayed like that for ages. Kara sat there, listening to his breath, burning inside, hoping he wouldn't move.

Five minutes passed before he spoke. "I gotta go get your ring. I'll be back."

Her chest fluttered. "Nope. Wait until they discharge me. We're going together. And Nidh confirmed last night. The stone is magic."

"What do you mean, confirmed? She told you the stone was magic?"

"No, but I threw that paperweight at her and—" Kara's heart sped up. Sweat sprung to her temples. Her throat clenched, her stomach flipped.

"Take your time." Alec leaned into her and gripped her elbow gently.

"Okay." Kara bit her bottom lip and breathed deep and slow through her nose. The nausea started to dissipate. "I couldn't get away, Alec. I was so scared. I couldn't stop her. I thought I was gonna die."

"How did you get away?"

"I threw the paperweight at her. You know. The one from the antique mall."

He stilled. Squeezed her elbow. "What did she do? Is she dead?"

"No. I don't think so. But she, like, spilled out of her suit."

"Spilled? Like water?"

"No. Like muscle. Like a mass of hard sentient red stuff. She ran, or crawled away, and took the suit with her."

"Jesus."

"Yeah."

"That's a lot."

"I know. And the whole stone and ring thing has me thinking."

Alec grew still again.

"Are you holding your breath?"

She felt his cheeks lift in a smile. "I was."

"The ring is a ring, but also kind of a tool, right?"

"Yeah, I guess you could say that, though I'm nervous where you're going with this."

"Hear me out. You said you'd go with the flow now, right?"

He made a short humming sound. "Right." He paused. "Within reason."

She smiled, elbowing him gently in the ribs. "If the ring is a tool, and the stone is magic, well, when you touched that horn of Gabriel in the workshop, it got windy. I think we have more tools we need to make use of."

"The horn," he whispered. "And at your mom's. That's the shape you saw in front of us when I drove."

"Yep," Kara said quietly. "And I can see stuff that other people can't. Which makes me think—"

"The eyes," Alec whispered. "The eyes of St. Lucy."

She nodded. "I saw Nidh that night. She took them from the cemetery. She didn't want us to have them."

"So how do we find them? Where would they be?"

"We don't have to. The one that made the wind blow, that was in the workshop, right? So we go get the replicas. They're made of the same 'magic' stone." Kara paused, looking straight ahead. Held up a pointer finger. "The ring first. Then, the replicas."

"Kara?"

"Yeah?"

"You're an unhinged genius."

She laughed, leaning toward him. "Nah. I don't know for sure that they work, or what they do."

"It all seems to make sense though, doesn't it? I mean, it doesn't, but it does. We'll figure it out, right?"

"I guess."

"So, we're doing this."

"I think we can." Kara nodded. "Yeah. We will."

"Are you sure you want to come with me to get the ring? What about my face?"

"Just stay on my blind side. Keep talking. As long as I hear your voice, I'll be fine."

"You sure?"

"The part of me that matters knows it's you."

<h1 style="text-align:center">23
STONE TOOLS</h1>

The last time they passed through this lobby, Kara had to stop herself from laughing.

Now, all was quiet. No heating system. Nothing.

They stood on the threshold, staring into the dark of Dino's workshop. The place stunk of stale air and iron. The memory of the attack, the death, was tangible. Without her permission, Kara's mind tried to place where Dino was lying just days ago when his slurried insides leaked out the holes of his eyes. Her skin stiffened; her throat constricted.

Alec flipped the light switch, and the sole green ceiling lamp illuminated the middle of the room in hard, yellow light, like a searchlight in the dark. Just like the last time they'd been there. Kara noticed fluorescent fixtures were set flush against the ceiling, but she couldn't locate a light switch for them. It was hard enough to see in there earlier when she had two working eyes. They both paused, taking everything in.

Whoever had been appointed to clean up had done a shit job.

The body was gone, of course. The red lake, too. Pale swoops of dried blood stained the shiny green-gray concrete. Like body-fluid watercolor. She stared at the busts along the back wall. Now their stillness seemed a conscious choice. To Kara's eye, the dark brick wall behind them vibrated and swirled, like black static. She looked down, willing herself to breathe slowly, evenly. A physical act of lying to her own body.

Alec cleared his throat and pointed to the table where the horn of Gabriel was. The horn, and the eyes. "Over there."

"Nobody moved it," Kara observed, gripping her ring and letting it drop against her chest.

"Nope." Like before, Alec was the first to advance deeper into the room. Kara followed him closely, glancing at the lobby entry every few seconds.

"Do you feel that charge in the room?" she whispered, realizing her mouth had gone dry. She licked her lips, touching Alec's bicep. "Or is that just me?" The charge that ran through her, that terrified nervousness warred with something that burned for him, all-encompassing. More real than she could deal with. Kara tightened her grip.

"I feel it too." Gently, Alec removed her hand from his arm and held it. "You okay?" His lips were tight, nervous. But the corners of his mouth teased themselves up, like he'd just received some really good news. He laced his fingers with hers and their hands hung, joined. All casual, like they were going for a stroll.

He's good with us doing this. He's even happy with it.

"As okay as I can be," she said. "Was I hurting you?"

"No," he said. Then his eyes doubled back to her. "Okay. Maybe a little, Captain Planet."

"Really? *That's* who you chose?" she said, chuckling in the back of her throat.

"I dunno. I'm nervous right now. For multiple reasons. Plus, you dyed your hair green once in high school and cut it real short. Remember?"

"Yeah." She forced another laugh. "I'm nervous, too." *Jesus, my stomach hurts.*

"I don't blame you. Or me. Don't blame us." Alec sighed, releasing her hand, gently, and walked over to the horn.

He closed his hands over the narrow part of it, hoisting it up. A stiff wind tousled his hair, then let go. Kara let out a deep breath.

Then, the moaning started. The air was deathly still, but a sound like tornado-speed gusts wrenched through the place. Kara covered her ears.

"What *is* that?" Alec shouted, still holding the thing. "Should I put it down?" His words were strung tightly together in fear. Rapidly, his shoulders rose, and fell, his breaths coming fast and short.

Kara held her hands out to him. "Can you feel anything different?"

"Yeah. I feel . . . charged up. Like I drank too much coffee."

"Otherwise, okay?"

Alec grimaced. "Ish?"

"If you can stand it, I think you should hang onto it. See if anything happens."

Alec bit his lip. "Okay."

Gradually, the moaning died down, and they looked around.

"That was really loud," Kara said.

"Do you think Nidh would have heard that?"

"Possibly." Kara bit her thumbnail. "I hope not."

"Do you think anything else happened?" Alec asked. "Anything that we can't see?"

Kara looked at his normal living human face, then remembered.

"I'm afraid to take my necklace off."

"Try holding the eyes without taking it off." Alec tried a reassuring smile but it was tight. "Baby steps."

"Baby steps, yeah." She grabbed the eyes of St Lucia. Unlike the originals, these were unnaturally large, half the size of billiard balls, and just as heavy, smooth, and slick in her hands. Immediately, the wind started up again, and she tilted her head to get her bangs off her face. Her own eyes tingled; her heart beat so fast and hard, it hurt. It felt wrong. Like, *medically* wrong. Kara gasped for breath.

"All okay?" Alec asked quietly.

"I think?" She shook her head. "Was your heart pounding a million miles a minute when you did this?"

Alec bit his lip again. "Yeah."

"Why didn't you tell me?"

"I didn't want to worry you." He put his hand on her shoulder. "It started to slow down for me after a minute or two. Otherwise I wouldn't have let you do it."

"Let me?" Kara took a deep breath and smiled. "That's cute." She was pretty sure it was slowing down for her, now. "My eyes are all pinpricks. It feels really weird. Like static electricity, stopping just shy of being painful."

"Try closing them?"

She took a few deep breaths and closed her eyes. The back of her eyelids lit up like a painting under a spotlight. Both eyes, not just the one she could see out of. How odd. "It hasn't been raining out, has it?"

"What do you mean?" Alec said. "No. Why?"

"I can see the quarry with my eyes closed! It's filled to the top with water. I can't even see the tall stone at the back."

"Huh."

"But that's not even possible. The stone at the far end is taller than the basin that holds it. Or, it is, now." She opened her eyes again. Her right eye was blind again when she opened them.

Alec ran to the front door and opened it, peering across the parking lot toward the quarry. "Kara, that's not at all what I'm seeing. Whatever you're seeing is definitely *not* happening right now."

"The scene when I close my eyes—this was just like the setting for the dream I had, right before I woke up in the hospital. Nidhogg had a body, with skin. Then the skin shed. Her muscles became these horrible red ropes, and this strange white metallic shape floated to the top of the water, the same thing she's wearing— or—no, driving right now."

Kara gasped when she realized it. "The body of water in the dream, that was the quarry."

She remembered the stuff that looked like ice, but marbled, creeping across the water's surface. "It was stone."

"Kara, it's still stone."

"No, I mean, first it was water. There was water here. And somehow, I think that water *became* stone."

"Whaaat."

"How long ago would this stone have formed?"

"God," Alec breathed. "I have no idea." He set down the horn and searched on his phone. "350 million years ago."

"Christ! So according to my vision she was here, shapeshifting, 350 million years ago."

"So she's actually the Norse god? Nidhogg, the dragon at the roots of the world tree. Only she's displaced."

"Holy shit." Kara raised her eyebrows. She placed the eyes into her bag and rubbed her face. "Yours has to do something, Alec. Mine helps me see things."

"Maybe it helps us get away faster, right? Like in the car?"

"Yeah, but you can already do that without the horn, right?"

"Oh yeah. Right."

"What does it do in the bible?" she asked.

"Uhhh, signal the apocalypse?"

"So what is it, just a get out of jail free card by taking the world all down with us?"

Alec looked down at the horn, thinking. "I don't think so. I feel like it has to be smaller scale than that."

"How so?"

"Well? The dead miners walk in Barre. These dog people are terrorizing Barre. This isn't a national or even a state-wide phenomenon."

"So we're thinking it's her? She's here in our town, so she's to blame for all this?"

"Either to blame, or involved somehow. What I was going to say is, whatever my horn does, it's probably only going to affect something local, right?"

"Oh," Kara bit her lip, thinking. "Right. That makes sense. And without the eyes, I can see past one layer of your skin. But when I hold them, I can see further, to the past. And without the horn, you travel to somewhere real across town."

"So where is it I'll travel with the horn?"

"I don't know. Somewhere Nidhogg doesn't want us to go."

Off to their right, the back door of the warehouse opened with a bang, then slowly creaked shut.

Kara's eyes shot open, and Alec moved up next to her. They stared into the black void beyond the workshop at the back of the warehouse.

Silently, Kara waited for the creaking door to shut itself. For the silence to swell in her ears. For the nothing to yawn and spit out the horrible, clawing inevitability.

They'd played with their tools, and some part of her knew what came next.

"We have to go," she whispered urgently.

A long, scraping step came from the dark of the room; the shadowed, hulking figure moved forward, out of the darkness.

Fear claimed Kara, anchoring her to the spot. "We can't let her take them this time." She spoke plainly, now. No more whispering. "They're the only ones left."

"Yes, I agree, so come on," Alec hissed between clenched teeth, taking her one hand with both of his.

"No, no, no, Alec!" she hissed. "When did you put the horn down?"

"Shit!" He was emphatic. "When I was checking my phone."

"Mm, I see you're wearing it now." Nidhogg's voice was a crackling robotic hiss. She advanced on them, feet pounding quickly against the concrete. "How fetching against the flesh of you."

"Kara?! You need to go."

"No."

"*Please.* Run. I'll get the horn."

Kara turned, blood rushing, heart pounding, and scrambled toward the lobby, but stopped at the entrance.

Alec ran toward where he had set the horn. Barely twenty yards stood between himself and Nidhogg, and she was advancing on him fast. She reached the end of the row of statues, rounding the corner to reach him, just as he lifted the horn. He strained to hold its weight. With his other arm, he heaved the long table over, the heavy granite toppling to the floor.

Nidhogg came around the table, reaching for Alec, just as a severed stone hand slid down the table's surface and grazed the flesh of her foot. Nidhogg let out a scream and dropped immediately to one knee. The red flesh rioted from her foot, shooting thin ropes out in all directions, like hair standing straight up before a lightning strike. The crimson ropes clung tightly to the calf of her armor and inched up the thing. A few tendrils braced themselves against the knee of the armor, and others tried to hoist the white leg back upright. Slowly, it righted the leg. But the foot was left completely crooked, the inside of it lying flat on its side.

Broken foot and all, it pressed its weight on the stump of its leg. Metal groaned as Nidh limped around the back of the table where Alec had gone, gaining speed, circling around the back of the fallen table and following him as he dragged the horn along, catching up with Kara.

"Go!" Alec shouted, dragging the horn with him.

"Just come on!" As soon as he reached Kara, she grabbed his wrist and dragged him along, limping with the weight of the horn.

The screeching metallic sound continued. "Return to me, child. Give me your ring, and I will return your father to you."

Kara's throat constricted. "Dad." Her eyes filled. But she kept moving.

"No way is that true," Alec growled as they reached the front door. He pushed the handle, but the door wouldn't budge.

"Did you lock it?" Kara hissed. She fumbled for the key, kneeling down, desperate. She knocked it to the floor. "Fuck!" she whispered, her heart slamming in her chest.

The scraping grew louder. Faster.

"Is she close?" Kara's breath was ragged as she located the keys.

"Yes." Alec's voice was quiet. Resigned. He backed up against Kara, shielding her.

She couldn't bear the way he sounded. Like he was done. Given up.

"The eyes, girl. Give them to me. Give them to me and you can have your father. Give them to me and you may leave," Nidhogg rasped.

Kara's blind eye throbbed, and the other one tingled. The lock glowed a warm gold. The metal teeth of the key scraped painfully against her fingers as she tried jabbing it in and failed. It was upside down. Cursing again, she flipped it.

Another scraping sound, this time the satisfying clunk of the key plunging in, and a sudden scream from Alec as she pushed the bar of the door, releasing the latch.

Kara pushed the door open with her back, and he collapsed against her.

Fear throttled her but her anger overcame it. "What did you do to him?" she spat. She tried to pull Alec's still form through the door.

Slowly, the blank white face tilted to the side, regarding Kara. An arm shot out, grabbing for her necklace. The chain was pulled tight against the back of her neck.

"No," Kara cried. "Please, no."

"You will join me," the voice groaned in excitement. "You will never be far from the ring! You will be reunited with your father!"

Kara tried to reach for the necklace, to hang on, to wrestle it back. The chain was strong, but Nidhogg was stronger. Kara's skin gave; the metal of the necklace stung her broken skin. "No," she sobbed weakly, struggling with everything to hang on to Alec, who slumped in her aching arms. "No!"

"Like goddamn fuck she will," Alec's voice was weak, but it was there. He heaved up the stone horn and bashed it against the hip of Nidh's suit.

A giant groan emanated from the thing, and it crashed to the ground. The red ropes that were Nidhogg howled, and shot out the side of the suit.

The horn skipped across the thin brown carpeting. Kara and Alec both stooped quickly to hoist it up. Kara slammed the door back open with her hip.

They rushed out the door, and into the dwindling light.

***

The streets were empty. Kara drove as quickly as she could toward the cemetery.

"She said I was going to join my father," she said. "I was going to join Dad."

Alec nodded slowly. "Let's get some distance." His voice was sober.

"I think she can control the miners," Kara continued. "From what she said, I think if she gets my ring, she can control the living, too."

"Let's hope not," Alec said. "Let's hope that was just an empty threat."

"Why else would she be so dead set on getting the necklace?"

"I don't know."

"And now that I had that vision in the quarry, I realized something." She chewed a fingernail. "The dream I had, Alec. There was something huge, black, triangular in the stone."

The lake made her think about the pond near the hospital. About what Ten told her. Birds depositing eggs in the pond from somewhere else.

"I dreamed the white suit was floating up from the bottom of the water. It wasn't there all along. It had to have come out of something else. It's the only thing that makes sense."

"So what does that mean?" Alec's voice was flat.

"That white suit. For her, I think it's protective. But remember when we talked about the bird in the world tree signifying Indrid Cold? An alien? That black triangular structure could be a ship, buried deep in the stone. At the time, submerged in water. And that suit could have floated up from it as the ship sunk."

Alec didn't say anything.

"Alec? Come on! Are you with me?" The traffic light washed them over in red, and she stopped. She thought about Mothman. Dog people. Did Nidhogg control them, too? Did she have influence over cryptids and undead humans?

"Alec?" she repeated, turning to him.

He was immobile. Bathed in red. His head rested gently against the passenger window, a rivulet of blood trailing down from his temple.

***

"I can't get the TV any louder," Alec grimaced. "And this machine won't stop beeping at me. I'm not even hooked up to it. The sensor's just hanging there, carrying on about being hooked up to nobody."

"I'm glad you're complaining. Maybe that means you're okay."

"So far, so good." A minute ago he'd said his head was still hurting him, but he'd seemed pretty alert again since they'd gotten out of the car. "I was really worried about all that blood, but the nurse informed me that even the smallest bump can cause lots of bleeding. So she didn't *say* I'm overreacting, but she didn't *not* say that, either."

"I'm gonna interpret that as a sign you have a chance of surviving instead of a suggestion that you're overreacting."

"And if it's both, I'll take an attack on my character if it comes with good news about my head trauma."

"I don't care what anyone says. You're my favorite character." Kara smiled warmly. Something about his brief spell of unconsciousness in the car had tapped a well of even more gushing emotions.

Alec blushed, and laughed quietly, looking at the TV, which was off.

His shyness made her bold, somehow. "I wanted to tell you something."

"Oh boy." He raised his eyebrows at her.

"What?" Now her cheeks were getting hot.

"Nothing, just, we've been fighting literal monsters for a few days and you haven't warned me you were gonna tell me something this whole time. So that's a pretty big preamble."

"Shut up, or I won't be able to tell you."

Alec inclined his head, suppressing his smile.

"This morning, you brought up that summer when Tyler locked me in the shed."

"Yeah?" He was serious, now. Eyes locked on her.

"Yeah, well. I never made a pass at him."

His face went slack with relief. "No?"

"He made a pass at me, and then he got mad I wouldn't reciprocate, so he locked me in there."

"Jesus." His face reddened.

"I was so fucking mad he made everything weird. I always felt like you and me were perfect, and I was really protective of that. And then your cousin came in and torched it all. When Tyler did that, I didn't know how to talk to you. I didn't know how to function."

"I was *so* worried, Kara."

"I'm sorry. I spent the rest of the summer thinking it'd just be weird forever. I was so glad when I came back and things were okay. I remember thinking it was the end of the world until I saw you again at school."

"Just goes to show. We always work things out. You know that."

The nurse came in and turned the beeping machine off. Kara thanked her and waited for her to leave before continuing.

"I know. I mean, I know that *now*. I didn't then. But the reason I wanted to tell you that was, um—" she paused. Her heart was pounding. "When you brought up the Tyler thing, you know, when *I* was in the hospital bed, mere hours ago? I just had to tell you. I didn't want anything to do with him. And then, earlier, in the car, before I drove you here like a bat out of Hell? I was really scared for your, uh, mortality. So this is my 'what if you died' confession. I'm team Alec. Always have been."

Alec rubbed his eyes slowly. "You're being so honest."

"You look like that pains you."

"No. It's a good thing. Honesty. I need to tell you something, too. I haven't been lying about anything. More like omitting something. For a long time."

"What?"

"I keep worrying we're closer in my mind than we really are. Or, closer than you'd want to be."

Her heart dropped into her guts. "What do you mean?"

"I mean, this is hard to say. Because I'm scared, Kara. I don't want you to feel like I've been pining for you. Because me feeling that way without you knowing or wanting that, it tarnishes our friendship. You shouldn't worry that while we're laughing about some stupid shit that I might be thinking 'wow, that weird choking sound she makes when she really gets laughing is just the most adorable sound I've ever heard.' You shouldn't worry that, if we're sitting close together on the couch just watching a movie, most of my energy is spent ignoring that all I want to do is get as close to you as physically possible." He reddened, rubbing his face. "Sorry."

Her heart thundered and she stared at him dumbly. She felt warm all over. "So . . . you've been pining for me?" The corners of her lips crept up into a smile she hadn't authorized. She covered her mouth with her palm to hide it, and bit her lip.

"I mean, I push it way down. I avoid it. Like, I've given it no hope. Just starved the feeling. I just love being with you. It's the best, Kara. And your friendship is everything. But lately I feel like you've given me reason to hope. And even then, I keep telling myself: 'no, she's just being nice.' But it just feels like there's been something more lately. Something coming from you that wasn't there before. And when we touched in the cemetery?"

"Yeah," she nodded in confirmation, her face flushing with heat.

Alec's face lit up. "Yeah? You too?"

"It was—" she paused. Was she really going to say it? "It was electric." Her face burned. She felt weird now, leaning against the wall of his hospital room after saying that. It'd felt natural a second ago, but now, awkward. She folded her hands in front of her, not knowing what else to do.

His face looked a little funny, like his eyes were boring into her, but like his thoughts were far away at the same time. Maybe trying to unearth everything after all this time.

She sighed. "I've been really scared of these feelings."

"When did it start for you?"

"The night of my dad's shiva, when I came to see you at work."

"God, really? That's so recent."

"Yeah. I mean, if I'm being honest, Tennyson has been on me forever, saying we belong together. Telling me I'm possessive of you and stuff. 'Cause I never liked any of those girls who would hang around you at school over the years. But she's too easy to shout down. A pushover." She laughed quietly. "I think it was there before, but suddenly, it's just way stronger, now. I don't know."

"Are you sure you're okay talking about this?" he asked. He was still watching her face, but all of him was back with her, now. Checking on her. Like always, but even better.

"I'm scared, too. It's so strong. So much, so fast. But I—"

"It's okay. We don't have to—"

"It's just that, I want it so much. The more I ignore it or deny it, the bigger it gets."

Alec cocked an eyebrow at that, but then seemed to bury that thought. "Sorry."

"Sorry for what?"

"Nothing. You're probably still processing. It's just this is the coolest thing I've ever heard." He shook his head slowly. "I really didn't know how this was gonna go."

She chortled, her stomach doing wild cartwheels. "Too bad we're gonna die."

"I don't want to talk about that now. For like five minutes, let's not talk about that."

***

"I can't believe there was no internal bleeding. No concussion." Kara shook her head, staring absently at the town from the cliff edge where they'd parked.

"Are you disappointed?" Alec asked, smiling. "It hardly hurts anymore, anyway."

"You're just saying that so I won't worry."

"Kara, seriously. I'm fine."

"You're fine." She sighed. "Except for the fact that you got clocked in the head by a god in a giant space suit."

Alec snorted, then looked at her sideways. "We both did," he reminded her. "How's your eye doing?"

She covered her good eye just to check. "Still can't see out of the bad one." She shook her head. "God, what a fucked up few days this has been." She could swear she felt the magic in the granite pieces in back. And some kind of vibrating tether that held her to Alec. She couldn't stand it when they were in the car together like this. It was all she could do to breathe evenly. Especially now that they'd talked about . . . that thing between them.

"What are we supposed to do?" Kara whispered, staring at the clock radio, then up at the darkening horizon.

"We're supposed to do what we're supposed to do." Alec picked at something on the side of his shoe, then returned his foot to the floor of the car. His knees touched the dashboard. He looked so uncomfortable, just shoehorned in. She loved that about him, though. His long legs. She thought about that a lot, actually.

"What's that supposed to mean? I don't think you're being as helpful as you think you're being."

"Yeah, I guess you're right." Alec pressed his palm to his mouth, in thought.

Kara shuddered.

"You okay?" Alec asked her.

Absolutely not. "Oh, sure," she chuckled quietly, shaking her head. Tears sprang to her eyes. She tried to focus on something else. Something besides the fact she was supposed to save herself. Alec. Her town's dead miners, including her own father. Something besides the fact they were almost certainly going to die. Besides the sound of her mom's heart breaking as she buried her in the same place she'd be stuck in forever if they failed. A song played on the speakers, deep and thick with jangling rock guitar and a steady drumbeat.

Focus on the drums, she thought. Something besides the fact that she wanted to rail the man in the car next to her. Besides the fact her fingers burned with electrical lust for her best friend and teenage Kara was shouting that it might wreck everything.

She picked at her nails. If she touched him, would she see his face all weird and skeletal? Or would she see his head tilted back, face relaxed, as she moved against him? Would he let her be that? Do that for him? She shook her head from side to side and pressed her hands to her head.

"Kara?"

"Huh?" Startled, she turned toward him, ripped from her thoughts.

Alec's eyes were soft. He reached for her, pressed his fingers gently against her neck, his thumb caressing her jaw. She let out a short gasp.

"It's okay to be scared," he said, his voice low. "At least we're together, right?"

She grinned. Her heart pressed against her throat, blood singing, surging against his fingers.

"Is this okay?" he asked.

Kara nodded, fervently. Her tears spilled out. "*Please,* yes."

"Good." Alec's eyes lit up. Like her answer was everything. "I just can't *not* do this anymore."

He bit the corner of his lip, his eyes caressing her face side to side in quick little motions. Reached to undo his seatbelt, automatically moving it up and over. Eyes hooded, he leaned in, returning his hands to her face, and she brought her own hands up, held his wrists gently. Her fingers awoke, little shoots of electricity igniting where they touched.

"Good god, Kara." Alec grazed his thumb slowly over her bottom lip, watching her. As though checking if she were real. "I've wanted this for so long."

His skin was coarse, and her world slowed. Nothing existed, other than the scrape of his thumb against her bottom lip. The texture. The pressure.

Kara's breath quickened. "Closer," she whispered, smiling, extending the "r" at the end, beckoning. There were inches between them, now. Any nearer and she'd feel his breath against her cheek. She rubbed her thumb against his cheekbone, brought her mouth to his.

They touched, and she felt him sigh against her. She knew how he felt because she felt it, too. Everything that had been coiled tightly inside for so long was unwinding slowly, gently. His mouth was warm and soft and she claimed it with hers. Shut her eyes. Let everything she'd kept inside so long press against him.

She slipped her hands through his hair. Watched his eyebrows relax. His breath hitched, and it made her skin heat all over, to see him react that way to her.

He cupped a hand over her bicep, his hand flattening, fingers spreading, traveling across her shoulder. The bare skin of his hand heating her neck, and up higher, each finger marrying with strands of her hair, cradling the nape of her neck with his palm. Kara tilted her head back, and Alec pressed his lips, full and warm, at the spot just below her earlobe. He hugged her tightly, the middle console still between them. He traveled down her neck with his mouth, kissing her neck slow and deep, taking his time.

Her breath was heavy. She motioned for him to move back. She moved to the center console, leaning over him.

He looked up into her eyes, grinning. "You're taller than me," he said, his voice still low and gravelly from what they'd been doing.

Kara leaned into him, kissing him again, her fingers tracing his jaw. She reached for the armrest on his door, transferring all her weight to that arm. Lowered herself to sit on his lap, and brought her face close to his.

"Hey," she whispered.

"What's up."

"Eh. Nothin'." She smiled.

Eyes closed again, she caressed his lips with her own. Telling him, wordlessly, everything she'd longed to say.

24

Into the Skirt of the Bell and Through

Kara and Alec parked at the small patch of gravel where the street ran against the opening of the field. Red Tree Hill sat maybe fifty yards back, shadowed by the gathering dark. As soon as they got out of the car and retrieved the horn, the sky broke open above them. Kara's arms ached, and her shoulders and back even more so. Every so often, she and Alec switched positions, one walking forward and the other backwards, but none of it seemed to really help.

Alec must have felt it too. "Not too far," he said, the strain eating at the way he pronounced the vowels.

"Yeah," Kara huffed. Her chest burned. Speaking wasted the little breath she had left. She wanted to set the thing down and take a break, but worried it'd be impossible to hoist it back up. She was soaked with rain and sweat, heavy tendrils of hair sticking to her face, and now they'd hit another humid patch.

"Should we stop when we get right in front of the tree?"

"Yeah, I think so," Kara said, unsure. "I'll keep looking and I'll tell you when we're almost at the hill."

They moved quicker now that they knew they were almost there. Kara had to look back often to make sure she didn't trip over the uneven ground. As it grew darker, they had to tell each other to wait so they could get their bearings. Each time they paused, Kara checked her purse to make sure the eyes of St. Lucy were still inside. Once she joked to Alec "don't worry, I still have my balls," and she couldn't tell if he was coughing or laughing.

As they reached the bottom of the hill, the inside of her purse began to burn hot against her leg, and her eyes began to ache. Like a migraine, but with hunger pangs.

"Uh, Alec?"

"Yeah?"

"Something's going on with my balls. Or, I mean, my eyeballs. The ones in my bag. They feel really, really hot."

Alec groaned. "What do you think we should do?"

"I don't know." Kara squeezed her eyes shut and shook her head. Her sockets growled. "My eyes feel funny, too."

"The ones in your head?"

"Yeah. I don't know how else to explain it." *Oh hell, just go for it.* "I know it doesn't make sense, but my eye sockets feel . . . hungry."

"I'd say that was weird, but for the past couple of weeks, everything's weird."

"I know, right?" She dried her hands off on her damp pants the best she could and pressed her blistered hand hard against the stone.

"Do you think it means something?"

"Everything seems to, lately."

"Yeah." Alec paused. "Are your balls too hot? Do we need to adjust where they're at before we start pushing again?"

She laughed dryly. "No, but they're super warm. I can feel them on my leg."

"Same here."

"TMI, babe."

Alec snorted. "I know."

"Ready to climb the hill?"

"Ready."

The hill was a gradual enough incline, but they were fatigued from dragging the horn up. Their directions to each other grew terse.

When they finally reached the top, Kara shuddered, and a tremor rocked her bicep. She rubbed it vigorously and sucked air through her teeth.

"You okay?" Alec reached for her gently, squeezing her arm, squinting at it in the near-dark as if he knew how to fix the damage. Somehow Kara's face grew even hotter.

"Yeah, thanks." She put her hand over his.

A green glow filled the space between them. "It's the ring," she whispered. The glow intensified until they had to shield their eyes.

For a while she just stared at him, watched the way the green light held his face. He was some combination of ghoulish and beautiful. A face that held all the answers. All the good answers, and the bad. Everything.

Her fingers itched suddenly, intensely. She grasped Alec's hands. Her hands burned with pleasure, as if her fingers were rewarding her for her correct choice. His eyes lit up in recognition.

"You too?" he asked.

Kara nodded.

As if in answer, the tree's base glowed red against the darkening sky. The glow climbed upwards and filled the branches, then the twigs.

"Do you see that?" Alec asked. Lights dropped down rapidly from the sky; all primary colors. Red, green, and blue.

"Oh god." Kara's eyes welled up and her heart pounded. "Alec, what is this? I'm scared." Some lights were dotted in triangular shapes; others glowed alone. They hovered above the trees, then shot down quickly and silently. As they settled themselves beyond the tree, they emitted a quiet humming sound. They gathered in a line at the edge of the forest.

"What should we do now?" Kara asked, her voice shaking.

"Maybe they're just here to watch?" Alec whispered. "Like why Indrid Cold said he was here."

"You think he told us the truth?"

"I think he was showing off his knowledge. I don't think he was trying to trick us. Look at them." He motioned with his head, gripping Kara's hands tighter. "They're not moving toward us. If there are bookies in space, I guarantee you Indrid Cold bet on whether we'd succeed or not."

"I dunno," she shuddered again. "What if they're waiting for us to make our next move?"

Alec sniffed. "We can't worry about that. We've got to follow through."

"We're both gonna worry about it, but you're right: we have to follow through." Kara's legs didn't want to move; but at least she was here with Alec. They were together. They were here. It was time.

She turned the clues over in her brain. They were paired. The horn of Gabriel was here, and so were the eyes of St. Lucy. She feared the way the eyes warmed her leg and how her eye sockets ached, so she figured they'd try the part that seemed easier first.

"Blow into the horn," she instructed Alec.

"It's huge," he replied.

"Yeah, but, why else would we have brought it here? We are supposed to wield them. You should blow it and see what happens."

"I'm not going to bring about Judgment Day, am I?"

Kara shook her head immediately. "No. You said yourself. This is all fantastical and crazy, but it's small-scale. This isn't a world-ending prophecy."

Alec looked at her, one eyebrow raised. "Okay. This feels super weird, though." Alec hoisted up the narrow end of the horn and Kara held the wider end. He pressed his mouth against it and Kara waited.

He moved his lips away. "Nothing?"

"You blew in it just now?"

"Yeah, nothing happened, did it?"

Kara shook her head slowly. "Well, it is a horn, right? Remember when I took French horn lessons in fifth grade? You can't just blow into it, you have to sort of vibrate your lips and *push* the breath out. Maybe it needs to be played that way."

He laughed quietly. "Hmm, it's worth a shot if you think it'll work."

"I do." Kara paused. "I think. Maybe." She crossed her arms, which vibrated with excitement and fear. She realized that, up until this point, they had just been *reacting* to everything. Finding stories from the generation before. Visits—hell, *conversations* with otherworldly beings. Her and Alec's relationship being tested. This was different. They were here on their own terms, now.

The horn sounded.

It was mournful and long. Multi-faceted and tight. Odd, like cable cords stretching and screaming. But organic, like the scream of an elk.

Immediately, Kara's aching eye sockets cringed. She felt her own eyes suck back and settle somewhere in the depths of her skull. Everything went black. She screamed but the horn drowned out her voice. She sucked in a million tiny desperate breaths.

The second the strange, alien call stopped, her ears began to ring. Two hands touched her cheeks, held her face. She took them in her own, and together she and Alec reached into her bag. Together they dug out the eyes of St. Lucia. Kara's breaths were still fast, desperate, but the warmth rolled in waves against her palms. Slow, and soothing, like bathing in the ocean. It felt right in her hands. She ducked her face down, down, toward the stone spheres. They were heavy but almost as small as her own eyes. The nearer they got to her face, the more she doubted what she was trying to do.

I can't, she thought. *I can't see, and I can't do it. We're both going to die.*

Her hands moved an inch closer, and the orbs left her hands, entering her eye sockets.

The warmth spread. She could feel it in a different way. The veins, the ventricles careening, celebrating, hugging the gray veins of the granite. She felt the new colors, they hummed to her their flavor. Like her flesh and bones could lick them, taste them. Thin little branches of sharp pain wrapped around the new eyes, then the same thin fingers gave her pleasure, in a quick little buzzing pattern, like being shocked. Then, explosions leapt through her skull, and other than a whining, ringing sort of sound, her hearing was gone. She held her head gently, let the taste writhe wildly in her head. Through her skull, she could hear herself groaning. As the vibrations grew harder, she started to come back to herself.

Finally, she could feel a voice in her ear.

"Kara," Alec's voice was muffled, but it was there. And he was speaking in a frantic whisper. He held her gently by the wrists. "What did it do, what happened to you?"

Kara hummed quietly, trying to find the words. But there weren't any. Nothing would come out. Since she couldn't speak, she smiled dreamily to try to show him she was okay.

"God, no. What have they done to you, Kara?"

She lifted her eyelids and Alec gasped, his mouth wide in horror. He looked like he wanted to run, but instead fell to his knees. "We can go." He touched her hand. His mouth was normal now, but his eyes were grave. "We'll leave this place. We'll figure something out." He waved his hand in front of her face. "Can you see me? Can you see anything?"

"You're made of light, Alec."

Tears wet her heavy stone eyes. Their heat had crept lower and thrummed in her chest now.

"You're still you, right, Kara? Please tell me you're still with me."

"It's me, I'm here! I just feel weird. Like I'm in a dream. I felt so happy for a second. So happy I could hardly stand it. But it's fading now."

"God, Kara," Alec hugged her, hard. "I'm so sorry."

Her heart tripped. "Was that there before?"

"What?"

"That opening, that hole, at the base of the tree." She pointed.

"Kara, there's no opening."

"Oh, it's there," she assured him. "All you're telling me is you don't see it."

"Huh."

"Your horn is smaller, now. It's glowing."

Alec looked at the thing lying on the ground and gasped. "It's changed! It looks like Gjallarhorn."

Kara stared at him.

"The one on my tattoo." He picked it up. "See? It even has this strap like you see in all the texts." He lowered it over his head and slung it over his shoulder. "It's glowing now? What color?"

"Whiteish, I guess?" The stone eyes were getting dry. Kara blinked rapidly. "Do you know what I'm going to say next?"

"I can't even begin to guess."

"Put the horn in the opening."

Alec raised his eyebrows. Turned the horn around so the wide end was facing out. Pushed it up against the opening.

Kara chewed her lip. "No, the other way, I think."

"You think?"

A voice spoke from high up in the tree. "Definitely the other way."

The white robotic body was there. Up in the boughs of the tree. The red tendrils sat against its chest, some part of it still up in the head, making the head move. Making it talk.

Kara screamed, grabbed Alec's shoulders and walked them back quickly. Alec fumbled with the horn, returning it to his shoulder.

"What the hell was that?" Alec asked

"It's her. We have to go," Kara said.

Alec ducked down, quick. "Is it above us?"

"Yeah," Kara hissed. "Come on."

He grabbed it and backed away, fast. "Where can we go?"

"Fuck, I don't know." Kara grabbed Alec's hand and yanked him in the direction of the forest. The stupid woods were a good three hundred yards off still, and the darkness seemed to eat everything before they even approached the trees.

They ran until Kara was gasping for breath. She slowed and turned around.

"What are you doing?" Alec hissed. "Don't stop!"

"She's not following us," Kara said, gasping for breath.

"Yeah, but it's close. Was even closer. And it *talked*—"

The sound of loud crying cut Alec off and stopped Kara dead. Not quite the mournful call of a coyote, and not quite the howling trill of a cat, but some ungodly union between the two.

"The trees," Kara whispered. "That's the sound I heard in the trees as a kid. I've never heard it while outside. It's sharper, now. It's not the trees. It's animals."

"That's where they found Sammy." Alec's hand rested protectively on Kara's shoulder. "Charlie said one of the dog people took him. Dragged him off to the woods. Let's go a different way."

"Yeah." Immediately, they changed course and headed straight for the cemetery. "If we can just make it over the fence."

They ran for another fifty yards. She was sure they were being followed. She could feel it.

Kara heard ragged breathing behind her.

"They're here," she growled at Alec, catching up to him, grabbing him by the arm.

Alec turned to look. "Oh my god." He doubled back and ran toward the fence.

"Alec, they're gonna get us." Kara squeezed his arm harder.

"No!" Alec wrapped his fingers around her bicep now, pulling her closer to the fence. "We can make it, we can climb."

Kara backed up abruptly, banging an elbow painfully against the fencepost. She could see them now. Four of them. Ugly hairless things, walking on hind legs. From the ground, they looked so tall. So close. Their lips curled back in a collective grimace. A low growl that meant *we've found you, now, you're ours*.

She wanted to climb the fence, but she was afraid of what they'd do if she turned away for even a moment.

"Kara! Let's go!" Alec shouted. He stepped up on the bottom rail and turned, reaching for her.

She grabbed his hand, hoisting herself up. Alec was already halfway over.

One of the things sank its teeth into Kara's calf. She screamed. She was stuck still, clinging to the fence, every muscle tight. The thing was as big as her, if not bigger.

It tugged hard at her leg, teeth still deep inside the flesh of it, trying to separate meat from bone. Kara screamed again. Some combination of the thing's spit and blood rolled down to her ankle, soaking her sock. She forced in a breath and held it, then pulled back, squeezing her thighs against the balusters. Groaning, she dragged herself hard and slow up against the cold metal.

Finally the thing let go of her calf, but another one grabbed her shoe. Its bite was sharp, the pressure agonizing. Muscles crunched against bone. Its jaws were locked tight. It had a short snout and its teeth stuck out, curving away from its gums. It stared at her with golden brown irises, its eyes yellowed and bloodshot. Kara kicked repeatedly at its face with her other foot, nothing landing, no more than a few pathetic swipes.

"Alec," she screamed. "Do something!"

Squinting, she looked down. Alec had been trying to help her, trying to shove back the one who had her by the foot with the small end of the horn.

The others had grabbed the horn with their claws, had hold of his arms, were pulling him up against the fence from her side.

Kara let out a frustrated shout. Holding her breath, she leaned back, gripped the fence with both hands, trying to topple backwards over it, force the thing to release her. Her foot felt ready to break between the thing's jaws, but finally it loosened its grip. Groaning, she tried again, but its jaws clamped back on, pulled her back toward its side of the fence. She leaned forward, trying to shove the other dogs back. They didn't do much more than flinch.

"Fuck!" she cried. Her hair was pasted to her face by her own spit and tears.

Alec groaned. Everything in him seemed focused on what he was doing. Three of the dogmen had hold of the horn through the fence now.

Kara's ears rang, and her vision blurred.

She didn't know how much longer she could hold on.

The horn was slipping from Alec's hands. Everything was slipping.

"Get it back," she cried.

Alec's eyes were exhausted. He was spent. He tried to grasp the thing, but he only had about an inch left of it in his hands. Suddenly he leaned forward, pressed his lips to the mouthpiece, and sounded the horn again.

The creature before the bell of the horn fell to the ground. A low whine sounded from its throat. Its skull collapsed like something unseen had stepped on it. Just uneven foggy eyes on an empty, oozing pelt.

The jaws clamped down on Kara's foot loosened. The creature still clung to her, but barely. Pain shot up her leg as she kicked at its teeth, and it fell. She scrambled up the fence and threw herself over the side, landing violently on her good foot before falling onto her side.

The other dog-things looked down at their sibling. The one who had had Kara's foot whimpered quietly. They stared up at her, then started to climb the fence.

The moment Kara stood, the ground shook again, harder than the first time.

***

Kara and Alec stumbled to their knees, holding each other. Waiting for the shaking to stop. Kara watched in horror as near-perfect rectangles of dirt crumbled. All the burial plots were collapsing, gravestones sinking, crooked, into the dirt. A faint smell, musty and wet, wafted over them.

Why, though?

What felt like endless minutes passed until finally, the shaking stopped.

"What's happening? Is that—" Kara tried, her face buried in Alec's shoulder. "Is that because you blew the horn?"

"Maybe," Alec said quietly.

A soft glow filtered up from the thirty-odd graves that were now gaping holes. It was the same turquoise as the water in the quarry.

Slowly, they stood. The braying of the dogmen started up again. They were at the top of the fence, now. Damn near about to touch down in the cemetery.

"Come on!" Kara shouted. They booked it toward a black stone mausoleum with wooden double doors. The only thing standing in this cemetery, it seemed, that wasn't made with Barre gray granite from the quarry. Every few graves they passed were sunken. Random rectangular openings dotted the landscape as far back as their eyes could see.

"Where did the bodies go," she whispered.

"Underneath."

"Underneath, where?"

Alec didn't answer. The frenzied grunting grew louder. The chase was back on.

"Hurry!" Kara shouted. Together, they yanked open the colossal double doors. They strained to pull the massive doors shut. Darkness swallowed them.

Kara and Alec gaped at the room around them, trying to ignore the snarling, splintering, nails-on-wood scraping at the door. The dark space had become a brilliant son et lumière. Bold green circles of light pulsed into view, tree rings insinuating themselves, etched deep into the giant wooden doors.

From the corner of the room, completely separate from the dog people, a second sound rose. Something slow, something dragging.

A six-foot humanoid shape emerged into the green glow and lumbered over to the doors, blocking them with its own form. Kara stared at the thing—all reddish-brown muscle.

"Alec," she whispered, backing up to the opposite wall.

Outside, the cryptids quieted. Everything stopped. A deep, shaking breath came from the figure, followed by a labored exhalation.

The red-brown colors of the thing looked like an anatomy poster of the muscular system. Like what Charlie had described that night in his house.

Nidh without her robotic body.

"Nidhogg," Kara whispered. "No." How had she gotten in there before them?

She grabbed Alec by the arm and pulled him back, away from the doors, behind one of the two stone coffins. This was worse, much worse a fate than what waited for them outside those doors.

"Wait," the voice was human, male. Not robotic, like Nidh's in the tree. "What's happening?"

Kara recognized the voice, now. "Cedro?" Her heart flooded with relief, then sank when she remembered the workshop. The attack. All that blood. And now here he stood, stripped of his flesh.

"Everyone went down," Cedro said. "I felt everyone go down to the underworld and leave me here."

"Everyone?" Kara asked.

"The dead miners and artisans here all had Barre Grey monuments. They were brought back at night. But not me. I didn't want a monument."

"Why?"

"The stone has magic. I knew the magic keeps them from resting."

"Why are you still up here, then? Still standing? Talking to us?"

"I don't know. It doesn't feel natural, though. Not like those eyes in your skull, or that horn you brought in here." Cedro gestured to Kara's face, then to the horn slung over Alec's shoulder. Kara stared at his big, bloodshot eyes embraced by red lids and shuddered.

"How can either of you see anything?" Alec started. It was quiet for a moment, until he realized. "Oh."

"You think this looks natural—" Kara started. Then redirected. "Do you think the dead are at peace, now? Down there?" Kara gestured to the doors. Outside, the dog people whined and scraped at the doors.

"I don't. Those eyes, the horn. Did you find the poem? At my booth in the antique mall?"

"Yes."

"So? There are tunnels underneath us. The workers there, that's their hell, but not everyone belongs there. The river from the poem, that's what takes the righteous to their final resting place. One of you started them on their journey when you blew the horn."

"So, how do we help them?"

"Who used the horn?"

"Alec."

"So that leaves you, with the eyes. What can you see?"

Kara squinted and looked around. She hadn't focused on anything but survival. "I can see everything that's here, but in different colors." She stared at Alec. His chest throbbed red. She looked up at his face. A pale greenish yellow. Alec grimaced, no doubt disturbed by her new eyes.

"Look harder," Cedro urged her.

She faced Cedro. His blood pooled inside him. Stagnant. It didn't churn like it did in a living person. Whatever sentient state he was in wouldn't last. A gentle wind entered the crypt, wafting with it the smell of rotted meat. Kara gagged. "You're—"

"—I know," he replied. "I can feel it. I will be gone soon."

Suddenly, the door handles rattled. Kara and Alec leaped forward to hang on. To keep them at bay. "They're figuring out how to get in," Cedro said. "You have to go. I'll hold them back."

"Go where?"

"The coffin next to mine, didn't you wonder who that was for?"

"Honestly?" Kara gulped, staring down at the blue coffin. The closed one. "I hadn't even had time to wonder." The coffin to the left of it was—of course—open. Cedro's. "What's in it?"

"Open it and your eyes will tell you. Follow the path of the Battered Bell."

Kara turned to him before moving toward the coffin. "I'm sorry this happened to you." She choked back a sob. "At least this is more of a goodbye?"

"There was nothing you could do, was there? Don't tell me you wanted us all to drink the Kool-Aid. Die together?"

Some laughter hiccupped between the sobs. Alec put his hands gently on Kara's shoulders. "You're very forward, you know that?" he said to Cedro.

"And I have a point, don't I?"

"Thanks," Kara whispered, smiling as tears ran down her face.

She and Alec tried moving the stone from the top of the coffin for a good few minutes. Counting to three and shoving, taking a breather, trying again. Kara groaned. It was immovable. Like it was all one fucking thousand-pound piece.

The doors pushed in with a bang, and Cedro pushed them shut again. "Hurry!"

They counted to three again. Kara pushed with everything she had. Nothing. Absolutely nothing.

A bigger bang. The doors whooshed open.

"Cedro!" Kara shouted. The largest dog ran in first, sinking its teeth into Cedro's forearm, yanking him down violently.

Cedro screamed in agony. "I'm already gone!" he shouted. "Go, now!"

Kara pulled Alec behind the unopened coffin and dropped to her knees, inspecting the lower back panels of the casket. Maybe the dogs hadn't seen her. Maybe they were stupid. Maybe they'd forgotten they were in there.

Maybe her new ability could help her get in.

"Kara, what are you doing?" Alec's voice was quick, shaking.

One of the creatures leapt up on Cedro's open coffin, mere feet away.

Kara pointed to the opposite side of the coffin, the side facing the opposite wall, then remembered that Alec couldn't see what she could. She yanked him in her direction, crawling as quietly as she could, dirt and rocks prickling her arms. A red glow shone against the opposite wall. She headed toward it and Alec followed.

Paws alit to the ground again, followed by the click, click, click of its claws.

Fuck. This. Kara crouched quietly, then pulled with all her weight to bring down the long narrow side panel that ran underneath the stone coffin. Alec crawled up next to her and pulled from the other side.

The panel wrenched down with a loud scrape and thudded heavily to the stone floor.

"Don't wait for me, get in!" Alec hissed, pulling Kara's arm, leading her underneath. The growling was upon them, now. Nothing had been easier than these creatures finding them in this small place. Alec cried out as Kara rolled underneath the crypt.

She scrambled into a space that was dark and wet. She tried to pull Alec inside, obscure them both enough so they couldn't be reached, but it was tight. Literally just enough space for two bodies. She pulled him closer, though one of the animals clearly had hold of his leg. Alec struggled against the thing, one of his arms still touching her; but with three of the dog people still out there? It was only a matter of time.

Amid the struggle, a color insinuated itself just above her head. Yellow with the most perfect ping of red warmth inked across the dark toward her. Sang to her eyes with its array.

She craned her neck to find a bell. Yes. Like poor Cedro had just told them.

Its opening faced her, and its mallet had an extension, ending with a small triangular handle. Perfectly hand-sized. *A triangle? Or an arrow pointing to its heading?* Kara thought about the ship in the stone in her dream. Also triangle-shaped.

She pictured the funnel shape that had appeared to her as Alec drove. She'd called it a tornado, but it had flared out a little at the end. And the surface was smooth. Just like the horn. Just like this bell. An opening that grew smaller, then flared out at the end.

So then, what would happen if I pulled? The implications that this device could move her to a different place seemed impossible; but what had she seen these past few days, if not the impossible? And what was her alternative? She thought about the shadows within the stone. Nidhogg directing her crew. *That* was impossible, but it was also real.

Alec's body started to pull away from her. "Kara, I'm sorry. I can't hang on anymore."

They hadn't come all this way for it all to end. There was no sense in that.

"Just stay in that corner," he said. "Maybe they won't reach you. I'm so sorry." A long scraping sound, and he was barely there anymore.

"Grab my hand," Kara shouted, no longer whispering. Because what was the point any longer? They were here, the worst was happening, now.

She grabbed him by the fingertips, as that was all she could reach now. Her only recourse. She would pull the triangle, and if nothing happened, then she supposed she'd be dog food. It would surely suck. But was there really any avoiding it?

Fuck. Alec was slipping. "I'm gonna do something!" Kara struggled, tightened her grip on the triangle. "Hang on, okay?" she shouted. "No matter what!"

"Okay," Alec said, breathlessly.

Kara closed her eyes tight, and pulled the triangle shape.

Slowly, they started to move in an impossible direction: into the skirt of the bell, and through.

25
NIDHOGG - NOW

My beautiful, broken bell.

I recognized it right away. Its call like the one I used at the quarry, but this one, imperfect. The steel in your fracture cries out to me.

If I'm honest, I loved the broken one more. All along, I had my transport back to hell available to me. But if I were to return, that muffled imperfect clanging announcing my arrival? After what I'd done? What would my people do to me? I'd thought of it more times than I could count, had I ever cared to count.

When I stood at the double doors of the crypt, I wondered: how did the humans find the place I'd been hiding it? And then I remembered: I'd felt her eyes when she was at the tree. Not her given eyes, but stone carved as eyes, like the ones I'd stolen once they'd paired. Those eyes would help her find it, wouldn't they.

The little monster had three sets, now. The ones she was given at birth, the stone ones, and *my* given eyes, lost to the granite when Indrid betrayed me, unearthed and then set in her stupid father's ring.

Fucking humans.

When people marry, they sound a pair of bells to signify a beginning. However, the song of a singular bell symbolizes an end. How funny that this single broken thing is ringing, now.

I cannot breach the dizzying bliss of space, without the town's dead to unearth my flying machine. I cannot have my revenge on Indrid if I cannot travel to his home planet. And anyhow, he is here on earth now, I'm told. I am left with no choice but to risk a return to where I came from, to retrieve my human dead.

My beautiful, broken bell, I thank you. For you've heralded their entry. You've signaled a new ending.

Theirs, at least.

26

KARA - NOW

That yellow light is still there, but the red keeps drinking it and growing from the center, out. Alec and I, we're suspended, like in water. And we're moving forward without moving our arms or legs.

I feel Alec's hand on mine, can feel him shaking, like an insurmountable pressure tethered to me. But no matter how hard I try, I can't turn my head to look at him. My hand screams out but I can't fathom letting go.

I wish this thing weren't so goddamned loud. I'm sure now that Nidh's going to follow. Right? This noise, this stupid loud call of the bell keeps reverberating. What's the sound bouncing off of? All I see is black, encircling the light ahead. I think this bell is sharp and permeates all the space around it, like the bells at the doors of a supermarket, announcing loudly "we've arrived."

Where are we going, anyway? Lately, it feels like we exit one situation, to slide straight into some new, fresh hell.

I really just said that, when I'm sure that's literally where we're headed.

27

HEL II

They emerged into a dark place with a glow that insinuated dawn. The place smelled like coal had pissed itself. She turned toward the glow, but she had to go slowly. The walls held her close; allowing maybe a foot of clearance on either side of her. The scrape of their jeans against the hard, cold stone sounded tightly around them. She looked up. The black stone ceiling was only three or four feet above their heads.

"Can you see anything?" Alec whispered to Kara, his voice echoing.

"Yeah," she said. "You can't?"

"No."

"Take my hand again." He was turned the wrong way, reaching out to nothing. "I'm right here." She guided him back toward her.

"What do we do now?" he asked, and reality came screaming back.

They were in hell. Probably. No, clearly. She had these special eyes. Great. Alec had a horn that made dead people sink further underground. Was it going to be enough? They were supposed to . . . what? Find her father and all the other miners, so that Alec could shepherd them to the banks of the river Seol, which would guide them to the abode of the dead?

Holy hedgehogs.

"Listen for any kind of running water," she instructed Alec lamely. "Like a river."

"Oh yeah," he said, his voice vague and dreamlike. *Like, of course we're going to do that next; but again, holy hedgehogs.*

After walking crouched for what felt like an hour, they finally turned left. Kara was thirsty. She had no idea if it was because she knew she had no access to water, but she was starting to panic.

"I really don't know if we're going to reach a taller area anytime soon, Kare." Alec spoke slowly, and she guessed he was avoiding addressing anything beyond their immediate future. "I think we should try crawling. We're going to hurt our backs and necks otherwise."

"Sounds good." After so long with no change in their surroundings, any option seemed like a good one.

"You don't think we should," she could hardly dare to say it, "go back the other way, do you? We haven't come across anything."

Alec didn't answer. Kara closed her eyes tight. Pictured her body drying up, dying slowly. Would Alec stay by her if she died first? Would they be here together? For eternity? She hadn't even gotten the chance to think about a possible future *living* together, and now dying together seemed more likely. The grim reality of it all burned sharp in her stomach; petals of acid opened up their colors to her.

A sob escaped her, quick and unexpected. She grabbed Alec by the ankle and held on for a second, squeezing him tight. Then, she sat back on her heels, the back of her hand pressed hard against her lips. More sobs racked her.

Alec sat down, knees to his chest, head against her shoulder. "It's okay," he said quietly. "It's okay. This has to be the way they went."

"How do we know," she whispered, rubbing her nose with the back of her hand.

He answered her, after a long pause. "I dunno. We just gotta keep going like we'll find them."

"I just feel like I can't right now."

"Don't give up. We can't give up."

"Okay. I just need a break. I need to rest a second."

"Kaaaaraaaa."

"What?" She stared at him. Her strange vision showed her his weird white eyes with a brighter white in the middle. She was almost sure his mouth hadn't moved.

"Kara?" He paused again, speaking slowly, carefully. "That wasn't me."

"Karaaaaaaa."

She stilled. The sound came from behind her.

It sounded like her dad, if her dad had been strung up and dried out until his vocal cords had cracked. A rapid scrabbling sound in the dirt threw her into a blind panic.

"Dad!" She spoke in a sharp whisper.

She saw his face now. Just ten yards beyond Alec. The same direction the voice had come from. She knew it had to be him. But still, she grabbed Alec by the waist, dragged him back, away from the thing that said her name.

"Is it him?" Alec said, panic choking his voice. "Jonathan?" he called out.

"I think," Kara said.

On instinct, they both crawled quickly away, their feet kicking up dirt. After a few feet, Kara shouted again, "Dad!"

The scrambling sound stopped.

"I'm so sorry, but can you stop . . . coming toward us for a second? We're really scared. I'm so sorry. I can't help it. I'm scared of you."

He didn't respond, but he didn't advance, either. She focused in on him. He looked emaciated. His cheeks were gaunt, his hair slick and pasted to his face. His eyes were white like Alec's in the dark. But they weren't glowing, like Charlie had described when he'd told the story of the Conovers finding the dead miners marching. Maybe they only glowed in headlights.

Kara's breath left her at the sight of her father like this, and she doubled over. "Dad," she gasped. "Is it really you?"

"I don't know how to answer that. I'm so sorry. I don't think I know you."

Kara's eyes filled. "Do you remember anything? From your life?"

"All I know from life is what the other men tell me. I worked with them. I had a wife and daughter. Lola and Kara."

"That's me. I'm your daughter. I'm Kara," she choked. "How do they remember and not you?"

"I don't know." He stared at her. His eyes were intense, like when they used to talk about something serious and she could tell he was really listening. But something in it was different. The glimmer was gone. Like some part of him was on autopilot. "I'm sorry. I wish there was a way I could comfort you." He frowned. "There was a part of me who knew you. I don't know where that part of me went."

Her stomach hurt. She tried to decide what was worse. Never seeing him again, or seeing him like this.

She wasn't sure what else to say. She still worried about whatever part of her dad this was. "Are you in pain?"

"I don't hurt. I feel . . . wrong."

"You don't belong here."

"No."

"Can you help us? Where are the other men? Are they down here?"

"Yes. They're not far behind. We are trapped."

"Is there any way out?"

"I'm not sure. We've been traveling for a while. We're making the same three left turns. We're stuck in a triangle."

"The vortex," Kara whispered. "Indrid said this is a vortex."

"What is that?" Alec asked.

Jonathan explained. "The men told me that there are three landmarks within the town. The quarry, the cemetery and the red tree, or world tree. I think we're in some kind of tunnel linking those three points from underneath. That would explain all the left turns and how long we've been moving down this tunnel."

"Assuming that's true, does knowing it help us?" Alec asked.

"Hm," said Kara. "Indrid said we should use our abilities."

"Isn't that what we're doing?"

"Only in the most obvious way. Hang on." Kara closed her eyes, tilted her head downward, trying to look beyond where they sat. "Maybe there's more I can see with these," she whispered.

She screamed as the floor dropped down from beneath her feet.

28

ALL-THE-WAY DOWN

"Kara!" Alec shouted. "Kara, are you okay?"

Alec held her face in his hands, and she lay back in his lap. A sheen of sweat coated her head and neck. She felt tired and cold. "I'm here. Hi. Where are we," was all she could think to say.

"What the hell happened?"

"Where are we," she repeated, weakly.

"We haven't gone anywhere. We're still stuck in the same place."

"Damn." She was nauseous. She spit in the dirt. Alec helped her to sit up. Her dad just watched, his mouth partly open. He was definitely not the dad she grew up knowing. Some of him was there, but most of him wasn't. Horrible.

Kara rubbed her face with the heels of her hands. "Well, I thought I was dropping through the floor just now. But I guess my eyes were just showing me what's . . . down below us."

"And what's down below us?"

"More Hel, I guess? A series of tunnels, then chutes slanting down, and more tunnels. Then a long set of steps. They go down and bend, then go down more and bend, again."

"But what about the river? Can you see the river?"

"Maybe. The stairs, and then, I think, solid ground, with some kind of curving, moving path. Hopefully that's where we need to take you, Dad."

"Thank you," her dad whispered.

"You're welcome," she replied quietly. Alec gripped her shoulder tightly, and she placed her hand over his. "Anyway, I think one of these corners of this triangle has a portal to go back home. So hopefully we can find our way back up here after. Would be nice to leave this place alive." Kara added that last part just to see if her dad reacted at all to the reality of her mortal peril.

He didn't.

She fought back tears and took a deep breath. "Dad, can you show us where the other miners are? I can check below again and figure out where we need to dig to find the first chute."

"Kara?" A different, dry, strung-out voice came from behind her father.

"Who's that?" Kara's breath grew short. She was just starting to get used to her dad being there, and now, that quick scrabbling sound had increased behind him. This tight space and all the dead sharing it with her sent little zaps of fear through her body.

"It's Gavin Conover," the new voice answered. The figure emerged from behind her dad.

"She—" Her dad paused, correcting himself. "Kara has found us a way out of here," he explained in his new, flat, devoid-of-humanity tone.

Gavin shuffled closer, which made Alec promptly move right up next to Kara. Her heart thundered, and she braced herself as Gavin came face to face with her. The first thing she noticed was that his eyes *were* glowing white, unlike her dad's. His skin was blue. To her, at least. Small clumps of flesh rotted away at the cheeks, and a fuzzy, thick substance; dark mold, maybe, ate at his ears. She could smell his breath, a sickening mix of vomit and fox shit.

"Why don't my dad's eyes glow?" she asked, holding her breath.

"They used to," Gavin said somberly. "Up until last night."

Kara took a sharp breath in. "I lit his Yartzeit candle last night."

"My god," Gavin whispered.

"That could be good, right?" Alec said. "You might have helped the 'real' Jonathan cross over. Might have gotten his soul, his essence, to where it was supposed to go."

"Oh my god," Kara whispered, and her heart leaped a little bit. "Maybe."

"That could be it." Gavin's eyes glowed intensely. "He is different, now. I think that's right."

"How will we know for sure?"

"I don't know," Gavin said.

The other miners talked excitedly behind her dad, the news traveling that she and Alec had come to rescue them. Gavin hugged her. As soon as she couldn't smell his breath anymore, the stench of mildew and rot overcame her. She held her breath, looking at Alec pleadingly. He pressed his lips together nervously, then moved even closer to Kara, making sure the embrace was short-lived.

"We worked together for years, but didn't get close until you were born," Gavin said. "We were talking shop right after he got back from leave. He asked if I had kids. I told him, yeah, but they're grown. Then I told him I had a six-month-old grandson. Jeremy, of course. You know Jeremy.

"I swear all we talked about was babies for a couple years. Anyway, he never stopped talking about you. Always showing people pictures of you. Soccer games, theater, first day of school. And when someone brought in donuts, he didn't eat 'em. He wrapped his up to bring home for you. So funny to see the big dude who worked the wire saw just smitten like that. He didn't care who knew it, either. But you know that. That's how he was."

Kara looked to her father for confirmation. An automatic reaction. He stared at them, unmoving. Listening, but with the same dazed expression as when she first found him. All of this was so weird. They were all here, but still, Gavin talked about him in past tense.

She couldn't look at those vacant eyes another second. Better to just keep moving.

With her eyes guiding them, they quickly found the place where the tunnel connected to the chute. The miners did a fine job of digging. One of them, almost comically, still had a pickaxe. She smiled to herself, picturing a family member burying him with it. She was sure that had provided some amusement to everyone at his funeral. Her gallows humor did little to steel her, though, against the realization that a horde of walking dead were voluntarily following her into the depths of Hel.

Light began to filter up from where the miners had dug. Alec held Kara's arm gently, and motioned her to the front. He placed a guiding hand on her back, as though they had always done things this way. Together, they moved to the front of the group. At first, nobody followed.

He and Kara sat side by side on the black stone floor, dangling their feet over the edge until they touched down on the first set of stairs toward the floor of Hel. "It's okay." Alec spoke loudly to the others behind him, but his voice was gentle.

She felt some sort of pull toward him. Those two words were comforting, somehow. Like he'd just talked her through everything. But he'd hardly said anything. It was an urge to follow him. To stay close. Like just wearing that horn slung over his shoulder made him some kind of Hellish pied piper, leading everyone to the river. Did the others feel it too?

"Do you feel that pull?" Gavin asked, and everyone nodded. "I think this is how it's supposed to be. Kara will lead Alec, and Alec will lead us down. We're finally going home," Gavin said. "Some of you miss your families, and others only remember them, but can't feel anything anymore. But we've all been held captive by Nidhogg. I don't know what's after this for us. Hopefully we can all find peace."

Slowly, they started to follow.

They traveled this way for a while, Kara seeing what only she could: a dizzying series of triangle shapes overlaid upon each other, growing smaller with each level down, with a kind of chute linking them together. Each miner remained accountable to the man behind them, guiding them on. Every so often, a message would travel to the front. The older ones needed help. Some were confused, stopping and looking around. It was like they'd forgotten why they were down there; why they weren't going to the mine like all the other nights. Others had trouble walking. Three men seemed to have the same problem. Their knees would lock up every so often, and they'd have to drag their leg along. Others slowed to shoulder their weight and help them keep up.

When they descended the final staircase, she took in the high, beautifully finished black stone arches directly above them, which opened up into a vast cavern as far as her eyes could see, its ceiling like a brown earthy stone sky. A riverbank extended in front of the steps. It was beautiful, full of glowing purples and blues that glimmered despite having no light source.

The reality of what they were doing hit her harder than before. The river seemed tranquil, but as they approached, the water sped up. Pale faces beneath the surface regarded them vacantly, their cavernous mouths making surprised little "o"s.

"It's okay," Gavin told them. "They look weird. But we still feel that pull, right? It's the right place. They're heading where they belong."

"Are you sure?" Kara asked.

"They're going to the good place." He sounded completely certain. And what was the alternative anyway? Staying here? Taking them back up to be undead? It was a leap of faith, and their only option.

"You are a long ways from home. My little rat and her pied piper," a feminine voice spoke from off to the side of the steps.

Kara gasped, stopping short.

"Slow down," Alec called. "Hold on." He scanned the area, his gaze settling to the area the sound had come from.

A long, slow dragging sound issued from the blind spot next to the stairs, each scrape followed by the skitter of tiny rocks.

Slowly, a hulking mess of raw, blood-red muscle dragged itself to the base of the stairs. It spoke. "Don't worry. I will return them to their rightful place."

Kara's heart climbed into her throat. "How—" She stared in disbelief.

Outside of that white suit, unruly was the only word for her shape. The legs were less legs than they were two stands propping her up. From the two hardened clusters of red tendrils that bunched together on the ground, the shape resembled a messy tangle of wires, but hard, dark red wires with striations running along each one. While most were bunched together, random groupings of these things protruded from the shape, dancing slowly to their own baffling rhythms. Some slow and smooth like cat tails, others quick and restless like maggots.

"How did I find you? I know a faster way down. I followed you to the crypt from the world tree. The dog people are stupid. They would not know to try the door handles. I helped them with that."

"Is that right?"

"Yes, did you know I made them? I crossed your human descendants with their own pets. Sometimes, when they are bored, they defile your livestock." Nidh grinned. "They prefer horses."

"That is disgusting. Are you just trying to shock me?"

"Yes, yes I am. And it worked, too. However, they are my children, and they need me. They do as I tell them."

"Good for you. You should go to them, then."

"I have other affairs, right now."

"Oh, right. Stealing our families from us."

"Precisely. Though you as a species are already ruined. And so now, I must stop you and your little fuck friend."

Kara reddened, bracing herself. "You'll never understand how much more than that he is."

"I'm done with you. It is night. Your dead have work to do." Nidh gestured to the miners. "Come, my wilted flowers. I'm here to take you home."

The miners made their way down the steps toward Nidh, Alec in front, along with them. He had no choice but to keep moving.

Kara came to the bottom of the steps and stood there, arms folded. "They won't come with you," she told Nidhogg. "You've withheld their destiny long enough. They have someplace else to be."

Alec held up his horn, preparing to bring the miners back to his side.

"It's preposterous. The idea that the universe elected you—*humans*, the ones who created this problem within the stone—to shepherd the dead to the underworld. *You* were chosen, not an eternal one, like me.

"Ridiculous how you took this stone and marred it. It is now an abomination. I cannot fathom how you are afforded forgiveness, and second, third, fifth— infinite chances.

"Well, darlings, you are finite. And when you expire, you will be buried. And buried you will remain. A morsel for the worms to fight over."

"But you won't be able to control me," Kara said. "When I'm dead, I'll stay dead."

"I hardly think that's something to brag about."

Kara pushed forward, having to fight her body at every step to continue toward this creature. "I've figured it out. It's not *just* the headstones that animate the bodies. It's also the granite dust they've breathed in, in life. Cedro, the one who carved these monuments: he inhaled the dust, but his monument was made of a different stone." *And, what?* She asked herself, panicked. *What now?* She had to believe these gifts had been given to them for some reason. They were supposed to be here, now. They were supposed to do *something*. Her mind wheeled desperately. Roving. Searching wildly for some kind of clue. Something that could stop this. And save them.

"Very clever observation. I knew this already."

"Good for you." She was so close now, only a few yards away. Fear lighting up her brain, trilling in her chest, seizing her legs. Resisting her body's four-alarm warning was like wading through deep water. What came next? What could they possibly do?

The long shadow of Nidhogg's form laid before her feet like a snake. Kara felt someone next to her, and she didn't have to look. She knew it was Alec.

Despite the uncertainty, her chest swelled with warmth.

She looked at him. The horn was still slung over his shoulder. She remembered what happened when Alec had turned it on the dogmen. They looked at each other, and she laid her hand on the horn behind him, wiggling it gently. "Try it," she mouthed, shielding the side of her face with her hand. She tried playing it off like she was rubbing her face.

She watched his eyes register her message. Her new eyes showed her the blood heating in his cheeks, from berry-red to scarlet. His mouth turned down and lips parted, like he was going to throw up. This was terror in the shape of acceptance. He nodded, almost imperceptibly.

Alec took a few steps back and in response, Nidhogg's thousands of dark red muscles shifted and creaked against each other, considering him.

Quickly, Alec brought the horn from over his shoulder, aimed the thing at her, and pressed it to his mouth.

Nidhogg shot a red tendril out, wrapped it around the horn, and pulled. Alec pitched forward violently, his arms yanked arrow-straight by the force. He hung onto the thing until he couldn't anymore, white-knuckled with gritted teeth. A second tendril issued from somewhere within her middle, and then a third. And unforgiving, like metal cables, they joined, tightening their grip on the horn and pulling, the long red appendages thinning and vibrating with the effort until the horn shot out of his hands.

A high strangled cry escaped him and echoed for what felt like half a minute. He'd lost his balance in the struggle and fought now to remain upright, watching as their only weapon splashed into the river. Then, shielding Kara, he backed them up a few steps, shepherding her away. Away from the river. Away from the monster.

She felt his hand shake as it touched her shoulder. He risked a glance her way, and his eyes seemed to say: *At what point should we just scrap this plan and go home?*

Kara stopped backing up.

"If your plan is to have a go at me, it's already failed." Nidhogg rushed at Kara, red shoots extending outwards and wrapping around her throat.

Alec took the appendage in both fists and pulled hard, the force shaking Kara off balance, tugging her down onto one knee. She grabbed onto the thick cabling of tendrils as Nidhogg dragged her away from Alec, drawing her closer. Kara tripped over her own feet, stumbling forward, trying desperately to stay upright.

"Your father has breathed in this dust. And so he'll remain in his coffin, kicking his cold dead feet and screaming to the stars he will never see again, lest I instruct him to look to the sky." Nidhogg's breath was hot, and stunk of spoiled fruit. The breath, the stench, all came from an orifice the size of a golf ball. "For all the trouble you've caused, I will make you and your father suffer as I see fit, and then I will feast on your heart." When Nidhogg spoke, her mouth flaps were pale pink, and vertical. They moved like vocal folds in a human throat.

Kara's stomach flipped, and she shut her eyes tight. "Let go of me. Please." Anything else Kara could think of to say died at the back of her skull. It was all true. What Nidhogg had said would come true. There was nothing stopping her. All she had to do was take control of everyone again and bring them back to the surface, leaving her and Alec behind. They were weaker. They had nothing.

Everyone rushed forward to help, some with their tools brandished as weapons and others with nothing but their hands. The solid thud of fists hitting flesh issued from Nidhogg's other side as she dragged Kara toward the river. Kara struggled, kicking, trying again to walk along with her. Her neck was still held fast, and she breathed in short gasps, now. She couldn't dare turn her head; it would only restrict her airway further. It was all she could do to stay upright, and keep breathing.

After a few bigger, lurching steps, they stopped. It was quiet a moment, and then she heard Alec shout, and the hitting sounds continued.

Kara felt herself lifted a little, then lowered down. Suddenly, she was dropped roughly to the hard, stony ground, and groaned in pain at the impact. Alec gave a quick scream and before she could get her arms behind her, prop herself up somehow, she was dragged roughly against the ground, her neck wrenched backwards, and Nidhogg plunged her headfirst into the river.

Before she realized what was happening, she took a quick breath in, and her throat spasmed. With her head submerged, the icy water biting her skin, she coughed out, out, out, struggling to keep from breathing in again.

The water burned in her nose, and she shook her head wildly from side to side, finding Nidhogg's grasp around her neck had loosened, just a little. But more appendages pinioned her middle, roughly and clumsily turning her over until she lay on her belly. Then she was dragged further into the river.

Her lungs burned. She'd explode if she couldn't get air. She refocused, forcing her fingers between her neck and the appendage coiled around it. She pried with all her strength, twisting her torso, wrenching her body from side to side, letting all her frustration, fear, and anger, power her every function. She shoved her body hard against the bank of the river to force herself up somehow. If she could just get a few good breaths, she could try to keep fighting.

Kara sputtered and coughed, working to expel everything. As she took what short ragged breaths she could, the river water coursed down the side of her face, gathering on her chin. It reminded her of what her father said in her dream, about her burning the Yahrzeit candle.

"You burned it late, but the important thing is you burned it. I can get to the river, now. You'll come for me, but when the river washes your face like tears, you'll know I'm where I'm supposed to be."

When she cried, he used to always say something like that. "When you cry, pay attention to your tears. Those feelings make you strong, show you things. If someone makes you cry because they don't care, guess what your body is trying to tell you. Get rid of 'em. If you cry over someone good, keep them close to you. Crying is your body cleaning your eyes. But you're the one who's gotta take care of the rest of you."

The red tendrils formed a makeshift hand, solid as a rock that plunged her back under the water. It shoved the base of her skull so hard, she gagged from the pain, then held her breath. The cold seized her again, but quickly, she thought about her dad, and about the eyes.

The eyes.

Turning her head sharply to the right, she forced her eyes open this time. The river was purple and blue to her new eyes. It carried her gaze, winding and turning, climbing and falling until it reached a land of black hills. Roots with leaves of brilliant purple extended down, glowing green. Thin, upright trees with white bark made a forest. This was where the river took its dead.

Shadowy, translucent humanoid shapes walked among the trees. Just shapes, with no definable features. At least not from what she could see. She couldn't hear them, but the set of their shoulders and their slow gait showed no tension. They walked in a group, some of them turning to look at each other, then returning to observe their heading.

What were the chances she'd see her dad here in this land of the dead? Did her new eyes know where to look? Was this part of what they could do?

As though reading her mind, one of them turned to face in her direction. This one had flames where their eyes belonged. They saw her, and held her gaze.

Dad.

He'd already moved on. Her heart thundered. He wanted her here so she could see.

She heard a man scream from above the water. Nidhogg yanked her up so hard she lurched out onto hands and knees.

She gulped in deep, gasping breaths. "Dad!" She half-screamed, half-sobbed. She was shaking all over. She had no time to process this. She looked up. Nidhogg had Alec now. Those things had wrapped themselves around his wrists. Alec was pulling, leaning all his weight against her, feet slipping against the stones. He must have pulled on those tentacles until he'd gotten Kara all the way out of the water, and then Nidh had gotten ahold of him. The other men were on the ground, some lying flat and others starting to pick themselves back up.

"Dad! Help!" she sobbed, shifting her weight to one knee to help Alec. Dad would have known what to do. He would have been able to fix this. But he was too far away. No way he could get here. And she didn't want him to. Because everyone on this side of the river was doomed, just like she'd known since the minute all of this started.

She stood up. If she could get Nidhogg to grab her again instead of Alec, at least he had another minute or so to live.

Dad, or not-dad had gotten himself up and walked over to her. *Not the best time,* she thought. Looking at his vacant face broke her all over again.

"You called me?" he said, holding out his hand to her. At least he remembered she'd *told* him he was her father.

She took his hand, and he helped her to her feet. She tried to smile, but grimaced instead, another sob forcing its way out. "Thank you."

Nidhogg spoke again. "This is getting tiring. I was eager to see you suffer, but these idiots are toying with me."

"Well, I'm right here," Kara shouted, her voice cracking. She felt weak, shaking all over, her neck tender, and her throat sore. She didn't know how much more of this she could take. She stood all the way, taking another step toward Alec.

"Yes. Right there, getting more time with your father when I could be feasting on your heart and reclaiming my miners."

Kara felt sick at the thought. But then remembered something her mom had said. "After the accident, I tried to get Jonathan to apply as a custodian at the university, but he refused. I told him the mine was poisoning him from the inside out."

Poisoning him. Kara thought about that. The sound of his cough was burned in her memory. The relentless struggle to breathe. His body weak, rail-thin, so fatigued he practically sunk into his hospital bed.

Kara squared her shoulders. "You think *you* were fit to take charge of these men?"

"Excuse me?"

"You think it should have been you. To fix our mistake? To do what our gods would do, if we had gods?"

"Child, we *are* the gods. And yes. It would be better if it had been me, or someone like me."

"Considering you've withheld all these people from their final rest, it doesn't seem to me as if you're worthy of the responsibility. Your goal is selfish. And it's the opposite of what needs to be done."

"Oh, that is precious. You of such little knowledge. You, no taller than a stalk of corn, have an opinion. Please. Tell me more, my half-drowned rat."

"You don't care for us. You would never help them gain passage to the underworld. What *you've* done is an abomination."

"The rat amuses me in that it is correct. I suppose using your dead to unearth the stone and leave this godforsaken planet *does* bring me more joy than accepting the way of things. Do you know what else would bring me joy right now?"

"I suppose you're going to tell me."

"Feasting on your vacuous little heart."

Something shook loose inside Kara. She trembled. It was all she could do to stay standing.

"I don't care what happens to me, as long as my father leaves this world while you're busy eating my heart." She ran to Alec, dropped the necklace over his head fast, before he could protest or ask questions. "I'll be fine," she told Alec, loudly, hoping Nidhogg would take the bait. "Make sure my dad's body gets to the water, whatever you do."

"You will not be fine, little hero. I'll take your father's heart first, and yours will be my second," Nidhogg threatened.

Kara froze. A humming sound came from deep within Nidh. It grew quickly, climbing exponentially louder, and higher, then surging into an earsplitting whine.

Nidhogg's muscles caressed each other. Shiny thick red worms, teeming together, as that humming vibrated from her chest. As the hum gave way to a whine, the red worms that were her muscles quivered rapidly, the sound shifting from the center of her, seeming to radiate out from the edges of her chaotic form.

The worms exploded outward in a burst of vermillion tentacles. Undulating, beckoning. At the same moment, the whine erupted into a deafening scream.

The scream died down, and Kara turned to her father. Jonathan's eyes were locked tight on the display. A sick squelching sound came from his chest cavity. Strangely, he didn't fully react until a second after the sound. After that agonizing second, the light in his eyes stamped out. Before, his essence seemed gone, and now, all agency had vacated.

Jonathan's head tilted back. Eyelids fluttering rapidly. Pupils, rolling back, lids, closing.

Jonathan dropped to his knees and fell to the ground.

A disgusting slurp and a gulping sound came from Nidhogg's direction. Her muscles retracted, coiling together again. The scream dipped down into a pleasured buzzing. The worms climbed over each other, shuddering.

Alec shouted out to Jonathan. Kara ran to his side. Touched his face. It was cold. Days and days cold.

"Dad," she whispered. Her throat tightened with grief. She was hurting and numb at the same time. Too upset even to cry. Fear churning violently through her, she looked up at Nidh.

From the top, down, the muscles hardened, waves of sickly pale red washing over Nidhogg's body. Strips of the living stuff reached toward its middle, as though that action could stop the granite-dust-infested heart that now slid into whatever Nidh owned that passed for a digestive tract.

The moaning of something that grappled with certain death climbed higher and louder until it was dry and brittle as barren soil. The sound rattled on and on until it ran itself down to nothing. Until the body was dry as ash. It kept its shape for a moment, then crumbled like dirt underneath a solid boot.

"What—" Alec just stared, moving to touch Kara's shoulder.

"It's clear that the stone in this quarry is her own personal hell," Kara whispered, her hand covering her dead father's. "I know she enjoys eating hearts. I thought a miner's heart, filled with granite dust, was something she had earned."

"I'm so sorry, Ms. Lenker," Gavin whispered, kneeling at Jonathan's side.

"It's okay. It's not him. I'm sure of it," Kara said. "I saw him, with these eyes. I saw him walking in the land of the dead. He was a shadow, but he had flames in his eyes, like in my dream. What you suspected is true."

"How did you know she wouldn't take *your* heart?" Alec spoke up. "I'll be honest, when you put that necklace on me, I thought you were saying goodbye to *me*."

"That was another leap of faith." Kara looked down at her feet. "I hope you can forgive me."

"Now that she's dead, I guess I can worry about your mortality a little bit less," Alec smiled at her, his eyes watering. "Even less so once we're out of here. However that's gonna happen."

He stepped toward the river, gesturing for the miners to follow him. "Who wants to go first?" He stepped around what remained of Nidh's body, gritting his teeth in an awkward smile. An adorable attempt at trying to comfort everyone.

Gavin was the last to go in. He thanked them profusely with tears in his eyes. "I'll tell him what happened when I see him."

"Are you afraid?" she asked him. She hadn't felt comfortable asking anybody else.

"A little. But mostly just so, so tired."

"Rest well, Gavin."

He slipped in like all the others, legs first, treading awkwardly, then taking off easily with the current.

They watched him float listlessly down the river, until he was too small to see.

Kara knew someone else was there with them. She'd seen them duck behind the stairs while Alec helped the miners into the river.

She waited to see if they'd make themselves known.

"Ready to make our way back up?" Alec asked her.

"Not just yet. I have someone else I need to talk to."

"There's nobody else here."

"Coward." She said the word loudly so it could reach the eavesdropping party.

"Let me guess. You're not talking to me."

"Nah."

"Kara. Who are you talking to?"

"Maybe he'll answer me. He's been following us this whole time. To see if we can defeat our enemy, here. His enemy, too. But he's avoided getting involved."

"What makes you think that?" Alec asked.

Kara shot Alec a look.

He quirked an eyebrow. "I mean, how did you figure it out?"

"That's better. I didn't know before, but now I can see him." Kara gestured to the spot. "Can we just have our chat now? I'd hate for you to jump out and surprise me in those dark tunnels. At this point, I don't think I could handle that."

As soon as she'd made her catty comments, she regretted it, as she noticed how dark it was behind those steps. A pair of red eyes regarded her from back there, and her soul all but froze.

"Is it just you back there?" she managed, though her voice had gone much, much lower.

"Not just him. I'm here, too." Indrid stepped out from behind the steps as well, walking in front of Mothman.

"Well that works. You're the one I was referring to."

"You called me a coward. And I'd say, that's not true, my dear. I'd argue I'm more of an opportunist." Kara hadn't noticed before that his walk was glitchy, his movements quick, then quick again, then slow. Like his new skin wasn't fitting quite right.

"That skin looked better on Cedro," she growled.

"You're judging me? You're the one who thought it might be best if I take Cedro's skin and not yours."

She decided to steer him away from this talk. Hopefully he was done borrowing skin for a while. "You and Mothman. Are you two kind of a package deal or something?"

"We do tend to turn up in the same places, don't we. Before, it was me following him, but now that

Nidhogg can't control him anymore, maybe he'll follow me."

"You're not planning to stay down here, are you?"

"I'm not. What are you getting at?"

"Well. You killed our friend. I killed your enemy. I'd say you owe me, big time."

"What could I possibly have to offer you?"

"You're the bird, and she's the serpent, yeah?"

"Where did you hear that?"

"It was in some reading material we picked up. Do you have a better way out of here than a ten-mile hike up?"

Indrid laughed. "Why didn't you just ask me?"

"Just wanted to butter you up first, I guess."

Her heart pounded as Mothman lifted his wings and rose straight up. She pointed. "That wasn't your—"

Indrid looked confused, then his eyes lit up. "My ride?" He snorted. "No. I don't ride on the Mothman's back. Ridiculous girl." He devolved into a fit of high-pitched laughter, then composed himself and snapped his fingers.

Kara blinked. When she opened her eyes, she was back in the cemetery.

"Oh my god," she gasped, then fell to her knees. Then looked quickly up. Indrid was there, but no Alec. "Alec. Alec! What have you done with Alec?" she shouted, hot tears welling up.

"All right, all right. Quiet down." He snapped his fingers again and Alec appeared next to her, looking completely panicked.

"Kara! I thought you—"

"I didn't know what to think either." Kara's breath was fast, her heart pounding. Alec helped her up. "Of all the—"

"I'm not a hero, clearly. You're lucky I helped you. Let's hope I don't think of you when I need to come back here for some fresh skin." He turned and headed toward the front of the cemetery.

Of all the insults that cycled through Kara's head, she couldn't think of one she felt like saying out loud. She was glad to see him leave.

She turned to Alec, who still wore the necklace. "You okay?" he asked. The sunrise crept up behind him. Little visible rays of sun, like a shot in a god-damned movie.

"You know? I can see your whole jaw when you smile at me."

He took her hand. It was warm. Hopefully from blood flow and living flesh, and not the warming fires of hell. "I can easily say nobody's ever said that to me before."

"So I'm your first, huh?"

"I wouldn't go *that* far." He grinned even wider.

Kara felt warm all over. Like whatever was in him had spread over to her. "Let's go back to my place. Maybe I can be your last?"

Alec's eyes glimmered a little, the old softy. "I'd like that."

29
ALL-THE-WAY HOME

Kara lay in a booth in the restaurant, blinking at the ceiling. She was a week out from the swath of near-death experiences, and her injured eye had been re-gifted with sight just that morning, hence the (disbelieving, relieved) blinking. She, Alec, Tennyson, and Charlie had planned a memorial hangout at the restaurant to re-memorialize Dad now that he'd really moved on, and honor Cedro at the same time. She'd just found out Ten had invited her mom, so in addition to the blinking, she was also moping.

"She's been texting and calling you, with no luck," Ten said. "You can't ignore her forever."

"You are correct in saying that she has been. You know what she said to me about the ring, right? You remember?"

"I do! It was highly fucked up. And now you can work it out. Or yell at her. Whatever it is you've been holding back? You can let it out."

Kara sat up. "I can choose any of those things? Now you're talking." Confronting her mom. That was something she should do, and could pretend she was happy to do. In truth, though, she loathed to actually carry any of that out. In fact, confrontation was possibly worse than forgiveness.

She got up, and Ten walked with her to the bar. Charlie played *Jeff Wayne's Musical Version of the War of the Worlds* a bit too loudly on his Samsung Galaxy S II. It rang high and tinny, the piss poor audio eviscerating any chance of it making a lasting impression on anyone. A piece of duct tape held in the sim card. Every so often a wind instrument would chime in and Molly would interject heated questions like "is that a *piccolo*?" or "is this fucking disco?!" and Charlie would just make a shooing motion at her in casual disregard.

Alec sat to Molly's right at the bar, grinning at the display. "We gotta get you some speakers, Charlie. Does that brick even have bluetooth?"

"As you can guess, young man, I got no fuckin idea what bluetooth is."

Alec rolled his eyes in Kara's direction and suppressed a smile. She grinned back at him.

The door swung open, squeaking on its hinges, and her mom walked in. Kara cringed and wanted to look away, but they'd already locked eyes. Lola's makeup was done up, and her gray streaks were striking against her dark hair. Her smile was warm, but her eyes looked pinched and sad.

"Hi, babe," she said, her voice hoarse, but otherwise just as warm and sweet as when Kara called her (which was rare). "Can we talk alone for a sec?" She held a jacket over her arm, hugging it to her stomach. Dad's green jacket.

"How did you get that?" Kara asked, her throat tightening, threatening to push all her anger and sad out right then and there. She swallowed. *Fuck.*

"You left it at the house when you came with Alec." Her mom gestured back to the same booth Kara had just left. "That one still your favorite?"

"Yeah."

They walked over and sat down together, Lola keeping an acceptable distance.

Lola gestured at the jacket. "This is my visual aid. Like I'm in school."

"Visual aid for what?"

"I want you to keep this with you."

That hurt. She knew what the aim was, now.

"Why? You want to trade? Want the necklace back?"

"No, Kara. No, I don't. You should keep it. You should keep it, *and* I owe you an apology."

"Right." Kara looked down, trying to put her hands in her pockets, but that was difficult since she was sitting down. She folded her hands in her lap and looked back up.

"The ring is yours. I've been very weird since dad died, and I hope you can forgive me."

Kara refused to fill the pause that followed.

Lola continued. "Do you remember when Dad gave you this jacket?"

"I do. Do you?" Kara flashed her eyes at Lola.

"He told us we need to take care of each other."

"And?"

"Well, you're not a kid anymore, but you're still my girl. And the truth is, I miss you." She sniffed a little bit, and tried smiling but her eyes had gone watery. "I want you to still come over even though Dad's not here anymore. I wanna see you once a week. Do you think we can make that happen?"

Kara stared at the table. This wasn't what she expected her mom to say. Not at all. Her mom was quirky and snarky. And did weird confusing shit. This was out of character.

Lola kept on. "You know, I don't think I ever told you this but when I start doing weird things, I *know* I'm being weird. This little voice in my head tells me so. But somehow, I find that I *still* can't stop myself. I'm not gonna say 'let's not fight.' We naturally push each other's buttons. We always have. But let's communicate. Let's fight, and make up. And fight, and make up again, and hold each other accountable. Your dad used to call me on my shit, and I think I need *you* to be that person, now."

Why did this sound like such a revelation if Kara had had most of these thoughts a million times already? A lot of the things that bugged her about herself were things she had in common with her mom. And her dad was the opposite. And that worked, the three of them like that. Dad offsetting Mom.

But *did* that actually work in a real way? Or was Kara just embracing her dad and ignoring her mom?

When Dad died, Kara had wondered what she'd feel if her mom had gone first, and now she thought she knew.

Regret. Over not spending enough time with her. Over not being as close as she wished she was with her. Her mom was just more work, and somehow she'd let that excuse be acceptable.

Maybe she should try to understand these things instead of resisting or repressing them.

"Yeah, I think we should make more of an effort," she said. "I mean—*I* should."

She scooted closer to her mom, laid her head on her shoulder.

"Hold on," Lola said. Lifting Kara's head, she set the jacket over Kara's shoulders, pulling the lapels toward her chest so it wouldn't slip back off. It felt like a hug. And that diesel oil smell hit Kara like a truck. She was transported back to the start of this when she was in her room, using the jacket as a blanket in her bed, wondering what the hell was happening to her dad, to Alec, to herself.

And the feelings all came back, but now they were bent and different. Because back then her dad wasn't at peace. And now he was. And Kara had a hand in that. And that was something to celebrate.

But for now it was just a bit too much.

All these things rushed through her, sharp and fresh like the smell of ripped grass, just as Lola put a hand to Kara's cheek, gently returning Kara's head to Lola's shoulder. Kara cried heavily, and freely, and her mom hugged her tight.

Her mom dried her tears, then cupped a mouth to Kara's ear so she could hear. "I want you to keep this with you, always. His coat, his ring, and my love."

Kara wanted that, too. More than anything.

MUSIC

I wanted to mention some bands like Ghost, Baroness, Car Seat Headrest, and Big Thief, whose music was in my ears while I wrote *The Barre Incidents*. Their work was fuel and mood music for me and it kept/keeps me company while I write, when it's too early to (constantly) blab about what I'm writing to my friends and family. Their work means a whole lot to me.

ACKNOWLEDGEMENTS

Gigantic thanks go to Alan Good. Thank you for the things you do for us authors, and for how you run the place. Working with you is as easy as something like this can be. Because in addition to the hard stuff, it's fulfilling and fun.

Thanks to Alex Woodroe, my fantastic editor whose edits I love reading because they're brilliant. You lay down what's gotta be done, while making the most delightful comments in the doc.

Thank you to my writing group: Alex Woodroe, Michael Bettendorf, Lauren and Jacob Coffin, Matthew Pritt, Sam Melville, Steven Patchett, David Corse, and Paul Husband. Our space is a salve for many things and for gushing about fun stuff. Thanks for always being there.

Thanks to Tim Davis and Eric Williams for beta reading and for your awesome notes. Unread manuscripts feel scary, like they're just floating out there, haunting you with your own feelings of inadequacy, so thank you for un-haunting mine. Love to talk Horror with you guys. Thanks to Ivy Grimes and Michael Bettendorf for taking the time to read the book early for blurbs. You guys rock.

Thanks to Matthew Revert for the badass cover.

Thank you to my husband Marty, and my kids, Hannah and Ryan for your patience, and for making me feel like you missed me instead of like I'm a jerk for being gone sometimes for book stuff. Mostly, though, thanks for loving me and caring for and about me because your support and silliness and love is everything. And thanks to our cats, Maggie and Rory, for being on 24/7 pet support duty.

Thanks to anyone who reads this, picks it up, or shares it. :)

About the Author

Lauren Bolger loves writing, music, and frightening herself and others. She has loved these things ever since her brain started telling her what kinds of things she liked. She drums, too, sometimes. Her debut novel, *Kill Radio*, an Occult Supernatural novel, was released in April 2023, also with Malarkey Books. *The Barre Incidents* is her second novel. She lives in the Midwest with her husband, two kids, and two cats. More info on published works and events can be found at www. laurenbolger.com.

Thunder From a Clear Blue Sky,
a novel by Justin Bryant
The Muu-Antiques, a novel by Shome Dasgupta
Backmask, a novel by OF Cieri
Gloria Patri, a novel by Austin Ross
Where the Pavement Turns to Sand,
stories by Sheldon Birnie
Still Alive, a novel by LJ Pemberton
I Blame Myself But Also You, stories by Spencer Fleury
Hope and Wild Panic, stories by Sean Ennis
Thumbsucker, poems by Kat Giordano
The Great Atlantic Highway & Other Stories,
by Steve Gergley
Sleep Decades, stories by Israel A. Bonilla
First Aid for Choking Victims, stories by Matthew
Zanoni Müller
Boxcutters, stories by John Chrostek
My Ardent Love for the Pencil, poems by Vi Khi Nao
Consumption & Other Vices, a novel by Tyler Dempsey
Awful People, a novel by Scott Mitchel May
Drift, a novel by Craig Rodgers
The Ghost of Mile 43, a novel by Craig Rodgers
One More Number, stories by Craig Rodgers
Francis Top's Grand Design, stories by Craig Rodgers
Detective Novel a novel by Craig Rodgers

Malarkeybooks.com